# Hawksbill Times Two

By Robert Silverberg

Three Ravens Publishing
Chickamauga, GA USA

HAWKSBILL TIMES TWO By Robert Silverberg
Published by Three Ravens Publishing
threeravenspublishing@gmail.com
P O Box 851, Chickamauga, Ga 30707
https://www.threeravenspublishing.com


HAWKSBILL TIMES TWO By Robert Silverberg/Foxacre Press – 1st edition, 2002
Robert Silverberg/Three Ravens Publishing – 2nd edition, 2023

For permission requests, contact the publisher listed above, addressed "Attention: Permissions".

Publishers Note: This is a work of fiction. Names, characters, places, and incidents are a product of the author's imagination. Locales and public names are sometimes used for atmospheric purposes. Any resemblance to actual people, living or dead, or to businesses, companies, events, institutions, or locales is completely coincidental.

**Credits:**

Hawksbill Station was written by Robert Silverberg

Cover art by J.F. Posthumus

Mass Market Paperback ISBN: 978-1-951768-81-2
Hardback ISBN: 978-1-951768-82-9
Audiobook ISBN: 978-1-951768-83-6

Selected books by Robert Silverberg:

DYING INSIDE
THE BOOK OF SKULLS
NIGHTWINGS
THORNS
UP THE LINE
TOWER OF GLASS
GILGAMESH THE KING
LORD VALENTINE'S CASTLE
TOM O'BEDLAM
THE MAN IN THE MAZE
DOWNWARD TO THE EARTH
THE WORLD INSIDE
SHADRACH IN THE FURNACE
AT WINTER'S END
BORN WITH THE DEAD
NIGHTFALL (with Isaac Asimov)
THE FACE OF THE WATERS
THE UGLY LITTLE BOY (with Isaac Asimov)
KINGDOMS OF THE WALL

THE POSITRONIC MAN  (with Isaac Asimov)

HOT SKY AT MIDNIGHT

SORCERERS OF MAJIPOOR

The Longest Way Home

# Contents

# Publication History of Hawksbill Station:

The novella:  copyright 1967, 1995 by Agberg, Ltd.

First published in Galaxy Science Fiction, August 1967.

The novel: copyright 1968, 1996 by Agberg, Ltd.

First published by Doubleday Books.

Avon Books edition, March 1970.

Berkley Books edition, May, 1978.

Warner Books edition, August, 1986.

# Dedication

For Frederik Pohl. . . . it's about time.

Robert Silverberg

# Foreword

In some confusion I had given up the writing of science fiction in the winter of 1958-59, after four or five years of frenzied activity in which I had written enough of the stuff to fill three or four average careers. Still only in my mid-twenties, puzzled about my place in a genre that I loved deeply but seemed unable to serve well, I turned away and wandered for a few years in a morass of hackerei that still gives me the creeps when I look at the titles of the things I was writing then — "I Was Eaten by Monster Crabs," "World of Living Corpses," "The Syndicate Moves In," and much godawful more.

And then Frederik Pohl, who had become editor of the important s-f magazine Galaxy, teased me back into science fiction on a now-and-then basis by making me an offer I couldn't refuse, and I did a few short stories for him at a rate of about one every six months, and then a series of novelets that became the book To Open the Sky, and by then — it was now 1965 — I was hooked on writing s-f all over again. Only this time, because Pohl had given me the space to write the stories exactly as I felt they ought to be written, because I was no longer (as I had been doing from 1955 to 1958) tailoring my product to some editor's notion of what was acceptable, I was far more satisfied with what I was writing: at last, stories which I as a critical reader would have been interested in reading. And so began the second phase of my career, the so-called "new Silverberg" that elicited so much surprised comment in the mid-1960s. After the To Open the Sky stories came a novel for Doubleday, The Time Hoppers, which

I finished in March of 1966, and in mid-April I wrote to Pohl about another ambitious project that had grown out of my own deep interest in paleontology and my almost obsessive fascination with the idea of traveling in time. What I told him was: "I'm thinking in very science-fictional terms these days and I want to get these stories written while the fit is still on me. This one would be a novella — 15,000 words, 20,000, somewhere within that range. I have it roughed out, though not solidly enough for me to want to talk much about the plot, except to say that the story takes place in a camp for political prisoners on Earth approximately two and a half billion years ago. If you can find room for a Silverberg story of this length, I'd like to write it some time in the next month."

Fred gave me the go-ahead; I set to work immediately, and wrote the story in one white-hot week, 20,000 words, mailing it to him on May 5. By May 11 I had word of its acceptance. It was published in the August, 1967 issue of Galaxy and brought me one of the most cherishable reader comments I have ever received: the famed science-writer Willy Ley, encountering me at a New York literary party, praised at great length the accuracy and richness of texture of my portrait of life in the early Paleozoic. I am not exactly indifferent to most people's praise of my work, but, although I absorb it with pleasure, I tend to forget it quickly; hearing Willy tell me in rumbling Teutonic tones how well I had brought the era of trilobites to life for him is a memory that still glows brightly for me three and a half decades later.

The story also brought me my first Hugo and Nebula nominations, though competition for both awards was stiff that year and I finished as a runner-up. At that point in my career, though, simply getting on the final ballot was exciting.

Despite Willy Ley's warm praise, there was at least one inaccuracy in the story. It takes place in the late Cambrian period, which according to modern geological theory was about 550 million years ago. Yet in my original proposal for Fred Pohl I placed the scene "approximately two and a half billion years ago," and even in the published story I set the Cambrian two billion years in the past. That was not a case of ignorance, but of a writer's outsmarting himself, for what I was doing was implying a revision, after the development of time travel, of our entire geological time scale. But I found no convenient way of working into the story a statement to the effect that scientists had once believed the Cambrian to be 550 million years ago but now knew it to be two billion, and in the end I just used the greater time scale without explaining what I was up to, and this, of course, brought some critical comments from present-day geologists otherwise pleased with the work. So when the story was reprinted in the first of its many anthology appearances I cut the time span in half, putting the late Cambrian at one billion years ago — still a revisionist notion, but one less likely to draw attack. And I have kept it that way in all further printings of the story, as well as in the expansion to novel form that I carried out in the spring of 1967.

I think it would be best to talk about that expansion in an afterword, though, instead of discussing it here, because I might otherwise give away some aspects of the plot that I'd like to deal with in these comments. So: read the novella. Read the novel. I'll be back with some further remarks at the end of the book.

Robert Silverberg

## The Novella

Barrett was the uncrowned King of Hawksbill Station. He had been there the longest; he had suffered the most; he had the deepest inner resources of strength. Before his accident, he had been able to whip any man in the place. Now he was a cripple, but he still had that aura of power that gave him command. When there were problems at the Station, they were brought to Barrett. That was axiomatic. He was the king.

He ruled over quite a kingdom, too. In effect it was the whole world, pole to pole, meridian to meridian. For what it was worth. It wasn't worth very much.

Now it was raining again. Barrett shrugged himself to his feet in the quick, easy gesture that cost him an infinite amount of carefully concealed agony, and shuffled to the door of his hut. Rain made him impatient: the pounding of those great greasy drops against the corrugated tin roof was enough even to drive a Jim Barrett loony. He nudged the door open. Standing in the doorway, Barrett looked out over his kingdom.

Barren rock, nearly to the horizon. A shield of raw dolomite going on and on. Raindrops danced and bounced on that continental slab of rock. No trees. No grass. Behind Barrett's hut lay the sea, gray and vast. The sky was gray too, even when it wasn't raining.

He hobbled out into the rain. Manipulating his crutch was getting to be a simple matter for him now. He leaned comfortably, letting his crushed left foot dangle. A rockslide had pinned him last year during a trip to the edge of the Inland Sea. Back home, Barrett would have been fitted with prosthetics and that would have been the end of it: a new ankle, a new instep, refurbished ligaments and tendons. But home was a billion years away, and home there's no returning.

The rain hit him hard. Barrett was a big man, six and a half feet tall, with hooded dark eyes, a jutting nose, a chin that was a monarch among chins. He had weighed two hundred fifty pounds in his prime, in the good old agitating days when he had carried banners and pounded out manifestos. But now he was past sixty and beginning to shrink a little, the skin getting loose around the places where the mighty muscles used to be. It was hard to keep your weight in Hawksbill Station. The food was nutritious, but it lacked intensity. A man got to miss steak. Eating brachiopod stew and trilobite hash wasn't the same thing at all. Barrett was past all bitterness, though. That was another reason why the men regarded him as the leader. He didn't scowl. He didn't rant. He was resigned to his fate, tolerant of eternal exile, and so he could help the others get over that difficult, heart-clawing period of transition.

A figure arrived, jogging through the rain: Norton. The doctrinaire Khrushchevist with the Trotskyite leanings. A small, excitable man who frequently appointed himself messenger whenever there was news at the Station. He sprinted toward Barrett's hut, slipping and sliding over the naked rocks.

Barrett held up a meaty hand. "Whoa, Charley. Take it easy or you'll break your neck!"

Norton halted in front of the hut. The rain had pasted the widely spaced strands of his brown hair to his skull. His eyes had the fixed, glossy look of fanaticism—or perhaps just astigmatism. He gasped for breath and staggered into the hut, shaking himself like a wet puppy. He obviously had run all the way from the main building of the Station, three hundred yards away—a long dash over rock that slippery.

"Why are you standing around in the rain?" Norton asked.

"To get wet," said Barrett, following him inside. "What's the news?"

"The Hammer's glowing. We're getting company."

"How do you know it's a live shipment?"

"It's been glowing for half an hour. That means they're taking precautions. They're sending a new prisoner. Anyway, no supplies shipment is due."

Barrett nodded. "Okay. I'll come over. If it's a new man, we'll bunk him in with Latimer."

Norton managed a rasping laugh. "Maybe he's a materialist. Latimer will drive him crazy with all that mystic nonsense. We could put him with Altman instead."

"And he'll be raped in half an hour."

"Altman's off that kick now," said Norton. "He's trying to create a real woman, not looking for second-rate substitutes."

"Maybe our new man doesn't have any spare ribs."

"Very funny, Jim." Norton did not look amused. "You know what I want the new man to be? A conservative, that's what. A black-souled reactionary straight out of Adam Smith. God, that's what I want."

"Wouldn't you be happy with a fellow Bolshevik?"

"This place is full of Bolsheviks," said Norton. "Of all shades from pale pink to flagrant scarlet. Don't you think I'm sick of them? Sitting around fishing for trilobites and discussing the relative merits of

Kerensky and Malenkov? I need somebody to *talk* to, Jim. Somebody I can fight with."

"All right," Barrett said, slipping into his rain gear. "I'll see what I can do about hocusing a debating partner out of the Hammer for you. A rip-roaring Objectivist, okay?" He laughed. "You know something, maybe there's been a revolution Up Front since we got our last man? Maybe the left is in and the right is out, and they'll start shipping us nothing *but* reactionaries. How would you like that? Fifty or a hundred storm troopers, Charley? Plenty of material to debate economics with. And the place will fill up with more and more of them, until we're outnumbered, and then maybe they'll have a putsch and get rid of all the stinking leftists sent here by the old regime, and—"

Barrett stopped. Norton was staring at him in amazement, his faded eyes wide, his hand compulsively smoothing his thinning hair to hide his embarrassment. Barrett realized that he had just committed one of the most heinous crimes possible at Hawksbill Station: he had started to run off at the mouth. There hadn't been any call for his little outburst. What made it more troublesome was the fact that *he* was the one who had permitted himself such a luxury. He was supposed to be the strong one of this place, the stabilizer, the man of absolute integrity and principle and sanity on whom the others could lean. And suddenly he had lost control. It was a bad sign. His dead foot was throbbing again; possibly that was the reason.

In a tight voice he said, "Let's go. Maybe the new man is here already."

They stepped outside. The rain was beginning to let up; the storm was moving out to sea. In the east, over what would one day be the Atlantic, the sky was still clotted with gray mist, but to the west a different grayness was emerging, the shade of normal gray that meant dry weather. Before he had come out here, Barrett had expected to find the sky practically black, because there'd be fewer dust particles to bounce the light around and turn things blue. But the sky seemed to be a weary beige. So much for *a priori* theories.

Through the thinning rain they walked toward the main building. Norton accommodated himself to Barrett's limping pace, and Barrett, wielding his crutch furiously, did his damndest not to let his infirmity slow them up. He nearly lost his footing twice, and fought hard not to let Norton see.

Hawksbill Station spread out before them.

Hawksbill Times Two

It covered about five hundred acres. In the center of everything was the main building, an ample dome that contained most of their equipment and supplies. At widely paced intervals, rising from the rock shield like grotesque giant green mushrooms, were the plastic blisters of the individual dwellings. Some, like Barrett's, were shielded by tin sheeting salvaged from shipments from Up Front. Others stood unprotected, just as they had come from the mouth of the extruder.

The huts numbered about eighty. At that moment, there were 140 inmates in Hawksbill Station, pretty close to the all-time high. Up Front hadn't sent back any hut-building materials for a long time, and so all the newer arrivals had to double up with bunkmates. Barrett and all those whose exile had begun before 2014 had the privilege of private dwellings, if they wanted them. (Some did not wish to live alone; Barrett, to preserve his own authority, felt that he was required to.) As new exiles arrived, they bunked in with those who currently lived alone, in reverse order of seniority. Most of the 2015 exiles had been forced to take roommates now. Another dozen deportees and the 2014 group would be doubling up. Of course, there were deaths all up and down the line, and there were plenty who were eager to have company in their huts.

Barrett felt, though, that a man who has to be sentenced to life imprisonment ought to have the privilege of privacy if he desires it. One of his biggest problems here was keeping people from cracking up because there was too little privacy. Propinquity could be intolerable in a place like this.

Norton pointed toward the big shiny-skinned green dome of the main building.

"There's Altman going in now. And Rudiger. And Hutchett. Something's happening!"

Barrett stepped up his pace. Some of the men entering the building saw his bulky figure coming over the rise in the rock, and waved to him. Barrett lifted a massive hand in reply. He felt mounting excitement. It was a big event at the Station whenever a new man arrived. Nobody had come for six months, now. That was the longest gap he could remember. It had started to seem as though no one would ever come again.

That would be a catastrophe. New men were all that stood between the older inmates and insanity. New men brought news from the future, news from the world that was entirely left behind. They contributed new personalities to a group that always was in danger of going stale.

And, Barrett knew, some men—he was not one—lived in the deluded hope that the next arrival might just be a woman.

That was why they flocked to the main building when the Hammer began to glow. Barrett hobbled down the path. The rain died away just as he reached the entrance.

Within, sixty or seventy Station residents crowded the chamber of the Hammer— just about every man in the place who was able in body and mind, and still alert enough to show curiosity about a newcomer.

They shouted their greetings to Barrett. He nodded, smiled, deflected their questions with amiable gestures.

"Who's it going to be this time, Jim?"

"Maybe a girl, huh? Around nineteen years old, blonde, built like—"

"I hope he can play stochastic chess, anyway."

## Hawksbill Times Two

"Look at the glow! It's deepening!"

Barrett, like the others, stared at the Hammer. The complex, involuted collection of unfathomable instruments burned a bright cherry-red now, betokening the surge of who knew how many kilowatts being pumped in at the far end of the line. The glow had spread to the Anvil now, that broad aluminum bedplate on which all shipments from the future were dropped. In another moment—

"Condition Crimson!" somebody yelled. "Here he comes!"

## Two

A billion years up the time-line, power was flooding into the real Hammer of which this was only the partial replica. A man—or something else—stood in the center of the real Anvil, waiting for the Hawksbill Field to unfold him and kick him back to the early Paleozoic. The effect of time travel was very much like being hit with a gigantic hammer and driven clear through the walls of the continuum: hence the governing metaphors for the parts of the machine.

Setting up Hawksbill Station had been a long, slow job. The Hammer had knocked a pathway and had sent back the nucleus of the receiving station first. Since there was no receiving station on hand to receive the receiving station, a certain amount of waste had occurred. It wasn't necessary to have a

Hammer and Anvil on the receiving end, except as a fine control to prevent temporal spread; without the equipment, the field wandered a little, and it was possible to scatter consecutive shipments over a span of twenty or thirty years. There was plenty of such temporal garbage all around Hawksbill Station: stuff that had been intended for the original installation, but which because of tuning imprecisions in the pre-Hammer days had landed a couple of decades (and a couple of hundred miles) away from the intended site.

Despite such difficulties, they had finally sent through enough components to the master temporal site to allow for the construction of a receiving station. Then the first prisoners had gone through: technicians who knew how to put the Hammer and Anvil together. Of course, it was their privilege to refuse to cooperate.

But it was to their own advantage to assemble the receiving station, thus making it possible for them to be sure of getting further supplies from Up Front. They had done the job. After that, outfitting. Hawksbill Station had been easy.

Now the Hammer glowed, meaning that they had activated the Hawksbill Field on the sending end, somewhere up around 2028 or 2030 A.D. All the sending was done there. All the receiving was done here. It didn't work the other way. Nobody really knew why, although there was a lot of superficially profound talk about the rules of entropy.

There was a whining, hissing sound as the edges of the Hawksbill Field began to ionize the atmosphere in the room. Then came the expected thunderclap of implosion, caused by an imperfect overlapping of the quantity of air that was subtracted from this era and the quantity that was being thrust into it. And then abruptly, a man dropped out of the Hammer and lay stunned and limp, on the gleaming Anvil.

He looked young, which surprised Barrett considerably. He seemed to be well under thirty. Generally, only middle-aged men were sent to Hawksbill Station. Incorrigibles, who had to be separated from humanity for the general good. The youngest man in the place now had been close to forty when he arrived. The sight of this lean, clean-cut boy drew a hiss of anguish from a couple of the men in the room, and Barrett understood the constellation of emotions that pained them.

The new man sat up. He stirred like a child coming out of a long, deep sleep. He looked around. His face was very pale. His thin lips seemed bloodless. His blue eyes blinked rapidly. His jaws worked as though he wanted to say something, but could not find the words.

There were no physiological harmful effects to time travel, but it could be a rough jolt to the consciousness. The last moments before the Hammer descended were very much like the final moments beneath the guillotine, since exile to Hawksbill Station was tantamount to a sentence of death. The departing prisoner took his last look at the world of rocket transport and artificial organs, at the world in which he had lived and loved and agitated for a political cause, and then he was rammed into an inconceivably remote past on a one-way journey. It was a gloomy business, and it was not very surprising that the newcomers arrived in a state of emotional shock.

Barrett elbowed his way through the crowd. Automatically the others made way for him. He reached the lip of the Anvil and leaned over it, extending a hand to the new man. His broad smile was met by a look of blank bewilderment.

"I'm Jim Barrett. Welcome to Hawksbill Station. Here—get off that thing before a load of groceries lands on top of you." Wincing a little as he shifted his weight, Barrett pulled the new man down from the Anvil. It was altogether likely for the idiots Up Front to shoot another shipment along a minute after sending a man.

Barrett beckoned to Mel Rudiger, and the plump anarchist handed the new man an alcohol capsule. He took it and pressed it to his arm without a word. Charley Norton offered him a candy bar. The man shook it off. He looked groggy—a real case of temporal shock, Barrett thought, possibly the worst he had ever seen. The newcomer hadn't even spoken yet. Could the effect really be that extremes?

Barrett said, "We'll go to the infirmary and check you out. Then I'll assign you your quarters. There's time for you to find your way around and meet everybody later on. What's your name?"

"Hahn. Lew Hahn."

"I can't hear you."

"Hahn," the man repeated, still only barely audible.

"When are you from, Lew?"

"2029."

"You feel pretty sick?"

"I feel awful. I don't even believe this is happening to me. There's no such place as Hawksbill Station, is there?"

"I'm afraid there is," Barrett said. "At least, for most of us. A few of the boys think it's all an illusion induced by drugs.

But I have my doubts of that. If it's an illusion, it's damned good. Look."

He put one arm around Hahn's shoulders and guided him through the press of prisoners, out of the Hammer chamber and toward the nearby infirmary.

Although Hahn looked thin, even fragile, Barrett was surprised to feel the rippling muscles in those shoulders. He suspected that this man was a lot less helpless and ineffectual than he seemed to be right now. He *had* to be: he had earned banishment to Hawksbill Station.

They passed the open door of the building. "Look out there," Barrett commanded.

Hahn looked. He passed a hand across his eyes as though to clear away unseen cobwebs, and looked again.

"A Late Cambrian landscape," said Barrett quietly. "This view would be a geologist's dream, except that geologists don't tend to become political prisoners, it seems. Out in front of you is what they call Appalachia. It's a strip of rock a few hundred miles wide and a few thousand miles long, running from the Gulf of Mexico to Newfoundland. To the east we've got the Atlantic Ocean. A little way to the west we've got a thing called the Appalachian Geosyncline, which is a trough five hundred miles wide full of water. Somewhere about two thousand miles to the west there's another trough that they call the Cordilleran Geosyncline. It's full of water too, and at this particular stage of geological history the patch of land between the geosynclines is below sea level, so where Appalachia ends we've got the Inland Sea, currently, running way out to the west. On the far side of the Inland Sea is a narrow north-south land mass called

Cascadia that's going to be California and Oregon and Washington someday. Don't hold your breath till it happens. I hope you like seafood, Lew."

Hahn stared, and Barrett, standing beside him at the doorway, stared also. You never got used to the alienness of this place, not even after you had lived here twenty years, as Barrett had. It was Earth, and yet it was not really Earth at all, because it was somber and empty and unreal. The gray oceans swarmed with life, of course. But there was nothing on land except occasional patches of moss in the occasional patches of soil that had formed on the bare rock. Even a few cockroaches would be welcome; but insects, it seemed, were still a couple of geological periods in the future. To land dwellers, this was a dead world, a world unborn.

Shaking his head, Hahn moved away from the door. Barrett led him down the corridor and into the small, brightly lit room that served as the infirmary. Doc Quesada was waiting. Quesada wasn't really a doctor, but he had been a medical technician once, and that was good enough. He was a compact, swarthy man with a look of complete self-assurance. He hadn't lost too many patients, all things considered. Barrett had watched him removing appendixes with total aplomb. In his white smock, Quesada looked sufficiently medical to fit the role.

Barrett said, "Doc, this is Lew Hahn. He's in temporal shock. Fix him up."

Quesada nudged the newcomer onto a webfoam cradle and unzipped his blue jersey. Then he reached for his medical kit. Hawksbill Station was well equipped for most medical emergencies, now. The people Up Front had no wish to be inhumane, and they sent back all sorts of useful things, like anesthetics and surgical clamps and medicines and dermal probes. Barrett could remember a time at the beginning when there had been nothing much here but the empty huts, and a man who hurt himself was in real trouble.

"He's had a drink already," said Barrett.

"I see that," Quesada murmured. He scratched at his short-cropped, bristly mustache. The little diagnostat in the cradle had gone rapidly to work, flashing information about Hahn's blood pressure, potassium count, dilation index, and much else. Quesada seemed to comprehend the barrage of facts. After a moment he said to Hahn, "You aren't really sick, are you? Just shaken up a little. I don't blame you. Here—I'll give you a quick jolt to calm your nerves; and you'll be all right. As all right as any of us ever are."

He put a tube to Hahn's carotid and thumbed the snout. The subsonic whirred, and a tranquilizing compound slid into the man's bloodstream. Hahn shivered.

Quesada said, "Let him rest for five minutes. Then he'll be over the hump."

They left Hahn in his cradle and went out of the infirmary. In the hall, Barrett looked down at the little medic and said, "What's the report on Valdosto?"

Valdosto had gone into psychotic collapse several weeks before. Quesada was keeping him drugged and trying to bring him slowly back to the reality of Hawksbill Station. Shrugging, he replied, "The status is quo. I let him out from under the dream juice this morning and he was the same as he's been."

"You don't think he'll come out of it?"

"I doubt it. He's cracked for keeps. They could paste him together Up Front, but—"

"Yeah," Barrett said. If he could get Up Front at all, Valdosto wouldn't have cracked. "Keep him happy, then. If he can't be sane, he can at least be comfortable. What about Altman? Still got the shakes?"

"He's building a woman," Quesada said.

"That's what Charley Norton told me. What's he using? A rag, a bone—"

"I gave him some surplus chemicals. Chosen for their color, mainly. He's got some foul green copper compounds and a little bit of ethyl alcohol and six or seven other things, and he collected some soil and threw in a lot of dead shellfish, and he's sculpting it all into what he claims is female shape and waiting for lightning to strike it."

"In other words, he's gone crazy," Barrett said.

"I think that's a safe assumption. But he's not molesting his friends any more, anyway. You didn't think his homosexual phase would last much longer, as I recall."

"No, but I didn't think he'd go off the deep end. If a man needs sex and he can find some consenting playmates here, that's quite all right with me. But when he starts putting a woman together out of some dirt and rotten brachiopod meat it means we've lost him. It's too bad."

Quesada's dark eyes flickered. "We're all going to go that way sooner or later, Jim."

"I haven't. You haven't."

"Give us time. I've only been here eleven years.',"

"Altman's been here only eight. Valdosto even less."

"Some shells crack faster than others," said Quesada. "Here's our new friend."

Hahn had come out of the infirmary to join them. He still looked pale, but the fright was gone from his eyes. He was beginning to adjust to the unthinkable.

He said, "I couldn't help overhearing your conversation. Is there a lot of mental illness here?"

"Some of the men haven't been able to find anything meaningful to do here," Barrett said. "It eats them away. Quesada here has his medical work. I've got administrative duties. A couple of the fellows are studying the sea life. We've got a newspaper to keep some busy. But there are always those who just let themselves slide into despair, and they crack up. I'd say we have thirty or forty certifiable maniacs here at the moment, out of 140 residents."

"That's not so bad," Hahn said. "Considering the inherent instability of the men who get sent here, and the unusual conditions of life here."

Barrett laughed. "Hey, you're suddenly pretty articulate, aren't you? What was in the stuff Doc Quesada jolted you with?"

"I didn't mean to sound superior," Hahn said quickly. "Maybe that came out a little too smug. I mean—"

"Forget it. What did you do Up Front, anyway?"

"I was an economist."

"Just what we need," said Quesada. "He can help us solve our balance-of-payments problem."

Barrett said, "If you were an economist, you'll have plenty to discuss here. This place is full of economic theorists who'll want to bounce their ideas off you. Some of them are almost sane, too. Come with me and I'll show you where you're going to stay."

# Three

The path from the main building to the hut of Donald Latimer was mainly downhill, for which Barrett was grateful even though he knew that he'd have to negotiate the uphill return in a little while. Latimer's hut was on the eastern side of the Station, looking out over the ocean. They walked slowly toward it. Hahn was solicitous of Barrett's game leg, and Barrett was irritated by the exaggerated care the younger man took to keep pace with him.

He was puzzled by this Hahn. The man was full of seeming contradictions—showing up here with the worst case of arrival shock Barrett had ever seen, then snapping out of it with remarkable quickness; looking frail and shy, but hiding solid muscles inside his jersey; giving an outer appearance of incompetence, but speaking with calm control. Barrett wondered what this young man had done to earn him the trip to Hawksbill Station, but there was time for such inquiries later. All the time in the world.

Hahn said, "Is everything like this? Just rock and ocean?"

"That's all. Land life hasn't evolved yet. Everything's wonderfully simple, isn't it? No clutter. No urban sprawl. There's some moss moving onto land, but not much."

"And in the sea? Swimming dinosaurs?"

Barrett shook his head. "There won't be any vertebrates for millions of years. We don't even have fish yet, let alone reptiles out there. All we can offer is that which creepeth. Some shellfish, some big fellows that look like squids, and trilobites. Seven hundred billion different species of trilobites. We've got a man named Rudiger—he's the one who gave you the drink—who's making a collection of them. He's writing the world's definitive text on trilobites."

"But nobody will ever read it in—in the future."

"Up Front, we say."

"Up Front."

"That's the pity of it," said Barrett. "We told Rudiger to inscribe his book on imperishable plates of gold and hope that it's found by paleontologists. But he says the odds are against it. A billion years of geology will chew his plates to hell before they can be found."

Hahn sniffed. "Why does the air smell so strange?"

"It's a different mix," Barrett said. "We've analyzed it. More nitrogen, a little less oxygen, hardly any $CO_2$ at all. But that isn't really why it smells odd to you. The thing is, it's pure air, unpolluted by the exhalations of life. Nobody's been respiring into it but us lads, and there aren't enough of us to matter."

Smiling, Hahn said, "I feel a little cheated that it's so empty. I expected lush jungles of weird plants, and pterodactyls swooping through the air, and maybe a tyrannosaur crashing into a fence around the Station."

"No jungles. No pterodactyls. No tyrannosaurs. No fences. You didn't do your homework."

"Sorry."

"This is the Late Cambrian. Sea life exclusively."

"It was very kind of them to pick such a peaceful era as the dumping ground for political prisoners," Hahn said. "I was afraid it would be all teeth and claws."

"Kind, hell! They were looking for an era where we couldn't do any harm. That meant tossing us back before the evolution of mammals, just in case we'd accidentally get hold of the ancestor of all humanity and snuff him out. And while they were at it, they decided to stash us so far in the past that we'd be beyond all land life, on the theory that maybe even if we slaughtered a baby dinosaur it might affect the entire course of the future."

"They don't mind if we catch a few trilobites?"

"Evidently they think it's safe," Barrett said. "It looks as though they were right. Hawksbill Station has been here for twenty-five years, and it doesn't seem as though we've tampered with future history in any measurable way. Of course, they're careful not to send us any women."

"Why is that?"

"So we don't start reproducing and perpetuating ourselves. Wouldn't that mess up the time-lines? A successful human outpost in One Billion B.C., that's had all that time to evolve and mutate and grow? By the time the twenty-first century came around, our descendants would be in charge and the other kind of human being would probably be in penal servitude, and there'd be more paradoxes created than you could shake a trilobite at. So they don't send the women here. There's a prison camp for women, too, but it's a few hundred million years up the time line in the Late Silurian, and never the twain shall meet. That's why Ned Altman's trying to build a woman out of dust and garbage."

"God made Adam out of less."

"Altman isn't God," Barrett said. "That's the root of his whole problem. Look, here's the hut where you're going to stay. I'm rooming you with Don Latimer. He's a very sensitive, interesting, pleasant person. He used to be a physicist before he got into politics, and he's been here about a dozen years, and I might as well warn you that he's developed a strong and somewhat cockeyed mystic streak lately. The fellow he was rooming with killed himself last year, and since then he's been trying to find some way out of here through extrasensory powers."

"Is he serious?"

"I'm afraid he is. And we try to take him seriously. We all humor each other at Hawksbill Station; it's the only way we avoid a mass psychosis. Latimer will probably try to get you to collaborate with him on his project. If you don't like living with him, I can arrange a transfer for you. But I want to see how he reacts to someone new at the Station. I'd like you to give him a chance."

"Maybe I'll even help him find his psionic gateway."

"If you do, take me along," said Barrett. They both laughed. Then he rapped at Latimer's door. There was no answer, and after a moment Barrett pushed the door open. Hawksbill Station had no locks.

Latimer sat in the middle of the bare rock floor, cross-legged, meditating. He was a slender, gentle-faced man just beginning to look old. Right now he seemed a million miles away, ignoring them completely. Hahn shrugged. Barrett put a finger to his lips. They waited in silence for a few minutes, and then Latimer showed signs of coming up from his trance.

He got to his feet in a single flowing motion, without using his hands. In a low, courteous voice he said to Hahn, "Have you just arrived?"

"Within the last hour. I'm Lew Hahn."

"Donald Latimer. I regret that I have to make your acquaintance in these surroundings. But maybe we won't have to tolerate this illegal imprisonment much longer."

Barrett said, "Don, Lew is going to bunk with you. I think you'll get along well. He was an economist in 2029 until they gave him the Hammer."

"Where did you live?" Latimer asked, animation coming into his eyes.

"San Francisco."

The glow faded. Latimer said, "Were you ever in Toronto? I'm from there. I had a daughter—she'd be twenty-three now, Nella Latimer—I wondered if you knew her."

"No. I'm sorry."

"It wasn't very likely. But I'd love to know what kind of a woman she became. She was a little girl when I last saw her. Now I guess she's married. Or perhaps they've sent her to the other Station. Nella

Latimer—you're sure you didn't know her?"

Barrett left them together. It looked as though they'd get along. He told Latimer to bring Hahn up to the main building at dinner for introductions, and went out. A chilly drizzle had begun again. Barrett made his way slowly, painfully up the hill. It had been sad to see the light flicker from Latimer's eyes when Hahn said he didn't know his daughter. Most of the time, men at Hawksbill Station tried not to speak about their families, preferring to keep those tormenting memories well repressed. But the arrival of newcomers generally stirred old ties. There was never any news of relatives, and no way to obtain any, because it was impossible for the Station to communicate with anyone Up Front. No way to ask for the photo of a loved one, no way to request specific medicines, no way to obtain a certain book or a coveted tape. In a mindless, impersonal way, Up Front sent periodic shipments to the Station of things thought useful—reading matter, medical supplies, technical equipment, food. Occasionally they were startling in their generosity, as when they sent a case of Burgundy, or a box of sensory spools, or a recharger for the power pack. Such gifts usually meant a brief thaw in the world situation, which customarily produced a short-lived desire to be kind to the boys in Hawksbill Station. But they had a policy about sending information about relatives. Or about contemporary newspapers. Fine wine, yes; a tridim of a daughter who would never be seen again, no. For all Up Front knew, there was no one alive in Hawksbill Station. A plague could have killed everyone off ten years ago, but there was no way of telling. That was why the shipments still came back. The government whirred and clicked with predictable continuity. The government, whatever else it might be, was not malicious. There were other kinds of totalitarianism beside bloody repressive tyranny. Pausing at the top of the hill, Barrett caught his breath. Naturally, the alien air no longer smelled strange to him. He filled his lungs with it. Once again the rain ceased. Through the grayness came the sunshine, making the naked rocks sparkle. Barrett closed his eyes a moment and leaned on his crutch, and saw as though on an inner screen the creatures with many legs climbing up out of the sea, and the mossy carpets spreading, and the flowerless plants uncoiling and spreading their scaly branches, and the dull hides of eerie amphibians glistening on the shores, and the tropic heat of the coal-forming epoch descending like a glove over the world.

All that lay far in the future. Dinosaurs. Little chittering mammals. Pithecanthropus in the forests of Java. Sargon and Hannibal and Attila, and Orville Wright, and Thomas Edison, and Edmond Hawksbill. And finally a benign government that would find the thoughts of some men so intolerable that the only safe place to which they could be banished was a rock at the beginning of time. The government was too civilized to put men to death for subversive activities, and too cowardly to let them remain alive. The compromise was the living death of Hawksbill Station. A billion years of impassable time was suitable insulation even for the most nihilistic idea. Grimacing a little, Barrett struggled the rest of the way back toward his hut. He had long since come to accept his exile, but accepting his ruined foot was another matter entirely. The idle wish to find a way to regain the freedom of his own time no longer possessed him; but he wished with all his soul that the blank-faced administrators Up Front would send back a kit that would allow him to rebuild his foot.

He entered his but and flung his crutch aside, sinking down instantly on his cot. There had been no cots when he had come to Hawksbill Station. He had come here in the fourth year of the Station, when there were only a dozen buildings and little in the way of creature comforts. It had been a miserable place then, but the steady accretion of shipments from Up Front had made it relatively tolerable. Of the fifty or so prisoners who had preceded Barrett to Hawksbill, none remained alive. He had held highest seniority for almost ten years. Time moved here at a one-to-one correlation with time Up Front; the

Hammer was locked on this point of time, so that Hahn, arriving here today more than twenty years after Barrett, had departed from a year Up Front more than twenty years after the time of Barrett's expulsion. Barrett had not had the heart to begin pumping Hahn for news of 2029 so soon. He would learn all he needed to know, and small cheer it would be, anyway.

Barrett reached for a book. But the fatigue of hobbling around the Station had taken more out of him than he realized. He looked at the page for a moment. Then he put it away, and closed his eyes and dozed.

# Four

That evening, as every evening, the men of Hawksbill Station gathered in the main building for dinner and recreation. It was not mandatory, and some men chose to eat alone. But tonight nearly everyone who was in full possession of his faculties was there, because this was one of the infrequent occasions when a newcomer had arrived to be questioned about the world of men.

Hahn looked uneasy about his sudden notoriety. He seemed to be basically shy, unwilling to accept all the attention now being thrust upon him. There he sat in the middle of the group, while men twenty and thirty years his senior crowded in on him with their questions, and it was obvious that he wasn't enjoying the session.

## Hawksbill Times Two

Sitting to one side, Barrett took little part in the discussion. His curiosity about Up Front's ideological shifts had ebbed a long time ago. It was hard for him to realize that he had once been so passionately concerned about concepts like syndicalism and the dictatorship of the proletariat and the guaranteed annual wage that he had been willing to risk imprisonment over them. His concern for humanity had not waned, merely the degree of his involvement in the twenty-first century's political problems. After twenty years at Hawksbill Station, Up Front had become unreal to Jim Barrett, and his energies centered around the crises and challenges of what he had come to think of as "his own" time—the late Cambrian.

So he listened, but more with an ear for what the talk revealed about Lew Hahn than for what it revealed about current events Up Front. And what it revealed about Lew Hahn was mainly a matter of what was not revealed.

Hahn didn't say much. He seemed to be feinting and evading.

Charley Norton wanted to know, "Is there any sign of a weakening of the phony conservatism yet? I mean, they've been promising the end of big government for thirty years, and it gets bigger all the time."

Hahn moved restlessly in his chair. "They still promise. As soon as conditions become stabilized——"

"Which is when?"

"I don't know. I suppose they're just making words."

"What about the Martian Commune?" demanded Sid Hutchett. "Have they been infiltrating agents onto Earth?"

"I couldn't really say."

"How about the Gross Global Product?" Mel Rudiger wanted to know. "What's its curve? Still holding level, or has it started to drop?"

Hahn tugged at his ear. "I think it's slowly edging down."

"Where does the index stand?" Rudiger asked. "The last figures we had, for '25, it was at 909. But in four years—"

"It might be something like 875 now," said Hahn. It struck Barrett as a little odd that an economist would be so hazy about the basic economic statistic. Of course, he didn't know how long Hahn had been imprisoned before getting the Hammer. Maybe he simply wasn't up on recent figures. Barrett held his peace.

Charley Norton wanted to find out some things about the legal rights of citizens. Hahn couldn't tell him. Rudiger asked about the impact of weather control—

whether the supposedly conservative government of liberators was still ramming programmed weather down the mouths of the citizens—and Hahn wasn't sure. Hahn couldn't rightly say much about the functions of the judiciary, whether it had recovered any of the power stripped from it by the Enabling Act of '18. He didn't have any comments to offer on the tricky subject of population control. In fact, his performance was striking for its lack of hard information.

"He isn't saying much at all," Charley Norton grumbled to the silent Barrett. "He's putting up a smokescreen. But either he's not telling what he knows, or he doesn't know."

"Maybe he's not very bright," Barrett suggested. "What did he do to get here? He must have had some kind of deep commitment. But it doesn't show, Jim!

He's an intelligent kid, but he doesn't seem plugged in to anything that ever mattered to any of us."

Doc Quesada offered a thought. "Suppose he isn't political at all. Suppose they're sending a different kind of prisoner back here now. Axe murderers, or something. A quiet kid who very quietly chopped up sixteen people one Sunday morning. Naturally he isn't interested in politics."

Barrett shook his head. "I doubt that. I think he's just clamming up because he's shy or ill at ease. It's his first night here, remember. He's just been kicked out of his own world and there's no going back. He may have left a wife and baby behind, you know. He may simply not give a damn tonight about sitting up there and spouting the latest word on abstract philosophical theory, when all he wants to do is go off and cry his eyes out. I say we ought to leave him alone."

Quesada and Norton looked convinced. They shook their heads in agreement; but Barrett didn't voice his opinion to the room in general. He let the quizzing of Hahn continue until it petered out of its own accord. The men began to drift away. A couple of them went in back to convert Hahn's vague generalities into the lead story for the next handwritten edition of the Hawksbill Station *Times*. Rudiger stood on a table and shouted out that he was going night-fishing, and four men asked to join him. Charley Norton sought out his usual debating partner, the nihilist Ken Belardi, and reopened, like a festering wound, their discussion of planning versus chaos, which bored them both to the point of screaming. The nightly games of stochastic chess began. The loners who had made rare visits to the main building simply to see the new man went back to their huts to do whatever it was they did in them alone each night.

Hahn stood apart, fidgeting and uncertain.

Barrett went up to him. "I guess you didn't really want to be quizzed tonight," he said.

"I'm sorry I couldn't have been more informative. I've been out of circulation a while, you see."

'But you were politically active, weren't you?"

"Oh, yes," Hahn said. "Of course." He flicked his tongue over his lips. "What's supposed to happen now?"

"Nothing in particular. We don't have organized activities here. Doc and I are going out on sick call. Care to join us?"

"What does it involve?" asked Hahn.

"Visiting some of the worst cases. It can be grim, but you'll get a panoramic view of Hawksbill Station in a hurry."

"I'd like to go."

Barrett gestured to Quesada and the three of them left the building. This was a nightly ritual for Barrett, difficult as it was since he had hurt his foot. Before turning in, he visited the goofy ones and the psycho ones and the catatonic ones, tucked them in, wished them a good night and a healed mind in the morning. Someone had to show them that he cared. Barrett did.

Outside, Hahn peered up at the moon. It was nearly full tonight, shining like a burnished coin, its face a pale salmon color and hardly pockmarked at all.

"It looks so different here," Hahn said. "The craters—where are the craters?"

"Most of them haven't been formed yet," said Barrett. "A billion years is a long time even for the moon. Most of its upheavals are still ahead. We think it may still have an atmosphere, too. That's why it looks pink to us. Of course, Up Front hasn't bothered to send us much in the way of astronomical equipment. We can only guess."

Hahn started to say something. He cut himself off after one blurted syllable.

Quesada said, "Don't hold it back. What were you about to suggest?"

Hahn laughed in self-mockery. "That you ought to fly up there and take a look. It struck me as odd that you'd spend all these years here theorizing about whether the moon's got an atmosphere, and wouldn't ever once go up to look. But I forgot."

"It would be useful if we got a commute ship from Up Front," Barrett said. "But it hasn't occurred to them. All we can do is look. The moon's a popular place in '29, is it?"

"The biggest resort in the System," said Halm. "I was there on my honeymoon. Leah and I—"

He stopped again.

Barrett said hurriedly. "This is Bruce Valdosto's hut. He cracked up a few weeks ago. When we go in, stand behind us so he doesn't see you. He might be violent with a stranger. He's unpredictable."

Valdosto was a husky man in his late forties, with swarthy skin, coarse curling black hair, and the broadest shoulders any man had ever had. Sitting down, he looked even burlier than Jim Barrett, which was saying a great deal. But Valdosto had short, stumpy legs, the legs of a man of ordinary stature tacked to the trunk of a giant, which spoiled the effect completely. In his years Up Front he had totally refused any prosthesis. He believed in living with deformities.

Right now he was strapped into a webfoam cradle. His domed forehead was flecked with beads of sweat, his eyes were glittering beadily in the darkness. He was a very sick man. Once he had been clear-minded enough to throw a sleet-bomb into a meeting of the Council of Syndics, giving a dozen of them a bad case of gamma poisoning, but now he scarcely knew up from down, right from left.

Barrett leaned over him and said, "How are you, Bruce?"

"Who's that?"

"Jim. It's a beautiful night, Bruce. How'd you like to come outside and get some fresh air? The moon's almost full."

"I've got to rest. The committee meeting tomorrow—"

"It's been postponed."

"But how can it? The Revolution—"

"That's been postponed too. Indefinitely."

"Are they disbanding the cells?" Valdosto asked harshly.

"We don't know yet. We're waiting for orders. Come outside, Bruce. The air will do you good."

Muttering, Valdosto let himself be unlaced. Quesada and Barrett pulled him to his feet and propelled him through the door of the hut. Barrett caught sight of Hahn in the shadows, his face somber with shock. They stood together outside the hut. Barrett pointed to the moon. "It's got such a lovely color here. Not like the dead thing Up Front. And look, look down there, Bruce. The sea breaking on the rocky shore. Rudiger's out fishing. I can see his boat by moonlight."

"Striped bass," said Valdosto. "Sunnies. Maybe he'll catch some sunnies."

"There aren't any sunnies here. They haven't evolved yet." Barrett fished in his pocket and drew out something ridged and glossy, about two inches long. It was the exoskeleton of a small trilobite. He offered it to Valdosto, who shook his head.

"Don't give me that cockeyed crab."

"It's a trilobite, Bruce. It's extinct, but so are we. We're a billion years in our own past."

"You must be crazy," Valdosto said in a calm, low voice that belied his wild-eyed appearance. He took the trilobite from Barrett and hurled it against the rocks. "Cockeyed crab," he muttered.

Quesada shook his head sadly. He and Barrett led the sick man into the hut again. Valdosto did not protest as the medic gave him the sedative. His weary mind, rebelling entirely against the monstrous concept that he had been exiled to the inconceivably remote past, welcomed sleep.

When they went out Barrett saw Hahn holding the trilobite on his palm and staring at it in wonder. Hahn offered it to him, but Barrett brushed it away.

"Keep it if you like," he said. "There are more where I got that one."

They went on. They found Ned Altman beside his hut, crouching on his knees and patting his hands over the crude, lopsided form of what, from its exaggerated breasts and hips, appeared to be the image of a woman. He stood up when they appeared. Altman was a neat little man with yellow hair and nearly invisible white eyebrows. Unlike anyone else in the Station, he had actually been a government man once, fifteen years ago, before seeing through the myth of syndicalist capitalism and joining one of the underground factions. Eight years at Hawksbill Station had done things to him.

Altman pointed to his golem and said, "I hoped there'd be lightning in the rain today. That'll do it, you know. But there isn't much lightning this time of year. She'll get up alive, and then I'll need you, Doc, to give her shots and trim away some of the rough places."

Quesada forced a smile. "I'll be glad to do it, Ned. But you know the terms."

"Sure. When I'm through with her, you get her. You think I'm a goddamn monopolist? Ill share her. There'll be a waiting list. Just so you don't forget who made her, though. She'll remain mine, whenever I need her." He noticed Hahn. "Who are you?"

"He's new," Barrett said. "Lew Hahn. He came this afternoon."

"Ned Altman," said Altman with a courtly bow. "Formerly in government service. You're pretty young, aren't you? How's your sex orientation? Hetero?"

Hahn winced. "I'm afraid so."

"It's okay. I wouldn't touch you. I've got a project going here. But I just want you to know, I'll put you on my list. You're young and you've probably got stronger needs than some of us. I won't forget about you, even though you're new here."

Quesada coughed. "You ought to get some rest now, Ned. Maybe there'll be lightning tomorrow." Altman did not resist. The doctor took him inside and put him to bed while Hahn and Barrett surveyed the man's handiwork. Hahn pointed toward the figure's middle.

"He's left out something essential," he said. "If he's planning to make love to this girl after he's finished creating her, he'd better—"

"It was there yesterday," said Barrett. "He must be changing orientation again." Quesada emerged from the hut. They went on, down the rocky path.

Barrett did not make the complete circuit that night. Ordinarily, he would have gone all the way down to Latimer's hut overlooking the sea, for Latimer was on his list of sick ones. But Barrett had visited Latimer once that day, and he didn't think his aching good leg was up to another hike that far. So after he and Quesada and Hahn had been to all of the easily accessible huts, and visited the man who prayed for alien beings to rescue him and the man who was trying to break into a parallel universe where everything was as it ought to be in the world and the man who lay on his cot sobbing for all his wakeful hours, Barrett said good night to his companions and allowed Quesada to escort Hahn back to his hut without him.

After observing Hahn for half a day, Barrett realized he did not know much more about him than when he had first dropped onto the Anvil. That was odd. But maybe Hahn would open up a little more after he'd been here a while. Barrett stared up at the salmon moon, and reached into his pocket to finger the little trilobite before he remembered that he had given it to Hahn. He shuffled into his hut. He wondered how long ago Hahn had taken that lunar honeymoon trip.

# Five

udiger's catch was spread out in front of the main building the next morning when Barrett came up for breakfast. He had had a good night's fishing, obviously. He usually did. Rudiger went out three or four nights a week, in the little dinghy that he had cobbled together a few years ago from salvaged materials, and he took with him a team of friends whom he had trained in the deft use of the trawling nets.

It was an irony that Rudiger, the anarchist, the man who believed in individualism and the abolition of all political institutions, should be so good at leading a team of fishermen: Rudiger didn't care for teamwork in the abstract. But it was hard to manipulate the nets alone, he had discovered. Hawksbill Station had many little ironies of that sort. Political theorists tend to swallow their theories when forced back on pragmatic measures of survival.

The prize of the catch was a cephalopod about a dozen feet long—a rigid conical tube out of which some limp squidlike tentacles dangled. Plenty of meat on that one, Barrett thought. Dozens of trilobites were arrayed around it, ranging in size from the inch-long kind to the three-footers with their baroquely involuted exoskeletons. Rudiger fished both for food and for science; evidently these trilobites were discards, species that he already had studied, or he wouldn't have left them here to go into the food hoppers. His hut was stacked ceiling-high with trilobites. It kept him sane to collect and analyze them, and no one begrudged him his hobby.

Near the heap of trilobites were some clusters of hinged brachiopods, looking like scallops that had gone awry, and a pile of snails. The warm, shallow waters just off the coastal shelf teemed with life, in striking contrast to the barren land. Rudiger had also brought in a mound of shiny black seaweed. Barrett hoped someone would gather all this stuff up and get it into their heat-sink cooler before it spoiled. The bacteria of decay worked a lot slower here than they did Up Front, but a few hours in the mild air would do Rudiger's haul no good.

Today Barrett planned to recruit some men for the annual Inland Sea expedition. Traditionally, he led that trek himself, but his injury made it impossible for him even to consider going any more. Each year, a dozen or so able-bodied men went out on a wide-ranging reconnaissance that took them in a big circle, looping northwestward until they reached the sea, then coming around to the south and back to the Station. One purpose of the trip was to gather any temporal garbage that might have materialized in the vicinity of the Station during the past year. There was no way of knowing how wide a margin of error had been allowed during the early attempts to set up the Station, and the scattershot technique of hurling material into the past had been pretty unreliable. New stuff was turning up all the time that had been aimed for Minus One Billion, Two Thousand Oh Five A.D., but which didn't get there until a few decades later. Hawksbill Station needed all the spare equipment it could get, and Barrett didn't miss a chance to round up any of the debris.

There was another reason for the Inland Sea expeditions, though. They served as a focus for the year, an annual ritual, something to peg a custom to. It was a rite of spring here. The dozen strongest men, going on foot to the distant rock-rimmed shores of the tepid sea that drowned the middle of North America, were performing the closest thing Hawksbill Station had to a religious function, although they did nothing more mystical when they reached the Inland Sea than to net a few trilobites and eat them. The trip meant more to Barrett himself than he had even suspected, also. He realized that now, when he was unable to go. He had led every such expedition for twenty years.

But last year he had gone scrabbling over boulders loosened by the tireless action of the waves, venturing into risky territory for no rational reason that he could name, and his aging muscles had betrayed him. Often at night he woke sweating to escape from the dream in which he relived that ugly moment: slipping and sliding, clawing at the rocks, a mass of stone dislodged from somewhere and crashing down with improbably agonizing impact on his foot, pinning him, crushing him. He could not forget the sound of grinding bones. Nor was he likely to lose the memory of the homeward march, across hundreds of miles of bare rock, his bulky body slung between the bowed forms of his companions. He thought he would lose the foot, but Quesada had spared him from the amputation. He simply could not touch the foot to the ground and put weight on it now, or ever again. It might have been simpler to have the dead appendage sliced off. Quesada vetoed that, though. "Who knows," he had said, "some day they might send us a transplant kit. I can't rebuild a leg that's been amputated." So Barrett had kept his crushed foot. But he had never been quite the same since, and now someone else would have to lead the march.

Who would it be, he asked himself?

Quesada was the likeliest. Next to Barrett, he was the strongest man here, in all the ways that it was important to be strong. But Quesada couldn't be spared at the Station. It might be handy to have a medic along on the trip, but it was vital to have one here. After some reflection Barren put down Charley Norton as the leader. He added Ken Belardi—someone for Norton to talk to. Rudiger? A tower of strength last year after Barrett had been injured; Barrett didn't particularly want to let Rudiger leave the Station so long; he needed able men for the expedition, true, but he didn't want to strip the home base down to invalids, crackpots, and psychotics. Rudiger stayed. Two of his fellow fishermen went on the list. So did Sid Hutchett and Arny Jean-Claude.

Barrett thought about putting Don Latimer in the group. Latimer was coming to be something of a borderline mental case, but he was rational enough except when he lapsed into his psionic meditations, and he'd pull his own weight on the expedition. On the other hand, Latimer was Lew Hahn's roommate, and Barrett wanted Latimer around to observe Hahn at close range. He toyed with the idea of sending both of them out, but nixed it. Hahn was still an unknown quantity. It was too risky to let him go with the Inland Sea party this year. Probably he'd be in next spring's group, though.

Finally Barrett had his dozen men chosen. He chalked their names on the slate in front of the mess hall, and found Charley

Norton at breakfast to tell him he was in charge.

It felt strange to know that he'd have to stay home while the others went. It was an admission that he was beginning to abdicate after running this place so long. A crippled old man was what he was, whether he liked to admit it to himself or not, and that was something he'd have to come to terms with soon.

In the afternoon, the men of the Inland Sea expedition gathered to select their gear and plan their route. Barrett kept away from the meeting. This was Charley Norton's show, now. He'd made eight or ten trips, and he knew what to do. Barrett didn't want to interfere.

But some masochistic compulsion in him drove him to take a trek of his own. If he couldn't see the western waters this year, the least he could do was pay a visit to the

Atlantic, in his own back yard. Barrett stopped off in the infirmary and, finding Quesada elsewhere, helped himself to a tube of neural depressant. He scrambled along the eastern trail until he was a few hundred yards from the main building, dropped his trousers, and quickly gave each thigh a jolt of the drug, first the good leg, then the gimpy one. That would numb the muscles just enough so that he'd be able to take an extended hike without feeling the fire of fatigue in his protesting joints. He'd pay for it, he knew, eight ours from now, when the depressant wore off and the full impact of his exertion hit him like a million daggers. But he was willing to accept that price.

The road to the sea was a long, lonely one. Hawksbill Station was perched on the eastern rim of Appalachia, more than eight hundred feet above sea level. During the first half dozen years, the men of the Station had reached the ocean by a suicidal route across sheer rock faces, but Barrett had incited a ten-year project to carve a path. Now wide steps descended to the Atlantic. Chopping them out of the rock had kept a lot of men busy for a long time, too busy to worry or to slip into insanity. Barrett regretted that he couldn't conceive some comparable works project to occupy them nowadays.

The steps formed a succession of shallow platforms that switch backed to the edge of the water. Even for a healthy man it was a strenuous walk. For Barrett in his present condition it was an ordeal. It took him two hours to descend a distance that normally could be traversed in a quarter of that time. When he reached the bottom, he sank down exhaustedly on a flat rock licked by the waves, and dropped his crutch. The fingers of his left hand were cramped and gnarled from gripping the crutch, and his entire body was bathed in sweat.

The water looked gray and somehow oily. Barrett could not explain the prevailing colorlessness of the Late Cambrian world, with its somber sky and somber land and somber sea, but his heart quietly ached for a glimpse of green vegetation again. He missed chlorophyll. The dark wavelets lapped against his rock, pushing a mass of floating black seaweed back and forth. The sea stretched to infinity. He didn't have the faintest idea how much of Europe, if any, was above water in this epoch. At the best of times most of the planet was submerged; here, only a few hundred million years after the white-hot rocks of the land had pushed into view, it was likely that all that was above water on Earth was a strip of territory here and there. Had the Himalayas been born yet? The Rockies? The Andes? He knew the approximate outlines of Late Cambrian North America, but the rest was a mystery. Blanks in knowledge were not easy to fill when the only link with Up Front was by one-way transport; Hawksbill Station had to rely on the random assortment of reading matter that came back in time, and it was furiously frustrating to lack information that any college geology text could supply.

As he watched, a big trilobite unexpectedly came scuttering up out of the water. It was the spike-tailed kind, about a yard long, with an eggplant-purple shell and a bristling arrangement of slender spines along the margins. There seemed to be a lot of legs underneath. The trilobite crawled up on the shore—no sand, no beach, just a shelf of rock and advanced until it was eight or ten feet from the waves.

## Hawksbill Times Two

*Good for you*, Barrett thought. *Maybe you're the first one who ever came out on land to see what it was like. The pioneer. The trailblazer.*

It occurred to him that this adventurous trilobite might well be the ancestor of all the land-dwelling creatures of the eons to come. It was biological nonsense, but Barrett's weary mind conjured a picture of an evolutionary procession, with fish and amphibians and reptiles and mammals and man all stemming in unbroken sequence from this grotesque armored thing that moved in uncertain circles near his feet.

And if I were to step on you, he thought?

A quick motion—the sound of crunching chitin—the wild scrabbling of a host of little legs—

And the whole chain of life snapped in its first link. Evolution undone. No land creatures ever developed. With the descent of that heavy foot all the future would change, and there would never have been any Hawksbill Station, no human race, no James Edward Barrett. In an instant he would have both revenge on those who had condemned him to live out his days in this place, and release from his sentence.

He did nothing. The trilobite completed its slow perambulation of the shoreline rocks and scuttered back into the sea unharmed.

The soft voice of Don Latimer said, "I saw you sitting down here, Jim. Do you mind if I join you?"

Barrett swung around, momentarily surprised. Latimer had come down from his hilltop hut so quietly that Barrett hadn't heard a thing. He recovered and grinned and beckoned Latimer to an adjoining rock. "You fishing?" Latimer asked.

"Just sitting. An old man sunning himself."

Hawksbill Times Two

You took a hike like that just to sun yourself?, Latimer laughed. "Come off it. You're trying to get away from it all, and you probably wish I hadn't disturbed you."

"That's not so. Stay here. How's your new roommate getting along?"

"It's been strange," said Latimer. "That's one reason I came down here to talk to you." He leaned forward and peered searchingly into Barren's eyes. "Jim, tell me: do you think I'm a madman?"

"Why should I?"

"The esping business. My attempt to break through to another realm of consciousness. I know you're tough-minded and skeptical. You probably think it's all a lot of nonsense."

Barrett shrugged and said, "If you want the blunt truth, I do. I don't have the remotest belief that you're going to get us anywhere, Don. I think it's a complete waste of time and energy for you to sit there for hours harnessing your psionic powers, or whatever it is you do. But no, I don't think you're crazy. I think you're entitled to your obsession and that you're going about a basically futile thing in a reasonably level-headed way. Fair enough?"

"More than fair. I don't ask you to put any credence in my research, but I don't want you to think I'm a total lunatic for trying it. It's important that you regard me as sane, or else what I want to tell you about Hahn won't be valid to you."

"I don't see the connection."

"It's this," said Latimer. "On the basis of one evening's acquaintance, I've formed an opinion about Hahn. It's the kind of an opinion that might be formed by a garden-variety paranoid, and if you think I'm nuts you're likely to discount my idea about Hahn."

"I don't think you're nuts. What's your idea?"

"That he's spying on us."

Barrett had to work hard to keep from emitting the guffaw that would shatter Latimer's fragile self-esteem. "Spying?" he said casually. "You can't mean that. How can anyone spy here? I mean, how can he report his findings?"

I don't know," Latimer said. "But he asked me a million questions last night. About you, about Quesada, about some of the sick men. He wanted to know everything."

"The normal curiosity of a new man."

"Jim, he was taking notes. I saw him after he thought I was asleep. He sat up for two hours writing it all down in a little book."

Barrett frowned. "Maybe he's going to write a novel about us."

"I'm serious," Latimer said. "Questions—notes. And he's shifty. Try to get him to talk about himself!"

"I did. I didn't learn much."

"Do you know why he's been sent here?"

"No."

"Neither do I," said Latimer. "Political crimes, he said, but he was vague as hell. He hardly seemed to know what the present government was up to, let alone what his own opinions were toward it. I don't detect any passionate philosophical convictions in Mr. Hahn. And you know as well as I do that Hawksbill Station is the refuse heap for revolutionaries and agitators and subversives and all sorts of similar trash, but that we've never had any other kind of prisoner here."

Barrett said coolly, "I agree that Hahn's a puzzle. But who could he be spying for? He's got no way to file a report, if he's a government agent. He's stranded here for keeps, same as the rest of us."

"Maybe he was sent to keep an eye on us—to make sure we aren't cooking up some way to escape. Maybe he's a volunteer who willingly gave up his twenty-first-century life so he could come among us and thwart anything we might be hatching. Perhaps they're afraid we've invented forward time travel. Or that we've become a threat to the sequence of the time-lines. Anything. So Hahn comes among us to snoop around and block any dangers before they arrive."

Barrett felt a twinge of alarm. He saw how close to paranoia Latimer was hewing, now: in half a dozen sentences he had journeyed from the rational expression of some justifiable suspicions to the fretful fear that the men from Up Front were going to take steps to choke off the escape route that he was so close to perfecting.

He kept his voice level as he told Latimer, "I don't think you need to worry, Don. Hahn's an odd one, but he's not here to make trouble for us. The fellows Up Front have already made all the trouble for us they ever will."

"Would you keep an eye on him, anyway?"

"You know I will. And don't hesitate to let me know if Hahn does anything else out of the ordinary. You're in a better spot to notice than anyone else."

"I'll be watching," Latimer said. "We can't tolerate any spies from Up Front among us." He got to his feet and gave Barrett a pleasant smile. "I'll let you get back to your sunning now, Jim."

Latimer went up the path. Barrett eyed him until he was close to the top, only a faint dot against the stony backdrop. After a long while Barrett seized his crutch and levered himself to his feet. He stood staring down at the surf, dipping the tip of his crutch into the water to send a couple of little crawling things scurrying away. At length he turned and began the long, slow climb back to the Station.

# Six

A couple of days passed before Barrett had the chance to draw Lew Hahn aside for a spot of political discussion. The Inland Sea party had set out, and in a way that was too bad, for Barrett could have used Charley Norton's services in penetrating Hahn's armor. Norton was the most gifted theorist around, a man who could weave a tissue of dialectic from the least promising material. If anyone could find out the depth of Hahn's Marxist commitment, if any, it was Norton. But Norton was leading the expedition, so Barrett had to do the interrogating himself. His Marxism was a trifle rusty, and he couldn't thread his path through the Leninist, Stalinist, Trotskyite, Khrushchevist, Maoist, Berenkovskyite and Mgumbweist schools with Charley

Norton's skills. Yet he knew what questions to ask.

He picked a rainy evening when Hahn seemed to be in a fairly outgoing mood. There had been an hour's entertainment that night, an ingenious computer-composed film that Sid Hutchett had programmed last week. Up Front had been kind enough to ship back a modest computer, and Hutchett had rigged it to do animations by specifying line widths and lengths, shades of gray, and progression of raster units. It was a simple but remarkably clever business, and it brightened a dull night.

Afterward, sensing that Hahn was relaxed enough to lower his guard a bit, Barrett said, "Hutchett's a rare one. Did you meet him before he went on the trip?"

"Tall fellow with a sharp nose and no chin?'

"That's the one. A clever boy. He was the top computer man for the Continental Liberation Front until they caught him in '19. He programmed that fake broadcast in which Chancellor Dantell denounced his own regime. Remember?"

"I'm not sure I do." Hahn frowned. "How long ago was this?"

"The broadcast was in 2018. Would that be before your time? Only eleven years ago—"

"I was nineteen then," said Hahn. "I guess I wasn't very politically sophisticated."

"Too busy studying economics, I guess."

Hahn grinned. "That's right. Deep in the dismal science."

"And you never heard that broadcast? Or even heard *of* it?"

"I must have forgotten."

"The biggest hoax of the century," Barrett said, "and you forgot it. You know the Continental Liberation Front, of course."

"Of course." Hahn looked uneasy.

"Which group did you say you were with?"

"The People's Crusade for Liberty."

"I don't know it. One of the newer groups?"

"Less than five years old. It started in California."

"What's its program?"

"Oh, the usual," Hahn said. "Free elections, representative government, an opening of the security files, restoration of civil liberties."

"And the economic orientation? Pure Marxist or one of the offshoots?"

"Not really any, I guess. We believed in a kind of—well, capitalism with some government restraints."

"A little to the right of state socialism, and a little to the left of *laissez faire*?" Barrett suggested.

"Something like that."

"But that system was tried and failed, wasn't it? It had its day. It led inevitably to total socialism, which produced the compensating backlash of syndicalist capitalism, and then we got a government that pretended to be libertarian while actually stifling all individual liberties in the name of freedom. So if your group simply wanted to turn the clock back to 1955, say, there couldn't be much to its ideas."

Hahn looked bored. "You've got to understand I wasn't in the top ideological councils."

"Just an economist?"

"That's it. I drew up plans for the conversion to our system."

"Basing your work on the modified liberalism of Ricardo?"

"Well, in a sense."

"And avoiding the tendency to fascism that was found in the thinking of Keynes?"

"You could say so," Hahn said. He stood up, flashing a quick, vague smile. "Look, Jim, I'd love to argue this further with you some other time, but I've really got to go now. Ned Altman talked me into coming around and helping him do a lightning-dance to bring that pile of dirt to life. So if you don't mind—"

Hahn beat a hasty retreat.

Barrett was more perplexed then ever, now. Hahn hadn't been "arguing" anything. He had been carrying on a lame and feeble conversation, letting himself be pushed hither and thither by Barrett's questions. And he had spouted a lot of nonsense. He didn't seem to know Keynes from Ricardo, nor to care about it, which was odd for a self-professed economist. He didn't have a shred of an idea what his own political party stood for. He had so little revolutionary background that he was unaware even of Hutchett's astonishing hoax of eleven years back.

He seemed phony from top to bottom.

How was it possible that this kid had been deemed worthy of exile to Hawksbill Station, anyhow? Only the top firebrands went there. Sentencing a man to Hawksbill was like sentencing him to death, and it wasn't done lightly. Barrett couldn't imagine why Hahn was here. He seemed genuinely distressed at being exiled, and evidently he had left a beloved young wife behind, but nothing else rang true about the man.

Was he—as Latimer suggested—some kind of spy?

Barrett rejected the idea out of hand. He didn't want Latimer's paranoia infecting him. The government wasn't likely to send anyone on a one-way trip to the Late Cambrian just to spy on a bunch of aging revolutionaries who could never make trouble again. But what *was* Hahn doing here, then?

He would bear further watching, Barrett thought.

Barrett took care of some of the watching himself. But he had plenty of assistance. Latimer. Altman. Six or seven others. Latimer had recruited most of the ambulatory psycho cases, the ones who were superficially functional but full of all kinds of fears and credulities.

They were keeping an eye on the new man.

On the fifth day after his arrival, Hahn went out fishing in Rudiger's crew. Barrett stood for a long time on the edge of the world, watching the little boat bobbing in the surging Atlantic. Rudiger never went far from shore—eight hundred, a thousand yards out but the water was rough even there. The waves came rolling in with X thousand miles of gathered impact behind them. A continental shelf sloped off at a wide angle, so that even at a substantial distance off shore the water wasn't very deep. Rudiger had taken soundings up to a mile out, and had reported depths no greater than 164 feet. Nobody had gone past a mile.

It wasn't that they were afraid of falling off the side of the world if they went too far east. It was simply that a mile was a long distance to row in an open boat, using stubby oars made from old packing cases.

Up Front hadn't thought to spare an outboard motor for them.

Looking toward the horizon, Barrett had an odd thought. He had been told that the women's equivalent of Hawksbill Station was safely segregated out of reach, a couple of hundred million years up the time-line. But how did he know that? There could be another Station somewhere else in this very year, and they'd never know about it. A camp of women, say, living on the far side of the ocean, or even across the Inland Sea.

It wasn't very likely, he knew. With the entire past to pick from, the edgy men Up Front wouldn't take any chance that the two groups of exiles might get together and spawn a tribe of little subversives. They'd take every precaution to put an impenetrable barrier of epochs between them. Yet Barrett thought he could make it sound convincing to the other men. With a little effort he could get them to believe in the existence of several simultaneous Hawksbill Stations scattered on this level of time.

Which could be our salvation, he thought.

The instances of degenerative psychosis were beginning to snowball, now. Too many men had been here too long, and one crackup was starting to feed the next, in this blank lifeless world where humans were never meant to live. The men needed projects to keep them going. They were starting to slip off into harebrained projects, like Altman's Frankenstein girlfriend and Latimer's psi pursuit.

Suppose, Barrett thought, I could get them steamed up about reaching the other continents?

A round-the-world expedition. Maybe they could build some kind of big ship.

That would keep a lot of men busy for a long time. And they'd need navigational equipment—compasses, sextants, chronometers, whatnot. Somebody would have to design an improvised radio, too. It was the kind of project that might take thirty or forty years. A focus for our energies, Barrett thought. Of course, I won't live to see the ship set sail. But even so, it's a way of staving off collapse. We've built our staircase to the sea. Now we need something bigger to do. Idle hands make for idle minds . . . sick minds. . . .

He liked the idea he had hatched. For several weeks, now, Barrett had been worrying about the deteriorating state of affairs in the Station, and looking for some way to cope with it. Now he thought he had his way.

Turning, he saw Latimer and Altman standing behind him.

"How long have you been there?" he asked.

"Two minutes," said Latimer. "We brought you something to look at."

Altman nodded vigorously. "You ought to read it. We brought it for you to read."

"What is it?"

Latimer handed over a folded sheaf of papers. "I found this tucked away in Hahn's bunk after he went out with Rudiger. I know I'm not supposed to be invading his privacy, but I had to have a look at what he's been writing. There it is. He's a spy, all right."

Barrett glanced at the papers in his hand. "I'll read it a little later. What is it about?"

"It's a description of the Station, and a profile of most of the men in it," said Latimer. He smiled frostily. "Hahn's private opinion of me is that I've gone mad.

His private opinion of you is a little more flattering, but not much."

Altman said, "He's also been hanging around the Hammer."

"What?"

"I saw him going there late last night. He went into the building. I followed him. He was looking at the Hammer."

"Why didn't you tell me that right away?" Barrett snapped.

"I wasn't sure it was important," Altman said. "I had to talk it over with Don first. And I couldn't do that until Hahn had gone out fishing."

Sweat burst out on Barrett's face. "Listen, Ned, if you ever catch Hahn going near the time-travel equipment again, you let me know in a hurry. Without consulting Don or anyone else. Clear?"

"Clear," said Altman. He giggled. "You know what I think? They've decided to exterminate us Up Front. Hahn's been sent here to check us out as a suicide volunteer. Then they're going to send a bomb through the Hammer and blow the Station up. We ought to wreck the Hammer and Anvil before they get a chance."

"But why would they send a suicide volunteer?" Latimer asked. "Unless they've got some way to rescue their spy—"

"In any case we shouldn't take any chance," Altman argued. "Wreck the Hammer. Make it impossible for them to bomb us from Up Front."

"That might be a good idea. But—"

"Shut up, both of you," Barrett growled. "Let me look at these papers."

He walked a few steps away from them and sat down on a shelf of rock. He unfolded the sheaf. He began to read.

## Seven

Hahn had a cramped, crabbed handwriting that packed a maximum of information into a minimum of space, as though he regarded it as a mortal sin to waste paper. Fair enough; paper was a scarce commodity here, and evidently Hahn had brought these sheets with him from Up Front. His script was clear, though. So were his opinions. Painfully so.

He had written an analysis of conditions at Hawksbill Station, setting forth in about five thousand words everything that Barrett knew was going sour here. He had neatly ticked off the men as aging revolutionaries in whom the old fervor had turned rancid; he listed the ones who were certifiably psycho, and the ones who were on the edge, and the ones who were hanging on, like Quesada and Norton and Rudiger. Barrett was interested to see that Hahn rated even those three as suffering from severe strain and likely to fly apart at any moment. To him, Quesada and Norton and Rudiger seemed just about as stable as when they had first dropped onto the Anvil of Hawksbill Station; but there was possibly the distorting effect of his own blurred perceptions. To an outsider like Hahn, the view was different and perhaps more accurate.

Barrett forced himself not to skip ahead to Hahn's evaluation of him.

He wasn't pleased when he came to it. "Barrett," Hahn had written, "is like a mighty beam that's been gnawed from within by termites. He looks solid, but one good push would break him apart. A recent injury to his foot has evidently had a bad effect on him. The other men say he used to be physically vigorous and derived much of his authority from his size and strength. Now he can hardly walk. But I feel the trouble with Barrett is inherent in the life of Hawksbill Station, and doesn't have much to do with his lameness. He's been cut off from normal human drives for too long. The exercise of power here has provided the illusion of stability for him, but it's power in a vacuum, and things have happened within Barrett of which he's totally unaware. He's in bad need of therapy. He may be beyond help."

Barrett read that several times. *Gnawed from within by termites . . . one good push . . . things have happened within him . . . bad need of therapy . . . beyond help.*

He was less angered than he thought he should have been. Hahn was entitled to his views. Barrett finally stopped rereading his profile and pushed his way to the last page of Hahn's essay. It ended with the words, "Therefore I recommend prompt termination of the Hawksbill Station penal colony and, where possible, the therapeutic rehabilitation of its inmates."

What the hell was this?

It sounded like the report of a parole commissioner! But there was no parole from Hawksbill Station. That final sentence let all the viability of what had gone before bleed away. Hahn was pretending to be composing a report to the government Up Front, obviously. But a wall a billion years thick made filing of that report impossible. So Hahn was suffering from delusions, just like Altman and Valdosto and the others. In his fevered mind he believed he could send messages Up Front, pompous documents delineating the flaws and foibles of his fellow prisoners.

That raised a chilling prospect. Hahn might be crazy, but he hadn't been in the Station long enough to have gone crazy here. He must have brought his insanity with him.

What if they had stopped using Hawksbill Station as a camp for political prisoners, Barrett asked himself, and were starting to use it as an insane asylum?

A cascade of psychos descending on them. Men who had gone honorably buggy under the stress of confinement would have to make room for ordinary bedlamites. Barrett shivered. He folded up Hahn's papers and handed them to Latimer, who was sitting a few yards away, watching him intently.

"What did you think of that?" Latimer asked.

"I think it's hard to evaluate. But possibly friend Hahn is emotionally disturbed. Put this stuff back exactly where you got it, Don. And don't give Hahn the faintest inkling that you've read or removed it."

"Right."

"And come to me whenever you think there's something I ought to know about him," Barrett said. "He may be a very sick boy. He may need all the help we can give."

The fishing expedition returned in early afternoon. Barrett saw that the dinghy was overflowing with the haul, and Hahn, coming into the camp with his arms full of gaffed trilobites, looked sunburned and pleased with his outing. Barrett came over to inspect the catch. Rudiger was in an effusive mood, and held up a bright red crustacean that might have been the great-

great-grandfather of all boiled lobsters, except that it had no front claws and a wicked-looking triple spike where a tail should have been. It was about two feet long, and ugly.

"A new species!" Rudiger crowed. "There's nothing like this in any museum. I wish I could put it where it would be found. Some mountaintop, maybe."

"If it could be found, it *would* have been found," Barrett reminded him. "Some paleontologist of the twentieth century would have dug it out. So forget it, Mel."

Hahn said, "I've been wondering about that point. How is it nobody Up Front ever dug up the fossil remains of Hawksbill Station? Aren't they worried that one of the early fossil hunters will find it in the Cambrian strata and raise a fuss?"

Barrett shook his head. "For one thing, no paleontologist from the beginning of the science to the founding of the Station in 2005 ever *did* dig up Hawksbill. That's a matter of record, so there was nothing to worry about. If it came to light after 2005, why, everyone would know what it was. No paradox there."

"Besides," said Rudiger sadly, "in another billion years this whole strip of rock will be on the floor of the Atlantic, with a couple of miles of sediment over it. There's not a chance we'll be found. Or that anyone Up Front will ever see this guy I caught today. Not that I give a damn. I've seen him. I'll dissect him. Their loss."

"But you regret the fact that science will never know of this species," Hahn said.

"Sure I do. But is it my fault? Science does know of this species. Me. I'm science. I'm the leading paleontologist of this epoch. Can I help it if I can't publish my discoveries in the professional journals?"

He scowled and walked away, carrying the big red crustacean.

Hahn and Barrett looked at each other. They smiled, in a natural mutual response to Rudiger's grumbled outburst. Then Barrett's smile faded.

*. . . termites . . . one good push . . . therapy . . .*

"Something wrong?" Hahn asked.

"Why?"

"You looked so bleak, all of a sudden."

"My foot gave me a twinge," Barrett said. "It does that, you know. Here. I'll give you a hand carrying those things. We'll have fresh trilobite cocktail tonight."

# Eight

A little before midnight, Barrett was awakened by footsteps outside his hut. As he sat up, groping for the luminescence switch, Ned Altman came blundering through the door. Barrett blinked at him.

"What's the matter?"

"Hahn!" Altman rasped. "He's fooling around with the Hammer again. We just saw him go into the building."

Barrett shed his sleepiness like a seal bursting out of water. Ignoring the insistent throb in his left leg, he pulled himself from his bed and grabbed some clothing. He was more apprehensive than he wanted Altman to see. If Hahn, fooling around with the temporal mechanism, accidentally smashed the hammer, they might never get replacement equipment from Up Front.

Which would mean that all future shipments of supplies—if there were any—would come as random shoots that might land in any old year. What business did Hahn have with the machine, anyway?

Altman said, "Latimer's up there keeping an eye on him. He got suspicious when Hahn didn't come back to the hut, and he got me, and we went looking for him. And there he was, sniffing around the Hammer."

"Doing what?"

"I don't know. As soon as we saw him go in, I came down here to get you. Don's watching." Barrett stumped his way out of the hut and did his best to run toward the main building. Pain shot like trails of hot acid up the lower half of his body. The crutch dug mercilessly into his left armpit as he leaned all his weight into it. His crippled foot, swinging freely, burned with a cold glow. His right leg, which was carrying most of the burden, creaked and popped. Altman ran breathlessly alongside him. The Station was terribly silent at this hour.

As they passed Quesada's hut, Barrett considered waking the medic and taking him along. He decided against it. Whatever trouble Hahn might be up to, Barrett felt he could handle it himself. There was some strength left in the old gnawed beam, after all.

Latimer stood at the entrance to the main dome. He was right at the edge of panic, or perhaps over the edge. He seemed to be gibbering with fear and shock. Barrett had never seen a man gibber before. He clamped a big paw on Latimer's thin shoulder and said harshly, "Where is he? Where's Hahn?"

"He—disappeared."

"What do you mean? Where did he go?"

Latimer moaned. His face was fish-belly white. "He got onto the Anvil," Latimer blurted. "The light came on—the glow. And then Hahn disappeared!"

"No," Barrett said. "It isn't possible. You must be mistaken."

"I saw him go!"

"He's hiding somewhere in the building," Barrett insisted. "Close that door! Search for him!"

Altman said, "He probably did disappear, Jim. If Don says he disappeared—"

"He climbed right on the Anvil. Then everything turned red and he was gone."

Barrett clenched his fists. There was a white-hot blaze just behind his forehead that almost made him forget about his foot. He saw his mistake, now. He had depended for his espionage on two men who were patently and unmistakably insane, and that had been itself a not very sane thing to do. A man is known by his choice of lieutenants. Well, he had relied on Altman and Latimer, and now they were giving him the sort of information that such spies could be counted on to supply.

"You're hallucinating," he told Latimer curtly. "Ned, go wake Quesada and get him here right away. You, Don, you stand here by the entrance, and if Hahn shows up I want you to scream at the top of your lungs. I m going to search the building for him."

"Wait," Latimer said. He seemed to be in control of himself again. "Jim, do you remember when I asked you if you thought I was crazy? You said you didn't. You trusted me. Well, don't stop trusting me now. I tell you I'm not hallucinating. I saw Hahn disappear. I can't explain it, but I'm rational enough to know what I saw."

## Hawksbill Times Two

In a milder tone Barrett said, "All right. Maybe so. Stay by the door, anyway. I'll run a quick check." He started to make the circuit of the dome, beginning with the room where the Hammer was located. Everything seemed to be in order there. No Hawksbill Field glow was in evidence, and nothing had been disturbed. The room had no closets or cupboards in which Hahn could be hiding. When he had inspected it thoroughly, Barrett moved on, looking into the infirmary, the mess hall, the kitchen, the recreation room. He looked high and low. No Hahn. Of course, there were plenty of places in those rooms where Hahn might have secreted himself, but Barrett doubted that he was there. So it had all been some feverish fantasy of Latimer's, then. He completed the route and found himself back at the main entrance. Latimer still stood guard there. He had been joined by a sleepy Quesada. Altman, pale and shaky-looking, was just outside the door.

"What's happening?" Quesada asked.

"I'm not sure," said Barrett. "Don and Ned had the idea they saw Lew Hahn fooling around with the time equipment. I've checked the building, and he's not here, so maybe they made a little mistake. I suggest you take them both into the infirmary and give them a shot of something to settle their nerves, and we'll all try to get back to sleep."

Latimer said, "I tell you, I saw—"

"Shut up!" Altman broke in. "Listen! What's the noise?"

Barrett listened. The sound was clear and loud: the hissing whine of ionization. It was the sound produced by a functioning Hawksbill Field. Suddenly there were goose-pimples on his flesh. In a low voice he said, "The field's on. We're probably getting some supplies."

"At this hour?" said Latimer.

"We don't know what time it is Up Front. All of you stay here. I'll check the Hammer."

"Perhaps I ought to go with you," Quesada suggested mildly.

*"Stay here!"* Barrett thundered. He paused, embarrassed at his own explosive show of wrath. "It only takes one of us. I'll be right back."

Without waiting for further dissent, he pivoted and limped down the hall to the Hammer room. He shouldered the door open and looked in. There was no need for him to switch on the light. The red glow of the Hawksbill Field illuminated everything.

Barrett stationed himself just within the door. Hardly daring to breathe, he stared fixedly at the Hammer, watching as the glow deepened through various shades of pink toward crimson, and then spread until it enfolded the waiting Anvil beneath it. An endless moment passed.

Then came the implosive thunderclap, and Lew Hahn dropped out of nowhere and lay for a moment in temporal shock on the broad plate of the Anvil.

Nine

In the darkness, Hahn did not notice Barrett at first. He sat up slowly, shaking off the stunning effects of a trip through time. After a few seconds he pushed himself toward the lip of the Anvil and let his legs dangle over it. He swung them to get the circulation going. He took a series of deep breaths. Finally he slipped to the floor. The glow of the field had gone out in the moment of his arrival, and so he moved warily, as though not wanting to bump into anything.

Abruptly Barrett switched on the light and said, "What have you been up to, Hahn?"

The younger man recoiled as though he had been jabbed in the gut. He gasped, hopped backward a few steps, and flung up both hands in a defensive gesture. "Answer me," Barrett said.

Hahn regained his equilibrium. He shot a quick glance at Barrett's bulky form toward the hallway and said, "Let me go, will you? I can't explain now."

"You'd better explain now."

"It'll be easier for everyone if I don't," said Hahn. "Please. Let me pass."

Barrett continued to block the door. "I want to know where you've been. What have you been doing with the Hammer?"

"Nothing. Just studying it."

"You weren't in this room a minute ago. Then you appeared. Where'd you come from, Hahn?"

"You're mistaken. I was standing right behind the Hammer. I didn't—"

"I saw you drop down on the Anvil. You took a time trip, didn't you?"

"No."

"Don't lie to me! You've got some way of going forward in time, isn't that so? You've been spying on us, and you just went somewhere to file your report—somewhere—and now you're back."

Hahn's forehead was glistening. He said, "I warn you, don't ask too many questions. You'll know everything in due time. This isn't the time. Please, now. Let me pass."

"I want answers first," Barrett said. He realized that he was trembling. He already knew the answers, and they were answers that shook him to the core of his soul. He knew where Hahn had been.

But Hahn had to admit it himself.

Hahn said nothing. He took a couple of hesitant steps toward Barrett, who did not move. He seemed to be gathering momentum for a rush at the doorway.

Barrett said, "You aren't getting out of here until you tell me what I want to know."

Hahn charged.

Barrett planted himself squarely, crutch braced against the doorframe, his good foot flat on the floor, and waited for the younger man to reach him. He figured he outweighed Hahn by eighty pounds. That might be enough to balance the fact that he was spotting Hahn thirty years and one leg. They came together, and Barrett drove his hands down onto Hahn's shoulders, trying to hold him, to force him back into the room.

Hahn gave an inch or two. He looked up at Barrett without speaking and pushed forward again. "Don't—don't —" Barrett grunted. "I won't let you—"

"I don't want to do this," Hahn said.

He pushed again. Barrett felt himself buckling under the impact. He dug his hands as hard as he could into Hahn's shoulders, and tried to shove the other man backward into the room, but Hahn held firm and all of Barrett's energy was converted into a backward thrust rebounding on himself. He lost control of his crutch, and it slithered out from under his arm. For one agonizing moment Barrett's full weight rested on the crushed uselessness of his left foot, and then, as though his limbs were melting away beneath him, he began to sink toward the floor. He landed with a reverberating crash.

Quesada, Altman, and Latimer came rushing in. Barrett writhed in pain on the floor. Hahn stood over him, looking unhappy, his hands locked together.

"I'm sorry," he said. "You shouldn't have tried to muscle me like that."

Barrett glowered at him. "You were traveling in time, weren't you? You can answer me now!"

"Yes," Hahn said at last. "I went Up Front."

An hour later, after Quesada had pumped him with enough neural depressants to keep him from jumping out of his skin, Barrett got the full story. Hahn hadn't wanted to reveal it so soon, but he had changed his mind after his little scuffle.

It was all very simple. Time travel now worked in both directions. The glib, impressive noises about the flow of entropy had turned out to be just noises. "How long has this been known?" Barrett asked.

"At least five years. We aren't sure yet exactly when the breakthrough came. After we're finished going through all the suppressed records of the former government—"

"The former government?"

Hahn nodded. "The revolution came in January. Not really a violent one, either. The syndicalists just mildewed from within, and when they got the first push they fell over."

"Was it mildew?" Barrett asked, coloring. "Or termites? Keep your metaphors straight."

Hahn glanced away. "Anyway, the government fell. We've got a provisional liberal regime in office now. Don't ask me much about it. I'm not a political theorist. I'm not even an economist. You guessed as much."

"What are you, then?"

"A policeman," Hahn said. "Part of the commission that's investigating the prison system of the former government. Including this prison."

Barrett looked at Quesada, then at Hahn. Thoughts were streaming turbulently through him, and he could not remember when he had last been so overwhelmed by events. He had to work hard to keep from breaking into the shakes again. His voice quavered a little as he said, "You came back to observe Hawksbill Station, right? And you went Up Front tonight to tell them what you saw here. You think we're a pretty sad bunch, eh?"

"You've all been under heavy stress here," Hahn said. "Considering the circumstances of your imprisonment—"

Quesada broke in. "If there's a liberal government in power, now, and it's possible to travel both ways in time, then am I right in assuming that the Hawksbill prisoners are going to be sent Up Front?"

"Of course," said Hahn. "It'll be done as soon as possible. That's been the whole purpose of my reconnaissance mission. To find out if you people were still alive, first, and then to see what shape you're in, how badly in need of treatment you are. You'll be given every available benefit of modern therapy, naturally. No expense spared to—"

Barrett scarcely paid attention to Hahn's words. He had been fearing something like this all night, ever since Altman had told him Hahn was monkeying with the

Hammer, but he had never fully allowed himself to believe that it could really be possible.

He saw his kingdom crumbling, now.

He saw himself returned to a world he could not begin to comprehend—a lame Rip van Winkle, coming back after twenty years.

He saw himself leaving a place that had become his home.

Barrett said tiredly, "You know, some of the men aren't going to be able to adapt to the shock of freedom. It might just kill them to be dumped into the real world again. I mean advanced psychos— Valdosto, and such."

"Yes," Hahn said. "I've mentioned them in my report."

"It'll be necessary to get them ready for a return in gradual stages. It might take several years to condition them to the idea. It might even take longer than that."

"I'm no therapist," said Hahn. "Whatever the doctors think is right for them is what'll be done. Maybe it will be necessary to keep them here. I can see where it would be pretty potent to send them back, after they've spent all these years believing there's no return."

"More than that," said Barrett. "There's a lot of work that can be done here. Scientific works. Exploration. I don't think Hawksbill Station ought to be closed down."

"No one said it would be. We have every intention of keeping it going. But not as a prison. The prison concept is out."

"Good," Barrett said. He fumbled for his crutch, found it, and got heavily to his feet. Quesada moved toward him as though to steady him, but Barrett shook him off. "Let's go outside," he said.

They left the building. A gray mist had come in over the Station, and a fine drizzle had begun to fall. Barrett looked around at the scattering of huts. At the ocean, dimly visible to the east in the faint moonlight. He thought of Charley Norton and the party that had gone on the annual expedition to the Inland Sea. That bunch was going to be in for a real surprise, when they got back here in a few weeks and discovered that everybody was free to go home.

Very strangely, Barrett felt a sudden pressure forming around his eyelids, as of tears trying to force their way out into the open.

Then he turned to Hahn and Quesada. In a low voice he said, "Have you followed what I've been trying to tell you? Someone's got to stay here and ease the transition for the sick men who won't be able to stand the shock of return. Someone's got to keep the base running. Someone's got to explain things to the new men who'll be coming back here, the scientists."

"Naturally," Hahn said.

"The one who does that—the one who stays behind—I think it ought to be someone who knows the Station well, someone who's fit to return Up Front, but who's willing to make the sacrifice and stay. Do you follow me? A volunteer." They were smiling at him now. Barrett wondered if there might not be something patronizing about those smiles. He wondered if he might not be a little too transparent. To hell with both of them, he thought. He sucked the Cambrian air into his lungs until his chest swelled grandly.

"I'm offering to stay," Barrett said in a loud tone. He glared at them to keep them from objecting. But they wouldn't dare object, he knew. In Hawksbill Station, he was the king. And he meant to keep it that way. "I'll be the volunteer," he said. "I'll be the one who stays."

He looked out over his kingdom from the top of the hill.

# The Novel

## ONE

BARRETT WAS THE uncrowned king of Hawksbill Station. No one disputed that. He had been there the longest; he had suffered the most; he had the deepest inner resources of strength. Before his accident, he had been able to whip any man in the place. Now, to be sure, he was a cripple; but he still retained that aura of power that gave him command. When there were problems at the Station, they were brought to Barrett, and he took care of them. That went without saying. He was the king.

He ruled over quite a kingdom, too. In effect it was the whole world, pole to pole, meridian to meridian, the entire blessed earth. For what it was worth. It wasn't worth very much.

Hawksbill Times Two

Now it was raining again. Barrett shrugged himself to his feet in that quick, easy gesture that cost him such an infinite amount of carefully concealed agony, and shuffled to the door of his hut. Rain made him tense and impatient, the sort of rain that fell here. The constant pounding of those great greasy drops against the corrugated tin roof was enough even to drive a Jim Barrett loony. The Chinese water torture wouldn't be invented for another billion years or so, but Barrett understood its effects all too well.

He nudged the door open. Standing in the doorway of his hut, Barrett looked out over his kingdom.

He saw barren rock, reaching nearly to the horizon. A shield of raw dolomite going on and on. Raindrops danced and bounced and splattered on that continental slab of glossy rock. No trees. No grass. Behind

Barrett's sun lay the heavy sea, gray and vast. The sky was gray too, even when it didn't happen to be raining.

He hobbled out into the rain.

Manipulating his crutch was getting to be a simple matter for him now. At first the muscles of his armpit and side had rebelled at the thought that he needed help at all in walking, but they had fallen into line, and the crutch seemed merely to be an extension of his body. He leaned comfortably, letting his crushed left foot dangle unsupported.

A rockslide had pinned him last year, during a trip to the edge of the Inland Sea. Pinned him and ruined him. Back home, Barrett would have been hauled to the nearest state hospital, fitted with prosthetics, and that would have been the end of it: a new ankle, a new instep, refurbished ligaments and tendons, a swathe of homogeneous acrylic fibers where the damaged foot had been. But home was a billion years away from Hawksbill Station, and home there's no returning. The rain hit him hard, thudding against his skull, plastering the graying hair across his forehead. He scowled. He moved a little farther out of his hut, just taking stock.

Barrett was a big man, six and a half feet tall, with hooded dark eyes, a jutting nose, a chin that was a monarch among chins. He had weighed better than two hundred fifty pounds in his prime, in the good old agitating days Up Front when he had carried banners and shouted angry slogans and pounded out manifestoes. But now he was past sixty and beginning to shrink a little, the skin getting loose around the places where the mighty muscles once had been. It was hard to keep your weight up to par in Hawksbill Station. The food was nutritious, but it lacked . . . intensity. A man came to miss steak passionately, after a while. Eating brachiopod stew and trilobite hash wasn't the same thing at all.

Barrett was past all bitterness, though. That was another reason why the men regarded him as the Station's leader. He was solid. He didn't bellow. He didn't rant. He had become resigned to his fate, tolerant of eternal exile, and so he could help the others get over that difficult, heart-clawing period of transition, as they came to grips with the numbing fact that the world they knew was lost to them forever.

A figure arrived, jogging awkwardly through the rain: Charley Norton. The doctrinaire Khrushchevist with the Trotskyite leanings, a revisionist from way back. Norton was a small excitable man who frequently appointed himself messenger when there was news at the Station. He came sprinting toward Barrett's hut, slipping and sliding over the naked rocks, elbows lashing wildly at the air.

Barrett held up a meaty hand as he approached. "Whoa, Charley. Whoa! Take it easy or you'll break your neck!"

Norton halted with difficulty in front of the hut. The rain had pasted the widely spaced strands of his brown hair to his skull in an odd pattern of stripes. His eyes had the fixed, glossy look of fanaticism—or perhaps it was just astigmatism. He gasped for breath and staggered into the hut, standing in the open doorway and shaking himself like a wet puppy. Obviously he had run all the way from the main building of the Station, three hundred yards away. That was a long dash in this rain, and a dangerous one; the rock shield was slippery.

"Why are you standing around out there in the rain?" Norton asked.

"To get wet," Barrett said simply. He stepped into the hut and looked down at Norton. "What's the news?"

"The Hammer's glowing. We're going to get some company pretty soon."

"How do you know it's going to be a live shipment?"

"The Hammer's been glowing for fifteen minutes. That means they're taking precautions with what they're shipping. Obviously they're sending us a new prisoner. Anyway, no supplies shipment is due right now."

Barrett nodded. "Okay. I'll come over and see what's up. If we get a new man, we'll bunk him in with Latimer, I guess."

Norton managed a rasping laugh. "Maybe he's a materialist. If he is, Latimer will drive him crazy with all that mystic nonsense of his. We could put him with Altman instead."

"And he'll be raped in half an hour."

"Altman's off that kick now, didn't you hear?" said Norton. "He's trying to create a real woman, instead of looking for second-rate substitutes."

"Maybe our new man doesn't have any ribs to spare."

"Very funny, Jim." Norton did not look amused. There was sudden new intensity in his glittering little eyes. "Do you know what I want the new man to be?" he asked hoarsely. "A conservative, that's what. A black-souled reactionary straight out of Adam Smith. God, that's what I want those bastards to send us!"

"Wouldn't you be just as happy with a fellow Bolshevik, Charley?"

"This place is full of Bolsheviks," said Norton. "We've got them in all shades from pale pink to flagrant scarlet. Don't you think I'm sick of them? Sitting around all day fishing for trilobites and discussing the relative merits of Kerensky and Malenkov? I need somebody to *talk* to, Jim. Somebody I can really fight with."

"All right," Barrett said, slipping into his rain gear. "I'll see what I can do about hocusing a debating partner out of the Hammer for you. Maybe a rip-roaring Objectivist, okay?" Barrett laughed. Then he said quietly, "You know something, Charley, maybe there's been a revolution Up Front since we got out last news from there. Maybe the left is in and the right is out, now, and they'll start shipping us nothing *but* reactionaries. How would you like that? Say, fifty or a hundred storm troopers coming here for a start, Charley? You'd have plenty of material for your economics debates. And the place will go on filling up with them as the heads roll Up Front, more and more of them shipped back here, until we're outnumbered, and then maybe the newcomers will decide to have a putsch and get rid of all the stinking leftists that were sent here by the old regime, and—"

Barrett stopped. Norton was staring at him in blank amazement, his faded eyes wide, his hand compulsively smoothing his thinning hair to hide his distress and embarrassment.

Barrett realized that he had just committed one of the most heinous crimes possible at Hawksbill Station: he had started to run off at the mouth. There hadn't been any call for his little outburst just now. What made it all the more troublesome was the fact that *he was the one* who had permitted himself such a luxury. He was supposed to be the strong man of this place, the stabilizer, the man of absolute integrity and principle and sanity on whom the others could lean when they felt themselves losing control. And suddenly he had lost control. It was a bad sign. His dead foot was throbbing again; possibly that was the reason.

In a tight voice Barrett said, "Let's go. Maybe the new man is here already."

They stepped outside. The rain was beginning to let up now; the storm was moving out to sea. In the east, over what would one day be called the Atlantic, the sky was still clotted with swirling wisps of gray mist, but to the west a different grayness was emerging, the shade of normal gray that meant dry weather. Before he had been sent back here, Barrett had expected to find the sky practically black, because this far in the past there ought to be be fewer dust particles to bounce the light around and turn things blue. But the sky had turned out to be a weary beige. So much for theories conceived in advance. He had never pretended to be a scientist, anyway.

Through the thinning rain the two men walked toward the main building of the Station. Norton accommodated himself subtly to Barrett's limping pace, and Barrett, wielding his crutch furiously, did his damnedest not to let his infirmity slow them up.. Twice he nearly lost his footing, and each time he fought hard not to let Norton see what had happened.

Hawksbill Station spread out before them.

The Station covered about five hundred acres in a wide crescent. In the center of everything was the main building, an ample dome that contained most of the prisoners' equipment and supplies. Flanking it at widely spaced intervals, rising from the sleek rock shield like grotesque giant green mushrooms, were the plastic blisters that were the individual dwellings. Some huts, like Barrett's, were shielded by tin sheeting that had been salvaged from shipments arriving from Up Front. Others stood unprotected, naked plastic, just as they had come from the mouth of the extruder.

The huts numbered about eighty. At the moment, there were a hundred forty inmates at Hawksbill Station, which was pretty close to the all-time high, and indicated a rising temperature on the political scene Up Front. Up Front hadn't bothered to send back any hut-building materials for a long time, and so all the newer arrivals had to double up with bunkmates. Barrett and the others whose exiles had begun before 2014 had the privilege of occupying private dwellings, if they wanted them. Some men did not wish to live alone; Barrett, to preserve his own authority, felt that he was required to.

As new exiles arrived, they bunked in with those who currently lived alone. Private huts were surrendered in reverse order of seniority. Most of the exiles sent back in 2015 had been forced to take roommates by now. If another dozen deportees arrived, the 2014 group would have to start doubling up. Of course, there were deaths all up and down the line of seniority, which eased things a little, and there were plenty of men who didn't mind having company in their huts—who were eager for it, in fact.

Barrett felt, though, that a man who has been sentenced to life imprisonment without hope of parole ought to have the privilege of privacy, if he desires it. One of his biggest problems at Hawksbill Station was keeping people from cracking up because there was too little privacy. Propinquity could be intolerable in a place like this.

Norton pointed toward the big shiny-skinned green dome of the main building. "There's Altman going in now. And Rudiger. And Hutchett. Something must be happening!"

Barrett stepped up his pace, wincing a little. Some of the men entering the administration building saw his bulky figure coming over the rise in the humpbacked rock shield, and waved to him. Barrett lifted a massive arm in reply. He felt a mounting throb of excitement. It was a big event at the Station whenever a new man arrived—practically the only kind of event they ever had here. Without new men, they had no clue to what might be happening Up Front. Nobody had come to Hawksbill for six months, now, after a cascade of new arrivals late last year. They had been getting five or six a day, for a while—and then the flow stopped. And stayed stopped. Six months, and no one exiled: that was the longest gap Barrett could remember. It had started to seem as though no one would ever be sent to the Station again.

Which would be a catastrophe. New men were all that stood between the older inmates and insanity. New men brought news from the future, news from the world that had been left behind for all eternity. And they contributed the interplay of new personalities to a tight group that was always in danger of going stale.

Then, too, Barrett was aware, some of the men—he was not one—lived in the deluded hope that the next arrival might just be a woman.

That was why they flocked to the main building to see what was happening when the Hammer began to glow. Barrett hobbled down the path. The last trickle of rain died away just as he reached the entrance.

Within the building, sixty or seventy of the Station's residents crowded the chamber of the Hammer just about every man in the place who was able in body and mind, and who was still alert enough to register curiosity about a newcomer. They shouted their greetings to Barrett as he moved toward the center of the group. He nodded, smiled, deflected their chattering questions with amiable gestures.

"Who's it going to be this time, Jim?"

"Maybe a girl, huh? Around nineteen years old, blond, built like—"

"I hope he can play stochastic chess, anyway."

Hawksbill Times Two

"Look at the glow! It's deepening!"

Barrett, like the others, stared at the Hammer, watching change come over the thick column that was the time-travel device. The complex, involuted collection of unfathomable instruments burned a bright cherry red now, betokening the surge of who knew how many kilowatts being pumped in by the generators at the far end of the line, Up Front. There was a hissing in the air; the floor rumbled faintly. The glow had spread to the Anvil now, that broad aluminum bedplate on which all shipments from the future were dropped. In another moment—

"Condition Crimson!" somebody yelled. "Here he comes!"

# TWO

A BILLION YEARS Up the time-line, a surge of power was flooding into the real Hammer of which this was only the partial replica. Potential was building up moment by moment in that huge grim room that everyone in Hawksbill Station remembered only too vividly. A man—or something else, perhaps just a shipment of supplies—stood in the center of the real Anvil in that room, engulfed by fate. Barrett knew what it was like to stand there, waiting for the Hawksbill Field to enfold you and kick you back to the early Paleozoic. Cold eyes watched you as you awaited your exile, and those eyes gleamed in triumph, telling you that they were glad to be rid of you. And then the Hammer did its work and off you went on your one-way journey. The effect of being sent through time was very much like being hit with a gigantic hammer and driven clear through the walls of the continuum: hence the governing metaphors for the functional parts of the machine.

Everything in Hawksbill Station had come via the Hammer. Setting up the Station had been a long, slow, expensive job, the work of methodical men who were willing to go to any lengths to get rid of their opponents in what was considered the humane, twenty-first-century way of doing it. The Hammer had knocked a pathway through time and had sent back the nucleus of a receiving station, first. Since there was no receiving station already on hand in the Paleozoic to receive the receiving station, a certain amount of unavoidable waste had occurred. It wasn't strictly necessary to have a Hammer and Anvil on the receiving end, except as a fine control to prevent temporal spread; without the receiving equipment, the field tended to wander a little, though. Shipments emanating from consecutive points along the time-line, sent back all in the same day or week, might easily get scattered over a span of twenty or thirty years of the past, without the receiving equipment to guide it in. There was plenty of such temporal garbage all around Hawksbill Station: stuff that had been intended for the original installation, but that because of tuning imprecisions in the pre-Hammer days had landed a couple of decades (and a couple of hundred miles) away from the intended site.

Despite such difficulties, the planning authorities had finally sent through enough components to the master temporal site to allow for the construction of a receiving station. It was very much like threading a needle by remote control using mile-long manipulators, but they succeeded. All this time, of course, the Station was uninhabited; the government hadn't cared to waste any of its own engineers by sending them back to set the place up, because they'd be unable to return. Finally, the first prisoners had gone through—political prisoners, naturally, but chosen for their technical backgrounds. Before they were shipped out, they were given instructions on how to put the parts of the Hammer and Anvil together. Of course, it was their privilege to refuse to cooperate, once they reached the Station. They were beyond the reach of authority there. But it was to their own advantage to assemble the receiving station, thus making it possible for them to get further supplies from Up Front. They had done the job. After that, outfitting Hawksbill Station had been easy.

Now the Hammer glowed, meaning that they had activated the Hawksbill Field on the sending end, somewhere up around A.D. 2028 or 2030. All the sending was done from there. All the receiving was done here. Time travel didn't work the other way. Nobody really knew why, although there was a lot of superficially profound talk about the rules of entropy and the infinite temporal momentum that you were likely to attain if you tried to accelerate along the normal axis of time flow, which is to say from past to future.

The whining, hissing sound in the room began to grow painfully louder as the edges of the Hawksbill Field began to ionize the atmosphere. Then came the expected thunderclap of implosion, caused by an imperfect overlapping of the quantity of air that was being subtracted from this era and the quantity that was being thrust into it from the future.

And then, abruptly, a man dropped out of the Hammer and lay, stunned and limp, on the gleaming Anvil.

He looked very young, which surprised Barrett considerably. He seemed to be well under thirty years old. Generally, only middle-aged men were condemned to exile at Hawksbill Station. They sent only the incorrigibles, the men who had to be separated from humanity for the general good of the greatest number. The youngest man in the place now had been close to forty when he first arrived. The sight of this lean, clean-cut boy drew a hiss of anguish from a couple of the men in the room, and Barrett understood the constellation of emotions that pained them.

The new man sat up. He stirred like a child coming out of a long, deep sleep. He looked around.

He was wearing a simple gray tunic, with an underlying fabric of iridescent threads. His face was wedge-shaped, tapering to a sharp chin, and right now he was very pale. His thin lips seemed bloodless. His blue eyes blinked rapidly. He rubbed his eyebrows, which were blond and nearly invisible. His jaws worked as though he wanted to say something, but could not find the words.

The sensations incurred in time travel were not physiologically harmful, but they could deliver a rough jolt to the consciousness. The last moments before the Hammer descended were very much like the final moments beneath the guillotine, since exile to Hawksbill Station was tantamount to a sentence of death. The departing prisoner took his last look at the world of rocket transport and artificial organs and visiphones, at the world in which he had lived and loved and agitated for a sacred political cause, and then came the Hammer and he was rammed instantaneously into the inconceivably remote post on an irreversible trajectory. It was a gloomy business, and it was not very surprising that the newcomers arrived in a state of emotional shock.

Barrett elbowed his way through the crowd toward the machine. Automatically, the others made way for him. He reached the lip of the Anvil and leaned over it, extending a hand to the new man. His broad smile was met by a look of glassy bewilderment.

"I'm Jim Barrett. Welcome to Hawksbill Station."

"I—it—"

"Here—get off that thing before a load of groceries lands on top of you. They may still be transmitting." Barrett, wincing a little as he shifted his weight, pulled the new man down from the Anvil. It was altogether likely that the idiots Up Front would shoot another shipment along a minute after sending a man, without worrying about whether the man had had time to get off the Anvil. When it came to prisoners, Up Front had no empathy at all.

Barrett beckoned to Mel Rudiger, a plump, freckled anarchist with a soft pink face. Rudiger handed the new man an alcohol capsule. He took it and pressed it to his arm without a word, and his eyes brightened.

"Here's a candy bar," Charley Norton said. "Get your glucose level up to par in a hurry."

## Hawksbill Times Two

The man shook it off, moving his head as though through a liquid atmosphere. He looked groggy—a real case of temporal shock, Barrett thought, possibly the worst he had ever seen. The newcomer hadn't even spoken yet. Could the effect really be that extreme? Maybe for a young man the shock of being ripped from his rightful time was stronger than for others.

Barrett said softly, "We'll take you to the infirmary and check you out, okay? Then I'll assign you your quarters. There'll be time later on for you to find your way around and meet everybody. What's your name?"

"Hahn. Lew Hahn."

His voice was just a raspy whisper. "I can't hear you," Barrett said.

"Hahn," the man repeated, still only barely audible.

"When are you from, Lew?"

"2029."

"You feel pretty sick?"

"I feel awful. I don't even believe this is happening to me. There isn't really such a place as Hawksbill Station, is there?"

"I'm afraid there is," Barrett said. "At least, for most of us. A few of the boys think it's all an illusion induced by drugs, that we're really still up there in Century Twenty-One. But I have my doubts of that. If it's an illusion, it's a damned good one. Look."

He put one arm around Hahn's shoulders and guided him through the press of Station men, out of the Hammer chamber, and down the corridor toward the nearby infirmary. Although Hahn looked thin, even fragile, Barrett was surprised to feel the rippling, steely muscles in those shoulders. He suspected that this man was a good deal less helpless and ineffectual than he seemed to be right now. He *had* to be, in order to merit banishment to Hawksbill Station. It was expensive to hurl a man this far back in time; they didn't send just anyone here.

Barrett and Hahn passed the open door of the building. "Look out there," Barrett commanded.

Hahn looked. He passed a hand across his eyes as though to clear away unseen cobwebs, and looked again. "A Late Cambrian landscape," said Barrett quietly. "This view would be a geologist's dream, except that geologists don't tend to become political prisoners, it seems. Out in front of you is what they call Appalachia. It's a strip of rock a few hundred miles wide and a few thousand miles long, running from the Gulf of Mexico to Newfoundland. To the east we've got a thing called the Appalachian Geosyncline, which is a trough five hundred miles wide full of water. Somewhere about two thousand miles to the west there's another trough, what they call the Cordilleran Geosyncline. It's full of water too, and at this particular stage of geological history the path of land between the geosynclines is below sea level, so where Appalachia ends we've got the Inland Sea, currently, running way out to the west. On the far side of the Inland Sea is a narrow north-south land mass called Cascadia, that's going to be California and Oregon and Washington someday. Don't hold your breath till it happens. I hope you like seafood, Lew."

Hahn stared, and Barrett, standing beside him at the doorway, stared also. Even now, he felt wonder at the sight of it. You never could get used to the sheer alienness of this place, not even after you had lived here twenty years, as Barrett had done. It was

Earth, and yet it was not really Earth at all, because it was somber and empty and unreal. Where were the swarming cities? Where were the electronic freeways? Where were the noise, the pollution, the garishness? None of it had been born yet. This was a silent, sterile place.

The gray oceans swarmed with life, of course. But at this stage of evolution there was nothing living on the land except the intrusive men of Hawksbill Station. The surface of the planet, where it jutted above the seas, was a raw shield of naked rock, bare and monotonous, broken only by occasional patches of moss in the occasional patches of soil that had managed to form. Even a few cockroaches would have been welcome; but insects, it seemed, were still a couple of geological periods in the future. To land dwellers, this was a dead world, a world unborn.

Shaking his head, Hahn moved away from the door. Barrett led him down the corridor and into the small, brightly lit room that served as the Station's infirmary. Doc Quesada was waiting for him there.

Quesada wasn't really a doctor, but he had been a medical technician once, and that was good enough. He was a compact, swarthy man with harsh cheekbones and a spreading wedge of a nose. In his infirmary he wore a look of complete self-assurance. He hadn't lost too many of his patients, all things considered. Barrett had watched him removing appendixes and suturing wounds and amputating limbs with total aplomb. In his slightly frayed white smock, Quesada looked sufficiently medical to carry off his role convincingly.

Barrett said, "Doc, this is Lew Hahn. He's in temporal shock. Fix him up."

# Hawksbill Times Two

Quesada nudged the new man onto a webfoam cradle and briskly unzipped his gray tunic. Then he reached for his medical kit. Hawksbill Station was well equipped for most medical emergencies, now. The people Up Front were not terribly concerned with what happened to the prisoners at the Station, but they had no wish to be inhumane to men who could no longer harm them, and they sent back from time to time all sorts of useful things, like anesthetics and surgical clamps and diagnostats and medicines and dermal probes. Barrett could remember a time at the beginning when there had been nothing much here but the empty huts, and a man who hurt himself was in real trouble.

"He's had a drink already," said Barrett. "I thought you ought to know."

"I see that," Quesada murmured. He scratched at his shortcropped, bristly reddish mustache. The little diagnostat in the cradle had gone rapidly to work, flashing information about Hahn's blood pressure, potassium count, dilation index, vascular flow, alveolar flexing, and much else. Quesada seemed to have no difficulty in comprehending the barrage of facts that flashed across the screen and landed on the confirmation tape. After a moment he turned to Hahn and said, "You aren't really sick, are you, fellow? Just shaken up a little. I don't blame you. Here—I'll give you a quick jolt to calm your nerves, and you'll be all right. As all right as any of us ever are, I guess."

He put a tube to Hahn's carotid and thumbed the snout. The subsonic whirred, and a tranquilizing compound slid into the man's bloodstream. Hahn shivered.

Quesada said to Barrett, "Let him rest for five minutes. Then he'll be over the hump."

They left Hahn slumped in the cradle and went out of the infirmary. In the hall, Quesada said, "This one's a lot younger than usual."

"I've noticed. And also the first in months."

"You think something funny's going on Up Front?"

"I couldn't really say. But I'll have a long talk with Hahn once he's got some energy back." Barrett looked down at the little medic and said, "I meant to ask you before. What's the report on Valdosto?"

Valdosto had gone into psychotic collapse several weeks before. Quesada was keeping him drugged and trying to bring him slowly back to an acceptance of the reality of Hawksbill Station. Shrugging, he replied, "The status is quo. I let him out from under the dream juice this morning, and he was the same as he's been."

"You don't think he'll come out of it?"

"I doubt it. He's cracked for keeps. They could paste him together Up Front, but—"

"Yeah," Barrett said. "If he could get Up Front at all, Valdosto wouldn't have cracked. Keep him happy, then. If he can't be sane, he can at least be comfortable."

"What's happened to Valdosto really hurts you, doesn't it, Jim?"

"What do you think?" Barrett's eyes flickered a moment. "He and I were together almost from the start. When the party was getting organized, when we were all full of jism and ideals. I was the coordinator, he was the bomb-thrower. He was so steamed up about the rights of man that he was ready to mutilate any so-and-so who didn't toe a proper liberal line. I had to keep calming him down. You know, when Val and I were kids, we had an apartment together in New York."

"You and Val weren't kids at the same time," Quesada reminded him.

"Well, no," Barrett said. "He was maybe eighteen and I was pushing thirty. But he always seemed older than his age. And we had this apartment, the two of us. And girls. Girls all the time, coming, going, sometimes living there for a few weeks. Val always said a true revolutionary needs lots of sex. Hawksbill would come there too, the bastard, only we didn't know then that he was working on something that would hang us all. And Bernstein. And we'd sit up all night drinking cheap filtered rum, and Valdosto would start planning terrorist raids, and we'd shut him up, and—" Barrett scowled. "To hell with it. The past is dead. Probably it would be better if Val was, too."

"Jim—"

"Let's change the subject," Barrett said. "What about Altman? Still got the shakes?"

"He's building a woman," Quesada said.

"That's what Charley Norton told me. What's he using? A rag, a bone—"

"I gave him some surplus chemicals to fool with. Chosen mainly for their color, matter of fact. He's got some foul green copper compounds and a little bit of ethyl alcohol and some zinc sulphate and six or seven other things, and he collected some soil and threw in a lot of dead shellfish, and he's sculpting it all into what he claims is female shape and waiting for lightning to strike it and bring it to life."

"In other words," Barrett said, "he's gone crazy."

"I think that's a safe assumption. But at least he's not molesting his friends any more, anyway. You didn't think Altman's homosexual phase would last much longer, as I recall."

"No, but I didn't think he'd go altogether off the deep end, Doc. If a man needs sex and he can find some consenting playmates here, that's quite all right with me, as long as they don't offend anybody out in the open. But when Altman starts putting a woman together out of some dirt and rotten brachiopod meat, it means we've lost him for keeps. It's too bad."

Quesada's dark eyes fell. "We're all going to go that way sooner or later, Jim."

"I haven't cracked up yet. You haven't."

"Give us time. I've only been here eleven years."

"Altman's been here only eight," said Barrett. "Valdosto even less."

"Some shells crack faster than others," said Quesada. "Well, here's our new friend."

Hahn had come out of the infirmary to join them. He still looked pale and shaken, but the fright was gone from his eyes. He was beginning, thought Barrett, to adjust to the unthinkable.

He said, "I couldn't help overhearing part of your conversation. Is there a lot of mental illness here?"

"Some of the men haven't been able to find anything meaningful to do at the Station," Barrett said. "The boredom eats them away."

"What's meaningful to do here?"

"Quesada has his medical work. I've got administrative duties. A couple of the fellows are studying the sea life, making a real scientific survey. We've got a newspaper that comes out every now and then and keeps some of the boys busy. There's fishing, and cross-continental hiking. But there are always those who just let themselves slide into despair, and they crack up. I'd say we have thirty or forty certifiable maniacs here at the moment, out of a hundred forty residents."

"That's not so bad," Hahn said. "Considering the inherent instability of the men who get sent here, and the unusual conditions of life here."

"Inherent instability?" Barrett repeated. "I don't know about that. Most of us thought we were pretty sane, and fighting on the right side. Do you think that because a man's a revolutionary, he's *ipso facto* nuts? And if you do think so, Hahn, what the hell are you doing here?"

"You're misinterpreting me, Mr. Barrett. I'm not drawing any parallel between antigovernmental activity and mental disturbance, God knows. But you have to admit that a lot of the people any revolutionary movement attracts are—well, a little unhinged somewhere."

"Valdosto," Quesada murmured. "Throwing bombs."

"All right," Barrett said. He laughed. "Hey, Hahn, you're suddenly pretty articulate, aren't you, for a man who couldn't even mumble a few minutes back? What was in the stuff Doc Quesada jolted you with?"

"I didn't mean to sound superior," Hahn said quickly. "Maybe that came out a little too smug and condescending. I mean—"

"Forget it. What did you do Up Front, anyway?"

"I was an economist."

"Just what we need," said Quesada. "He can help us solve our balance-of-payments problem."

Barrett said, "If you were an economist back there, you'll have plenty to talk about here. This place is full of nutty economic theorists who'll want to bounce their ideas off you. Some of them are almost sane, too. The ideas, that is. Come with me and I'll show you where you're going to stay."

# THREE

HE PATH FROM the main building to the hut where Donald Latimer lived was mainly downhill, for which Barrett was grateful even though he knew that he'd have to negotiate the uphill return in a little while, anyway. Latimer's but was on the eastern side of the Station, looking out over it. Hahn and Barrett walked slowly toward it. Hahn was solicitous of Barrett's game leg, and Barrett was irritated by the exaggerated care the younger man took to keep pace with him.

He was puzzled by this Hahn. The man was full of seeming contradictions. Such as showing up here with the worst case of temporal shock on arrival Barrett had ever seen, then snapping out of it with remarkable quickness. Or looking frail and shy, but hiding solid muscles inside his tunic. Giving an outer appearance of general incompetence, but speaking with calm control. Barrett wondered what it was this sleek young man had done to earn him the trip to Hawksbill Station. But there was time for such inquiries later. All the time in the world.

Hahn swept his hand across the horizon and said, "Is everything like this? Just rock and ocean?"

"That's all. Land life hasn't evolved yet. Won't for quite a while. Everything's wonderfully simple here, isn't it? No clutter. No urban sprawl. No traffic jams. There's some moss moving up onto the land, but not much."

"And in the sea? Dinosaurs swimming around?"

Barrett shook his head. "There won't be any vertebrates for thirty, forty million years. They'll be arriving in the Ordovician, and we're in the Cambrian. We don't even have fish yet, let alone reptiles out there. All we can offer is that which creepeth. Some shellfish, some big ugly fellows that look like squids, and trilobites. We've got seven hundred billion different species of trilobites, more or less. And we've got a man named Mel Rudiger—he's the one who gave you the drink when you got here—who's making a collection of them. Rudiger's writing the world's definitive text on trilobites. His masterpiece."

"But nobody will ever have a chance to read it—in the future."

"Up Front, we say."

"Up Front."

That's the pity of it," said Barrett. "All that brilliant work, and it's wasted, because nobody else here gives a damn about the life and hard times of the trilobite, and nobody Up Front will ever know about it.

We told Rudiger to inscribe his book on imperishable plates of gold and hope that it's found by paleontologists later on. But he says the odds are against it. A billion years of geology will chew his plates to hell before they can be found. And if they ever did turn up, they'd probably be used to start a new religion, or something."

Hahn sniffed. "Why does the air smell so strange?"

"It's a different mix," Barrett said. "We've analyzed it. More nitrogen, a little less oxygen, hardly any carbon dioxide at all. But that isn't really why it smells odd to you. The thing is, it's pure air, unpolluted by the exhalations of life. Nobody's been respiring into it except us lads, and there aren't enough of us to matter."

Smiling, Hahn said, "I feel a little cheated that it's so empty. I expected lush jungles of weird plants, and pterodactyls swooping through the air, and maybe a tyrannosaur crashing into a fence around the Station."

"No jungles. No pterodactyls. No tyrannosaurs. No fences. You didn't do your homework."

"Sorry."

"This is the Late Cambrian. Sea life exclusively."

"It was very kind of them to pick such a peaceful era for their dumping ground for political prisoners," Hahn said. "I was afraid it would be all teeth and claws."

Barrett spat. "Kind, hell! They were looking for an era where we couldn't do any harm to their environment. That meant they had to toss us back before the evolution of mammals, just in case we'd accidentally get hold of the ancestor of all humanity and snuff him out. And while they were at it, they decided to stash us so far in the past that we'd be beyond all land life, on the theory that maybe even if we slaughtered a baby dinosaur it might affect the entire course of the future. *Their* world."

"They don't mind if we catch a few trilobites?"

"Evidently they think it's safe," Barrett said. "It looks as though they were right. Hawksbill Station has been here for twenty-five years, and it doesn't seem as though we've tampered with future history in any measurable way. There's still a continuity, despite our presence here. Of course, they're careful not to send us any women."

"Why is that?"

"So we don't start reproducing and perpetuating ourselves. Wouldn't that mess up the time-lines! Say, a successful human outpost planted here in one billion B.C., that's had all that time to evolve and mutate and grow?"

"A separate evolutionary line."

"You bet," Barrett said. "By the time the twenty-first century came around, our descendants would be in charge, whatever kind of creatures they'd be by then, and the other kind of human being would probably be in penal servitude, and there'd be more paradoxes created than you could shake a trilobite at. So they don't send the women here."

"But they send women back in time."

"Oh, yes," Barrett said. "There's a prison camp for women, too, but it's a few hundred million years up the time-line in the Late Silurian, and never the twain shall meet. That's why Ned Altman is trying to build a woman for himself out of dust and garbage."

"God made Adam out of less."

"Ned Altman isn't God," Barrett pointed out. "That's the root of his whole problem. Look, here's the hut where you're going to stay, Hahn. I'm rooming you with Don Latimer. He's a very sensitive, interesting, pleasant person. He used to be a physicist before he got into politics, and he's been here about a dozen years, and I might as well warn you that he's developed a strong and somewhat cockeyed mystic streak lately. The fellow he was rooming with killed himself last year, and since then Don's been trying to find some way out of the Station through the application of extrasensory powers."

"Is he serious?"

"I'm afraid he is. And we try to take him seriously, too. We all humor each other's quirks at Hawksbill Station; it's the only way we avoid an epidemic of mass psychosis. Latimer will probably try to get you to collaborate with him on his psi project. If you don't like living with him, I can arrange a transfer for you. But I want to see how he reacts to someone who's new at the Station. I'd like you to give bunking with him a chance."

"Maybe I'll even help him find that psionic gateway he's looking for."

"If you do, take me along," said Barrett. They both laughed. Then Barrett rapped at Latimer's door. There was no answer, and after a moment he pushed the door open. Hawksbill Station got along without locks.

Latimer sat in the middle of the bare rock floor, cross-legged, meditating. He was a slender, gentle-faced man with parchment-like skin and a somber, downturned mouth, and he was just beginning to look old. Right now he seemed at least a million miles away, ignoring them completely. Hahn shrugged. Barrett put a finger to his lips. They waited in silence for a few minutes, and then Latimer showed signs of coming up from his trance.

Hawksbill Times Two

He got to his feet in a single flowing motion, without using his hands. In a low, courteous voice he said to Hahn, "Have you just arrived?"

"Within the last hour. I'm Lew Hahn."

"Donald Latimer." He did not offer to shake hands. "I regret that I have to make your acquaintance in these surroundings. But perhaps we won't have to tolerate this illegal condition of imprisonment much longer."

Barrett said, "Don, Lew is going to bunk with you. I think you'll get along well. He was an economist in 2029 until they gave him the Hammer."

Animation came into Latimer's eyes. "Where did you live?" he asked.

"San Francisco."

The glow faded as if doused. Latimer said, "Were you ever in Toronto?"

"Toronto? No," Hahn said.

"I'm from there. I had a daughter—she'd be twenty-three years old now, Nella Latimer—I wondered if you knew her—perhaps you knew her—"

"No. I'm sorry."

Latimer sighed. "It wasn't very likely that you did. But I'd love to know what kind of a woman she became. She was a little girl when I last saw her. She was—let's see—she was ten, going on eleven. Now I suppose she's married. I might have grandchildren. Or perhaps they've sent her to the other Station. She might have come to be politically active, and—" Latimer paused. "Nella Latimer—you're sure that you didn't know her?"

Barrett left them together, Hahn looking concerned and sympathetic, Latimer trusting, open, hopeful. It seemed as though they'd get along pretty well. Barrett told Latimer to bring the new man up to the main building at dinnertime to be introduced around, and went out. A chilly drizzle had begun to fall again. Barrett made his way slowly, painfully up the hill, grunting faintly every time he put his weight on the crutch.

It had been sad to see the light flicker from Latimer's eyes when Hahn said he didn't know his daughter. Most of the time, men at Hawksbill Station tried not to speak about their families. They preferred—wisely—to keep those tormenting memories well repressed. To think about loved ones was to feel the ache of amputation, desperate and incurable. But the arrival of newcomers generally stirred old ties. There was never any news of relatives, and no way ever to obtain any, because it was impossible for the men of the Station to communicate with anyone Up Front. Nothing could be sent forward in time so much as a thousandth of a second.

No way to ask for the photo of a loved one, no way to request specific medicines or equipment, no way to obtain a certain book or a coveted tape. In a mindless, impersonal way, the authorities Up Front sent periodic shipments to the Station of things that might be useful to the inmates—reading matter, medical supplies, technical equipment, food. But always it was a random scoop, unpredictable, bizarre. Occasionally they were startling in their generosity, as when they sent a case of Burgundy, or a box of sensory spools, or a recharger for the power pack. Such gifts usually meant that they were having a brief thaw in the world situation. A relaxation of tension customarily produced a short-lived desire to be kind to the boys in Hawksbill Station.

# Hawksbill Times Two

But they had a strict policy about sending information about relatives. Or about sending contemporary newspapers and magazines. Fine wine, yes; a tridim of a daughter who would never be embraced again, no.

For all Up Front knew, there was no one alive in Hawksbill Station. A plague could have killed everyone in the place off ten years ago—but *they* had no way of telling that. They couldn't even be sure that any of the exiles had survived the trip to the past. All they had determined from Hawksbill's experiments was that a pastward trip of less than three years was not likely to be fatal; it had been impractical to extend the duration of experiments past that point. What would a billion years across time do? Not even Edmond Hawksbill had known that for certain.

So they went on sending shipments back to the prisoners in the blind assumption that there were prisoners alive to receive them. The government whirred and clicked with predictable continuity, looking after those whom it had condemned to eternal separation from the State. The government, whatever else it might be, was not malicious. Barrett had learned long ago that there were other kinds of totalitarianism besides bloody repressive tyranny.

Barrett paused at the top of the hill to catch his breath. Naturally, the alien air no longer smelled strange to him. He filled his lungs with it until he was a little dizzied by it. Once again the rain ceased. Through the grayness came thin shafts of sunshine, making the naked rocks sparkle and glow. Barrett closed his eyes a moment and leaned on his crutch, and saw as though on an inner screen in his mind the creatures with many legs climbing up out of the sea, and the broad mossy carpets spreading, and the flowerless plants uncoiling and extending their scaly grayish branches, and the dull hides of eerie flat-snouted amphibians glistening on the shores, and the tropic heat of the coal-forming epoch descending like a glove to smother the world.

All that lay far in the future. Dinosaurs.

Little chittering mammals.

Pithecanthropus hunting with hand-axes in the forests of Java.

Sargon and Hannibal and Attila, and Orville Wright, and Thomas Edison, and Edmond Hawksbill. And finally a benign government that would find the thoughts of certain men so intolerable that the only safe place to which those men could be banished was deemed to be a rock at the beginning of time.

The government was too civilized to put men to death for subversive activities, and too cowardly to let them remain alive and at large. The compromise was the living death of Hawksbill Station. A billion years of impassable time was suitable insulation even for the most nihilistic ideas.

Grimacing a little, Barrett struggled the rest of the way back to his hut. He had long since come to accept the fact of his exile, but accepting his ruined foot was another matter entirely. He had always been strong physically. He had feared old age because it might mean a withering of his strength; but now the age of sixty had come upon him, and the years had not sapped him as much as he feared they might, although they had certainly sapped him; but he would still have had most of his strength, except for this absurd accident that might have happened to him at any age. The idle wish to find a way to regain the freedom of his own time no longer possessed him; but Barrett wished with all his soul that the blank-faced authorities Up Front would send back a kit that would allow him to rebuild his foot.

He entered his hut and flung his crutch aside, sinking down instantly on his cot. There had been no cots when Barrett had come to Hawksbill Station. You slept on the floor, then, and the floor was solid rock. If you felt ambitious, you went out and scrabbled together some soil, looking in the crevices and creases of the rock shield, collecting the fledgling earth a handful at a time, and you made yourself an inch-deep bed of soil to lie on. Things were a little better here now.

Barrett had been sent to the Station in its fourth year of operation, when there had been only a dozen buildings, and little in the way of creature comforts. That had been A.D. 2008, Up Front time. The Station had been a raw, miserable place, then, but the steady accretion of shipments from Up Front had made it a relatively tolerable place to live.

Of the fifty or so exiles who had preceded Barrett to Hawksbill, none remained alive. He had held highest seniority in the camp for almost ten years, since the death of white-bearded old Pleyel, whom Barrett had regarded as a saint. Time here moved at a one-to-one correlation with time Up Front; the Hammer was locked on this single point of time, forever moving forward in perfect step, so that Lew Hahn, arriving here today more than twenty years after Barrett had come, had departed from Up Front at a spot on the calendar exactly twenty years and some months along from the date of Barrett's expulsion. Hahn came from 2029—a whole generation past the world Barrett had left. Barrett had not had the heart to begin pumping Hahn for news of that generation so soon. He would learn all he needed to know in Time, and small cheer it would be, anyway.

Barrett reached for a book. But the fatigue of hobbling around the Station had taken more out of him than he realized. He looked at the page for a moment. Then he put it away and closed his eyes.

Faces swam behind his lids. Bernstein. Pleyel. Hawksbill. Janet. Bernstein. Bernstein. Bernstein.

He dozed.

# FOUR

JIMMY BARRETT WAS sixteen years old, and Jack Bernstein was saying to him, "How can you be so big and ugly and not care a damn about what's happening to the weak people of this world?"

"Who says I don't care a damn?"

"It doesn't even need saying. It's obvious. Where's your commitment? What are you doing to keep civilization from falling apart?"

"It isn't—"

"It *is*," Bernstein said scornfully. "You big lummox, you don't even read the papers, do you? Do you realize that there's a constitutional crisis in this country, and that unless people like you and me start taking action, there's going to be a dictatorship here in the United States before this time next year?"

"You're exaggerating," Barrett said. "As usual."

"See? You don't give a damn!"

Barrett was exasperated, but that was nothing new. Jack Bernstein had been exasperating him ever since they had met, four years back in 1980. They had both been twelve years old then. Barrett was already close to six feet tall, husky and powerful; Jack was skinny and waxen-looking, undersized for his age, even smaller when he stood beside Barrett. Something had drawn the two of them together: the attraction of opposites, perhaps. Barrett valued and respected the smaller boy's quick, nimble mind, and he suspected that Jack had sought him out as a protector. Jack needed protection. He was the sort of fellow you wanted to hit for no particular reason at all, even when he hadn't said anything, and when he finally did open his mouth you wanted to hit him even harder.

Now they were sixteen, and Barrett had reached what he hoped was his full growth, six feet five, well over two hundred pounds, and he had to shave every day and his voice was deep and black. Jack Bernstein still looked as though he were on the wrong side of puberty. He was five feet five, five seven at best, with no shoulders at all, arms and legs so thin Barrett thought he could snap them with one hand, a high reedy voice, a sharp, aggressive nose. His face was scarred by some skin disease, and his thick, tangled eyebrows made a solid line across his forehead, visible half a block away. Jack had grown more waspish, more excitable in adolescence. There were times when

Barrett could hardly stand him at all. This was one of them.

"What do you want from me?" Barrett asked. "Will you come to one of our meetings?"

"I don't want to get into anything subversive."

"*Subversive!*" Bernstein shot back at him. "A label. A stinking semantic tag. Anyone who wants to patch the world up a little, he's a subversive in your book, right, Jimmy?"

"Well—"

"Take Christ. Would you call him a subversive?"

"I think I would," Barrett said cautiously. "Besides, you know what happened to Christ."

"He wasn't the first martyr to ideas, and he won't be the last. Do you want to play it safe all your life? Do you want to sit there wrapped in muscles and fat and let the wolves eat the world? What's it going to be like when you're sixty years old, Jimmy, and the world is one big slave camp, and there you sit in chains saying, Well, I'm alive, so everything turned out pretty fair?"

Barrett said coolly, "Better a live slave than a dead subversive."

"If you believe that, you're more of a moron than I think you are."

"I ought to swat you. You buzz, Jack. Like a mosquito."

"Do you believe that thing you just said to me about a live slave? Do you? Do you?"

Barrett shrugged. "What do you think?"

"Then come to a meeting. Get out of your cocoon and *do* something, Jimmy. We need men like you." Jack's voice had shifted pitch and timbre. It had lost its reedy, querulous tone, and suddenly was lower, more assured, more commanding.

"Someone of your size, Jimmy—of your natural authority. You'd be terrific. If I could only get you to see that what we're doing is important—"

"How can a bunch of high school kids save the world?" Jack's thin lips quirked and clamped; but he seemed to choke back whatever quick burst of reply had offered itself. After a pause he said, still in that same strange new voice of his, "Not all of us are high school kids, Jimmy. Most kids our age are like you—they lack commitment. We have older people, in their twenties, thirties, some even older than that. If you'd meet them, you'd see what I mean. Talk to Pleyel, if you want to know what true dedication is like. Talk to Hawksbill." Mischief flared in Jack's eyes. "You might even want to come just to meet the girls. We've got some girls in the group. They're pretty, liberated girls,

I might as well tell you. Just in case you care about such things, and maybe you do."

"Is this a Communist group, Jack?"

"No. Definitely not. We've got our Marxists, sure, but we run right through the political spectrum. As a matter of fact, our basic orientation is anti-Communist, because we believe in a minimum of State interference with individual life and thought, and you know that Marxists are planners. In that sense we're virtually anarchists. We might even be termed Radical Rightists, since we'd like to dismantle a lot of the government apparatus. You see how meaningless these political tags are? We're so far to the left that we're right-wingers, and we're so far to the right that we're left-wingers. But we do have a program. Will you come to a meeting?"

"Tell me about the girls."

"They're attractive and intelligent and sociable. Some of them might even be interested in an apolitical boor like you, simply because you're such a big hunk of meat."

Barrett nodded. "The next time there's a meeting, maybe I'll go."

He was tired of Bernstein's nagging, more than anything else. Large issues of politics had never interested him in a really passionate way. But it pained him to be told that he had no conscience, or that he was sitting idly by while the world went to hell, and in his whining, persistent way, Jack had goaded him into making a move. He would go to a meeting of this underground group. He would get a firsthand look. He expected that he would find it full of embittered nuts and futile dreamers, and he'd never go to a second meeting, but at least Jack would never be able to throw in his face again the accusation that he had rejected the movement out of hand.

A week later, Jack Bernstein told him that a meeting had been called for the following night. Barrett went. The date was April 11, 1984.

It was a cold, windy, rainy night, with more than a hint of snow in the air. Typical 1984 weather. There was a hex on the year, people said. That man had written a book about 1984, long ago, predicting all sorts of terrible things, and though none of those particular terrible things had come to pass in the United States, there were other troubles in the land, and everything seemed typified by the weather. Spring was not going to come this year: that looked certain. Mounds of dull gray snow lay heaped everywhere in New York, here in mid-April, except on those streets that had the heating filaments embedded in the pavement, downtown. The trees were still bare, and not even the buds were stirring. A bad year for people, tense and stormy. Not such a bad year for revolution, perhaps.

Jimmy Barrett met Jack Bernstein at the subway station near the edge of Prospect Park, and they rode into Manhattan, getting off at Times Square. The train they rode on had a shabby, tattered look to it, but that was nothing unusual. Everything was tattered and shabby, here in the ninth year of what was being called the Permanent Depression.

They walked down Forty-second Street to Ninth Avenue and entered the lobby of a golden tower eighty stories high, one of the last skyscrapers to go up before the Panic. An elevator door creaked open for them. Jack pressed the button for the basement, and down they went. "What am

I supposed to say when they ask me who I am?" Barrett wondered.

"Leave everything to me," Jack said. His pale, blotchy face was transfigured with importance. He was in his element now. Jack the conspirator. Jack the subversive. Jack the plotter in basement corridors. Barrett felt uncomfortable, awkwardly big and naïve.

They emerged from the elevator, passed through a low-vaulted passageway, and appeared before a closed green door with a chair propped against it. A girl stood in the hallway beside the chair. She was nineteen or twenty years old, Barrett guessed: short and fat, with thick legs visible beneath her short skirt. She wore her hair short too, in the current fashion, but that was the only fashionable thing about her. Heavy breasts sagged unsupported within a red woolen sweater. Her only makeup was a smear of luminescent blue across her lips, unevenly applied. A cigarette dangled loosely from one corner of her mouth. She looked deliberately slovenly, coarse, cheap, as though she saw some virtue in hunching her shoulders in and pretending she was a peasant. She seemed a caricature of all the left-wing girls who marched in protest demonstrations and waved petitions. Was this sleazy tramp the sort of girl typical of the group? "Attractive, intelligent, and sociable," Jack had said, cunningly baiting his trap with the promise of passion. But of course Jack's idea of an attractive girl didn't necessarily match his. To Jack—unpopular, scrawny, sharp-tongued—any girl who would let him paw her a little would seem like Aphrodite. Grubby boys found virtues in grubby girls that Barrett, not so limited by nature, tended not to see.

"Evening, Janet," Jack said. His voice was edgy again. The girl surveyed him coolly, then made a show of staring up at Barrett's full height.

"Who's that?"

"Jimmy Barrett. Classmate of mine. He's all right. Politically naïve, but he'll learn."

"You tell Pleyel you were asking him here?"

"No. But I'll vouch for him." Jack moved closer to her. In a possessive way he put his hand across her wrist. "Stop acting like a commissar and let us in, will you, lover?"

Janet disengaged herself. "You wait here. I'll see if it's okay."

She slipped within the green door. Jack turned to Barrett and said, "That's a marvelous girl. Sometimes she plays tough, but she's got real spirit. And sensuality. She's a very sensual girl."

"How would you know?" Barrett asked.

Jack colored and his lips compressed into a flat, angry line. "Believe me. I know."

"You mean you're not a virgin, Bernstein?"

"Knock it off, will you?"

The door opened again. Janet was back, and with her was a slim, reserved-looking man whose stubby hair was wholly gray, but whose face was unlined, so that he could have been fifty or thirty, and there was no telling. His eyes were gray too, and managed to be gentle and penetrating at the same time. Barrett saw Jack Bernstein stiffen to attention. "It's Pleyel," Bernstein whispered.

The girl said, "His name's Jim Barrett. Bernstein says he vouches for him."

Pleyel nodded amiably. The gray eyes moved quickly across Barrett's face, and it was a struggle not to flinch as those eyes excavated him. "Hello, Jim," Pleyel said: "My name's Norman Pleyel."

Barrett nodded. It sounded strange, hearing Janet and Pleyel calling him *Jim*. All his life, he had been *Jimmy* to everyone.

Jack blurted, "He's in my class. I've been working on him, getting to see his responsibilities to humanity. He finally decided to come down and attend a meeting. He—"

"Yes," Pleyel said. "We're glad to have you here, Jim. But you must understand one thing before you step inside. You're running risks by attending this meeting, even as an observer. This organization has met with official opposition. Your presence here may be held against you at some future time. Is that quite clear?"

"—yes."

"And also, since the rest of us live under constant risk, I'll have to remind you that everything that takes place here tonight is confidential. If we learn that you've taken advantage of your privilege as a guest to divulge anything you've heard, we'll be forced to take action against you. So if you step inside, you're exposing yourself to danger both from the presently constituted government and from ourselves. This is your chance to leave without stigma, if you wish."

Barrett hesitated. He glanced at Jack, whose face clearly registered distress; obviously Bernstein expected him to sidestep the risks and go home, undoing all the proselytizing work. Barrett considered the idea seriously. They were asking him to make an advance commitment before he knew anything about them; the moment he stepped through that door, he was placing himself in a matrix of responsibilities. To hell with the risks. "I'd still like to go inside, sir," he murmured.

Pleyel looked pleased. He opened the door. As Barrett stepped past the short, sullen-looking girl, he was surprised to see her staring at him with warm approval and even, perhaps, desire. She remained outside, guarding the door. Pleyel led the way within. Entering, Jack murmured to him, That man is one of the most remarkable human beings of all time." He might have been speaking of Goethe or Leonardo.

The room was large and cavernous and cold, and had not been painted for at least eight years. Rows of bare wooden benches were lined up facing an empty stage. About a dozen people had pushed some of the benches into a rough circle. They included two or three girls, a balding man, and a group of what looked like college students.

One of them was reading aloud from a long yellow slip of paper, and the others were punctuating his words with comments every few seconds.

"-in this present moment of crisis, we feel that—"

"No, it ought to be *all men must feel that—*"

"I don't think so. You make it sound stiff and—"

"Can we go back to the previous sentence, where you talk of the threat to liberty posed by—"

Barrett watched the wrangling without pleasure. It all seemed impossibly dull and dreary to him, this quibbling over the phraseology of a manifesto. That was essentially what he had expected to find here; a bunch of futilitarian hairsplitters in a drafty basement room, battling furiously over minute semantic differences. Were these the revolutionaries who would hold back the world from chaos? Hardly. Hardly.

In a moment, the discussion had turned into a scramble, with five people shouting suggestions for revision of the leaflet all at once. Pleyel stood by, looking pained but making no effort to salvage the meeting. There was a wounded and apologetic look on Jack Bernstein's face. The door opened again, and as a man in his twenties entered the meeting room, Bernstein nudged Barrett and said, "That's Hawksbill!"

The famous mathematician was an unimpressive sight. He was plump, frowsily dressed, and needed a shave. He wore thick glasses, no necktie, and a bulky blue pullover; his brown hair was curly but thinning, baring the crown of his scalp, but despite this he had the look of a college sophomore. There had to be more to the man than this, Barrett thought. Last year the newspapers had been full of the doings of Hawksbill; he had been a momentary hero of science, a nine-days' wonder when he stood up before that scientific congress in Zurich or Basel or wherever and read the text of his paper on the time equations. The newspapers had compared the work of twenty-five-year-old Edmond Hawksbill with the work of twenty-six-year-old Albert Einstein, and not to Hawksbill's disadvantage. So here he was, a member of this seedy revolutionary cell; and all his brilliance was on the inside. How could a man with such piggish little eyes be a genius?

Hawksbill put down his briefcase and said without preamble, "I ran the distribution vectors through the NYU computer while no one was looking. The indicated outcome is a breakup of *both* political parties, an inconclusive Presidential election, and the formation of a wholly different and nonrepresentative political system."

"When?" Pleyel asked.

"Within three months after the election, plus or minus fourteen days," said Hawksbill. The voice that came out of the stocky body was entirely lacking in resonance and inflection; it was a pale stream of flaccid sound. "We can expect persecution to begin by next February as the new administration attempts to stifle dissent in the name of restoring order."

"Show us the parameters!" snapped the man who had been reading the draft of the yellow-paper manifesto. "Step by step, lay it out for us, Hawksbill!"

Pleyel said, "Surely that isn't necessary. If we—"

Hawksbill Times Two

"No, I'll explain," the mathematician said, looking unruffled. He started to haul papers from his briefcase. "Item one. The election of President Delafield on the new American Conservative Party ticket in '72, resulting in fundamental changes in the economic role of the government, leading to the Boom of '73. Item two, the Panic of '76, ushering in the Permanent Depression. The victory of the National Liberal Party in '76, with the American Conservatives carrying only two states, that's item three. Now, if we cross-index the 1980 election, with its extremely subtle currents of disruption—"

"We know all that," came a bored voice.

Hawksbill shrugged. "It becomes possible to demonstrate mathematically, taking analog blocks of voter power, that neither major party is likely to achieve an electoral-vote majority this November, forcing the election into the House of Representatives, where, as a result of the situation that developed in the Congressional election of 1982, it will become impossible even to elect a President by that method. Whereupon—"

"The country will be in a mess."

"Precisely," said Hawksbill.

Barrett was aware that that last comment had come from a point not far from his left elbow. He looked down and saw Janet standing there. Absorbed in Hawksbill's droning' words, he had not even noticed her enter the room, but there she was beside him, quite close, in fact.

Jack Bernstein seemed annoyed by that, judging by the glare on his face.

The girl said, "Don't you find what they're saying terrifying?"

Barrett realized that she was speaking to him. He said tensely, "I knew things were bad, but I hadn't realized they were *that* bad. If it really happens—"

"It will. If Ed Hawksbill's computer says it'll happen, it'll happen. The Second American Revolution, we're calling it. Norm Pleyel is in contact with important men all over the country, trying to head it off."

It seemed unreal to Barrett. Oh, he knew there were strikes, protest parades, sabotage incidents. He knew there were millions of people out of work, that the dollar had been devalued four times since 1976, that the Communist countries were keeping up the pressure even though their economies weren't in such good shape themselves. And that the nation's political structure was all snarled up, with the old parties extinct and the new ones split into minority blocs. Yet it had always seemed to him and to everyone he knew that things would settle down after a while. These people seemed to be taking a deliberately pessimistic view. A revolution? An end to the present constitution?

Janet offered him a cigarette. He took it, nodding his thanks, and flipped the ignition cap. They sat down on the bench together. Her warm thigh pressed against his. Jack was on the far side of her, looking more and more annoyed. Barrett found himself thinking that this Janet wouldn't be so bad-looking if she lost twenty pounds, got herself a decent brassiere, washed her face more often, put some makeup on . . . and then he smiled at his own easy acceptance. At first glance she had seemed to be a pig, but he had begun to edit that opinion already.

Sitting quietly in a corner of the room, he tried to follow the sense of the meeting.

## Hawksbill Times Two

The focal points were Hawksbill and his hecklers. Pleyel, supposedly the leader of the group, remained to the side. Yet Barrett noticed that whenever the talk got too seriously astray, Pleyel cut in and rescued things. The man had the art of leading without seeming to lead, and Barrett was impressed.

He was not impressed at all with the rest of what was going on, though.

Everyone here seemed fundamentally sure that the country was in a bad way, and fundamentally agreed that Something Ought To Be Done About It. But beyond that point all was in haze and chaos. They couldn't even agree on the text of a manifesto to be distributed outside the White House, let alone on a program for rescuing the constitution. These people seemed as fragmented as a high school chess club, and about as capable of exerting political force. Did Bernstein expect him to take this group seriously? What was their goal? What were their methods? Politically naïve he might be, but he was at least able to assess this committee of dedicated revolutionaries and find them wanting.

The talk droned on for nearly two hours. Sometimes it grew passionate; mostly it was dull, all dialectics and hollow theory. Barrett noticed that Jack Bernstein, who surely was the youngest in the group, talked longest and loudest, shooting off cascades of verbal fireworks. Jack seemed in his element here. But all the talk came to very little. Barrett was taken by Pleyel's obvious dedication to his cause, by Hawksbill's obvious penetration of mind, and by Jack's obvious love for fiery rhetoric, but he was convinced that he had wasted his time by coming here.

Toward eleven, Janet said, "Where do you live?"

"Brooklyn. You know where Prospect Park is?"

"I'm from the Bronx. You work?"

"School."

"Oh. Yes. Right. You're in Jack's class." She seemed to be measuring him. "Does that mean you're the same age he is?"

"Sixteen, yes."

"You look a lot older, Jim."

"You're not the first to say that."

"Maybe we could get together sometime," she said. "I mean, for nonrevolutionary purposes. I'd like to know you better."

"Sure," he said. "Fine idea."

Very quickly, he found himself arranging a date. He rationalized it by telling himself that it was the decent thing to do, letting this fat, homely girl enjoy a little glamor once in her life. No doubt she'd be an easy make. It did not occur to him then that he was casually disemboweling Jack Bernstein by picking up Janet this way, but later, when he thought about it, he decided that he had done nothing wrong. Jack had nagged him into coming here, promising him that he'd meet girls, and was it his fault that the promise had been fulfilled?

On the train back to Brooklyn that night Jack was taut and cheerless. "It was a dull meeting," he said. "They aren't all that bad."

"Perhaps not."

"Sometimes a few of them get carried away with dialectics. But the cause is a good one."

"Yes," Barrett agreed. "I suppose."

He did not then plan ever to attend another meeting. But he was wrong about that, as he would prove to be wrong about so many other things in those years. Barrett did not realize then that the pattern of his adult life had been fixed in that drafty basement room, or that he had involved himself in a binding commitment, or that he had begun a lasting love affair, or that he had been face to face with his nemesis that evening. Nor did he imagine that he had transformed a friend into a savage, vindictive enemy who would one day hurl him to a strange fate.

# FIVE

ON THE EVENING of Lew Hahn's arrival, as on every evening, the men of Hawksbill Station gathered in the main building for dinner and recreation. It was not mandatory—very little was, here—and some men usually chose to eat alone. But tonight nearly everyone who was in full possession of his faculties showed up, because this was one of the infrequent occasions when a newcomer was on hand, available to be questioned about events Up Front in the world of mankind.

Hahn looked uneasy about his sudden notoriety. He seemed to be basically a shy man, unwilling to accept all the attention now being thrust upon him. There he sat in the middle of the group of exiles, while men who were twenty and thirty years his senior crowded in on him with their questions. It was obvious that he wasn't enjoying the session.

Sitting to one side, Barrett took little part in the talk. His curiosity about the ideological shifts of the world Up Front had ebbed a long time ago. It was an effort for him to recall that he had once been furiously concerned about concepts like syndicalism and the dictatorship of the proletariat and the guaranteed annual wage. When he was sixteen, and Jack Bernstein was dragging him to cell meetings, he had hardly cared about such things. But the virus of revolution had infected him, and when he was twenty-six and even when he was thirty-six he had still been so deeply involved in burning issues that he had been willing to risk imprisonment and exile over them. Now he had come full circle again, back to the political apathy of his adolescence.

It was not that his concern for the sufferings of humanity had waned—merely the degree of his involvement in the political difficulties of the twenty-first century. After two decades at Hawksbill Station, Up Front had become misty and faint to Jim Barrett, and his energies centered around the crises and challenges of what he had come to think of as "his own" time—the Late Cambrian.

So he listened, but more with an ear for what the talk revealed about Lew Hahn than for what it might reveal about current events Up Front. And what it revealed about Lew Hahn was mainly a matter of what was not revealed.

Hahn didn't say much at all. He seemed to be feinting and evading.

Hawksbill Times Two

Charley Norton wanted to know, "Is there any sign of a weakening of the phony conservatism yet? I mean, they've been promising the end of big government for thirty years, and it gets bigger all the time. When does the dismantling process begin, anyway?"

Hahn moved restlessly in his chair. "They still promise. As soon as conditions become stabilized—"

"Which happens when?"

"I don't know. I suppose they're just making fancy words."

"What about the Martian Commune?" demanded Sid Hutchett. "Have they been infiltrating agents onto Earth?"

"I couldn't really say," Hahn murmured. "We don't hear much news about Mars."

"How about the Gross Global Product?" Mel Rudiger wanted to know. "What's its curve? Still holding level, or has it started to drop?"

Hahn tugged thoughtfully at his ear. "I think it's slowly edging down. Yes, down."

"But where does the index stand?" Rudiger asked. "The last figures we had, for '25, it was at 909. But in four years' time—"

"It might be something like 875 now," said Hahn. "I'm not really sure."

It struck Barrett as a little odd that an economist would be so hazy about the basic economic statistic. Of course, he didn't know how long Hahn had been imprisoned before getting the Hammer. Maybe he simply wasn't up on the recent figures. Barrett held his peace.

Charley Norton jabbed a stubby forefinger forward and said, "Tell me about the basic legal rights of citizens nowadays. Is habeas corpus back? Search warrants?

Hawksbill Times Two

Where do they stand on gathering evidence through data channels without the knowledge of the accused?" Hahn couldn't tell him.

Rudiger asked about the impact of weather control—whether the supposedly conservative government of liberators, dedicated to upholding the rights of the governed against the abuses of the rulers, was still ramming programmed weather down the mouths of the citizens.

Hahn wasn't sure.

Hahn couldn't rightly say much about the functions of the judiciary, whether it had recovered any of the power stripped from it by the Enabling Act of '18. He didn't have any comments to offer on the tricky subject of population control. He didn't know much about tax rates. In fact, his performance was striking for its lack of hard information.

Charley Norton came over to the silent Barrett and grumbled, "He isn't saying a damned thing that's worth anything. First man we've had here in six months, and he's a clam. He's putting up a good smokescreen. Either he's not telling what he knows, or he doesn't know."

"Maybe he's just not very bright," Barrett suggested. "What did he do to get sent here, then? He must have had some kind of deep commitment. But it doesn't show, Jim! He's an intelligent kid, but he doesn't seem plugged in to anything that ever mattered to any of us."

Doc Quesada offered a thought. "Suppose this boy isn't a political at all! Suppose they're sending a different kind of prisoner back here now. Ax murderers, or something. A quiet kid who very quietly hauled out a laser and chopped up sixteen people on Sunday morning. Naturally he isn't interested in politics."

"And he's pretending to be an economist," Norton said, "because he doesn't want us to know why he really got sent here. Eh?"

Barrett shook his head. "I doubt that. I think he's just clamming up on us because he's shy or ill at ease. This is his first night here, remember. He's just been kicked out of his own world; and there's no going back, and it hurts. He may have left a wife and baby behind, you know. Or he may simply not give a damn tonight about sitting up there in the midst of you characters and spouting the latest word on abstract philosophical theory, when all he wants to do is go off and cry his eyes out. I say we ought to leave him alone. He'll talk when he feels like talking."

Quesada looked convinced. After a moment, Norton furrowed his forehead and said, "All right. Maybe." Barrett didn't spread his thoughts about Hahn any further. He let the quizzing of Hahn continue until it petered out of its own accord as the new man proved an unsatisfactory subject. The men began to drift away. A couple of them went into the back room to convert Hahn's vague generalities and evasive comments into the lead story for the next handwritten editions of the Hawksbill Station *Times*. Mel Rudiger stood on a table and shouted out that he was going night-fishing, and four men stepped forward to join him. Charley Norton sought out his customary debating partner, the nihilist Ken Belardi, and reopened, like a festering wound, their discussion of planning versus *laissez faire*, a discussion which by now bored them both to the point of screaming, but which they could not end. The nightly games of stochastic chess began. The loners who had broken their routine by making visits to the main building this evening, simply to see the new man and hear what he had to say, went back to their huts to do whatever it was they did in them alone each night.

Hahn stood apart, fidgeting and uncertain.

Barrett went up to him and drew a quick, uneasy smile. "I guess you didn't really want to be quizzed tonight, eh?" he said.

Hahn looked unhappy. "I'm sorry I couldn't have been more informative. I've been out of circulation a while, you see."

"Of course. I understand." Barrett had been out of circulation too, for quite a while, before they had decided to send him to Hawksbill Station. Sixteen months in a maximum-security interrogation chamber, and only one visitor during those sixteen months. Jack Bernstein had come to see him quite frequently. Good old Jack. After more than twenty years, Barrett hadn't forgotten a syllable of those conversations. Good. Old. Jack. Or Jacob, as he had liked to be called then. Barrett said, "You were politically active, I take it?"

"Oh, yes," Hahn said. "Of course." He flicked his tongue over his lips. "What's supposed to happen now?"

"Nothing in particular. We don't have organized activities here. It's every man for himself, essentially: the compleat anarchist community. In theory."

"Does the theory hold up?"

"Not very well," Barrett admitted. "But we try to pretend it does, and lean on each other when we need support, all the same. Doc Quesada and I are going out on sick call now. Care to join us?"

# Hawksbill Times Two

"What does it involve?" Hahn asked.

"Visiting some of the worst cases. Aid and comfort for hopeless causes, mostly. It can be grim, but you'll get a panoramic view of Hawksbill Station in a hurry. But if you prefer, you can—"

"I'd like to go."

"Good." Barrett gestured to Quesada, who came across the room to meet them. The three of them left the building. It was a mild, humid night. Thunder sounded in the distance, somewhere out over the Atlantic, and the dark ocean slapped at the obstinate ridge of rock that separated it from the waters of the Inland Sea.

Sick call was a nightly ritual for Barrett, difficult as it was for him since he had hurt his foot. He hadn't missed his rounds in years. Before turning in he stomped through the Station, visiting the goofy ones and the psycho ones and the catatonic ones, tucking them in, wishing them a good night's sleep and a healed mind in the morning. Someone had to show them that someone cared. Barrett did.

Outside, Hahn peered up at the moon. It was nearly full tonight, shining like a burnished coin, its face a pale salmon color and hardly pockmarked at all.

"It looks so different here," Hahn said. "The craters—where are the craters?"

"Most of them haven't been formed yet," Barrett told him. "A billion years is a long time even for the moon. Most of its upheavals are still ahead. We think it may still have an atmosphere, too. That's why it looks pink to us. And if it's got an atmosphere, why, it'll vaporize most of the meteors smashing into it, so there won't be so many craters gouged out. Of course, Up Front hasn't bothered to send us much in the way of astronomical equipment. We can only guess."

Hahn started to say something. He cut himself off after one blurted syllable.

Quesada said, "Don't hold it back. What were you about to suggest?"

Hahn laughed, a self-mocking snort. "That you ought to fly up there and take a look. It struck me as odd that you'd spend all these years theorizing about whether the moon's got an atmosphere, and wouldn't ever once go up there to look. But I forgot."

"It would be useful if we got a commute ship from Up Front," Barrett agreed. "But it hasn't occurred to them to send us one. All we can do is to look and guess. The moon's a popular place in '29, is it?"

"The biggest resort in the System."

"They were just starting to develop it when I came here," Barrett said.

"Government personnel only. A rest camp for bureaucrats in the middle of the big military complex up there."

Quesada said, "They opened it to selected nongovernmental elite before my trial. That was in '17, '18."

"Now it's a commercial resort," said Hahn. "I was there on my honeymoon. Leah and I—"

He stopped again.

Barrett said hurriedly, "This is Bruce Valdosto's hut. Val's a revolutionary from way back, grew up with me, more or less. He stayed under cover longer. They didn't send him here till '22." As he opened the door, Barrett went on, "He cracked up a few weeks ago, and he's in bad shape. When we go in, Hahn, stand behind us so he doesn't see you. He might be violent with a stranger. Val's unpredictable."

Valdosto was a husky man in his late forties, with swarthy skin, coarse curling black hair, and the broadest shoulders any man had ever had. Sitting down, he looked even burlier than Jim Barrett, which was saying a great deal. But Valdosto had short, stumpy legs, the legs of a man of ordinary stature tacked wantonly to the trunk of a giant, which spoiled the effect completely when he stood up. It would have been possible, while he was still living Up Front, for Valdosto to have a different pair of legs fitted to his body. But in his years Up Front he had totally refused to go in for prosthetics. He wanted his own true legs, gnarled and malproportioned though they were. He believed in living with deformities and adjusting to them. Right now he was strapped tightly into a webfoam cradle. 'His domed forehead was flecked with beads of sweat, and his eyes were glittering like mica in the darkness. Valdosto was a very sick man. Once he had been clear-minded enough to throw a sleet-bomb into a meeting of the Council of Syndics, giving a dozen of them a bad case of gamma poisoning, but now he scarcely knew up from down, right from left. It chilled Barrett to see Valdosto come apart this way. Barrett had known him more than thirty years, and hoped that he was not seeing in Valdosto's collapse a prefiguring of his own eventual decay.

The air in the hut was moist, as if a cloud of perspiration hovered below the roof. Barrett leaned over the sick man and said, "How are you, Val?"

"Who's that?"

"Jim. It's a beautiful night tonight, Val. We had some rain, but it's over, and the moon is out. How'd you like to come outside and get some fresh air? It's almost a full moon."

"I've got to rest. The committee meeting tomorrow—"

"It's been postponed."

"But how can it? The Revolution—"

"That's been postponed too. Indefinitely."

The muscles of Valdosto's cheeks writhed. "Are they disbanding the cells?" he asked harshly.

"We don't know yet. We're waiting for orders, and until they come we've just got to sit tight. Come outside, Val. The air will do you good."

"Kill all those bastards, that's the only way," Valdosto muttered. "Who told them they could run the world? A bomb right in their faces—a good little sleet-bomb, a fragmentation job loaded with hard radiation—"

"Easy, Val. There'll be time for throwing bombs later. Let's get you out of the cradle."

Still muttering, Valdosto allowed himself to be unlaced. Quesada and Barrett pulled him to his feet and let him get his balance. He was terribly unsteady, shifting his weight again and again, flexing his massive twisted calves. After a moment Barrett took him by the arm and propelled him through the door of the hut. He caught sight of Hahn standing in the shadows, his face somber with distress.

They all stood together just outside the hut. Barrett pointed to the moon. "There it is. It's got such a lovely color here, eh? Not like the dead thing that shines Up Front. And look, look down there, Val. The sea breaking on the rocky shore. Rudiger's out fishing. I can see his boat by the moonlight."

"Striped bass," said Valdosto. "Sunnies. Maybe he'll catch some sunnies."

"There aren't any sunnies here. They haven't evolved yet." Barrett reached into his pocket and drew out something ridged and hard and glossy, about two inches long. It was the exoskeleton of a small trilobite. He offered it to Valdosto, who shook his head brusquely. "Don't give me that cockeyed crab."

"It's a trilobite, Val. It's extinct, but so are we. We're living a billion years in our own past."

"You must be crazy," Valdosto said in a calm, low voice that belied his wild-eyed appearance. He took the trilobite from Barrett and hurled it against the rocks. "Cockeyed crab," he muttered. Then he said, "Look, why are we here? Why do we have to keep on waiting? Tomorrow, let's get some stuff and go get them. First we get

Bernstein, right? He's the dangerous one. And then the others. One by one, we pick them off, get all the goddam murderers out of the world so it's a safe place again. I'm sick of waiting. I hate it here, Jim. Jim? That's who you are, yeah? Jim Barrett."

Quesada shook his head sadly as Valdosto let a trickle of saliva run down his chin. The terrorist folded into a tight crouch, keening softly to himself, pressing his swollen knees against the rock. His hands clutched at the barrenness, searching for and not finding even enough dirt to make a decent handful. Quesada lifted him to his feet, and he and Barrett led the sick man into the hut again. Valdosto did not protest as the medic pressed the snout of the sedative capsule against his arm and activated it. His weary mind, rebelling entirely against the monstrous concept that he had been exiled forever to the inconceivably remote past, welcomed sleep.

When they went outside again, Barrett saw Hahn holding the trilobite on his palm and staring at the strange thing in wonder. Hahn offered it back to him, but Barrett brushed it away.

"Keep it if you like," he said. "There are more where I got that one. Plenty."

They went on.

They found Ned Altman beside his hut, crouching on his knees and patting his hands over the crude, lopsided form of what, from the exaggerated mounds where breasts and hips might be, appeared to be the image of a woman. He stood up smartly when they appeared. Altman was a neat little man with yellow hair and transparent-looking light blue eyes. Unlike anyone else in the Station, he had actually been a government man once, fifteen years ago, before seeing through the myth of syndicalist capitalism and joining one of the underground factions. With his insider's perspective on governmental operations, Altman had been invaluable to the underground, and the government had worked hard to find him and send him here. Eight years at Hawksbill Station had done things to him.

Altman pointed to his earthen golem and said, "I hoped there'd be lightning in the rain today. That'll do it, you know. The breath of life. But there isn't much lightning this time of year, I guess, even when it rains."

"There'll be electrical storms soon," said Barrett.

Altman nodded eagerly. "And lightning will strike her, and she'll get up alive and walk, and then I'll need your help, Doc. I'll need you to give her shots and trim away some of the rough places."

Quesada forced a smile. "I'll be glad to do it, Ned. But you know the terms."

"Sure. When I'm through with her, you get her. You think I'm a goddam monopolist? Fair is fair. I'll share her. There'll be a waiting list, everything in order of application. Just so you guys don't forget who made her, though. She'll remain mine, whenever I need her." He noticed Hahn for the first time. "Who are you?"

"He's new," Barrett explained. "Lew Hahn. He came this afternoon."

"My name's Ned Altman," said Altman with a courtly, mincing bow. "Formerly in the government service. Hey, you're pretty young, aren't you? Still got the bloom on the cheeks. How's your sex orientation, Lew? Hetero?"

Hahn winced. "I'm afraid so."

"It's okay. You can relax. I wouldn't touch you. I've got a project going, here, and I'm off that kind of stuff. But I just want you to know, if you're hetero, I'll put you on my list. You're young and you've probably got stronger needs than some of us. I won't forget about you, even though you're new here, Lew."

"That's kind of you," Hahn said.

Altman knelt. He ran his hands delicately over the curves of the clumsy figure, lingering at the tapering conical breasts, shaping them, trying to make them smooth. He might have been caressing a real woman's quivering flesh.

Quesada coughed. "I think you ought to get some rest , now, Ned. Maybe there'll be lightning tomorrow."

"Let's hope so."

"Up, now. Up."

Altman did not resist. The doctor took him inside and put him to bed. Barrett and Hahn, remaining outside, surveyed the man's handiwork. Hahn pointed toward the figure's middle.

"He's left out something essential, hasn't he?" he asked. "If he's planning to make love to this girl after he's finished creating her, he'd better—"

"It was there yesterday," said Barrett. "He must be changing orientation again."

Quesada emerged from Altman's hut, looking gloomy. The three of them went on, down the rocky path. Barrett did not make the complete circuit that night. Ordinarily, he would have gone all the way down to Don Latimer's hut overlooking the sea, for Latimer, with his obsession for finding a psionic gateway through which he could flee Hawksbill Station, was on his list of sick ones who needed special attention.

But Barrett had visited Latimer once that day, to introduce him to Hahn, and he didn't think his aching good leg was up to another hike that far so soon.

So after he and Quesada and Hahn had been to all of the easily accessible huts, he called it a night. They had visited Gaillard, the man who prayed for alien beings to come from another solar system and rescue him from the loneliness and misery of Hawksbill Station. They had visited Schultz, the man who was trying to break into a parallel universe where everything was as it ought to be in the world, a true Utopia. They had visited McDermott, who had not elaborated any imaginative and fanciful psychosis, but simply lay on his cot sobbing for all his wakeful hours, day after day. Then Barrett said good night to his companions and allowed Quesada to escort Hahn back to his but without him.

"You're sure you don't want us to walk up with you?" Hahn asked, eyeing Barrett's crutch.

"No. No, I'm fine. I'll make it."

They walked away. Barrett set out up the rocky slope. He had observed Hahn for half a day, now. And, Barrett realized, he did not know much more about him than when the man had first dropped onto the Anvil. That was odd. But maybe Hahn would open up a little more, after he'd been here a while and came to realize that these were the only companions he was ever going to have.

Barrett stared up at the salmon moon, and reached into his pocket by habit to finger the little trilobite, before he remembered that he had given it to Hahn. He shuffled into his hut. He wondered how long ago Hahn had taken that lunar honeymoon.

# SIX

IT WAS A couple of years of pretty hard work before Jim Barrett had succeeded in remaking Janet to the proper image. He was unwilling to push her to change, because he knew right away that that would guarantee failure. He was more subtle about it, borrowing some of Norm Pleyel's tactics of indirect persuasion. They worked. Janet never actually became beautiful, but at least she stopped making a cult out of slovenliness. And the change was considerable. Barrett left home and started living with her when he was nineteen. She was twenty-four, but that didn't really matter.

By then the revolution had come, and the counter-revolution was getting under way.

The upheaval took place right on schedule in late 1984, fulfilling the prediction of Edmond Hawksbill's computer, and putting to rest a political system that had celebrated a very grim bicentennial only eight years earlier. The system had simply ceased to work, and into the vacuum had moved, as expected, those who had long mistrusted the democratic process anyway. The Constitution of 1985 was ostensibly intended as a stopgap document, creating a caretaker government that would supervise the restoration of civil liberties in the United States, then wither away. But stopgap constitutions and caretaker governments sometimes fail to wither when the time for withering comes.

Under the new setup, a sixteen-man Council of Syndics led by a Chancellor performed most of the governmental functions. The names were strange ones to a country long accustomed to Presidents, Senators, Secretaries of State, and the like.

It had seemed that all those posts were eternal and immutable, and suddenly they were not, for an entire new rhetoric of command had been inserted where the familiar words had been. The change was most emphatic at the highest levels; the bureaucracy and civil service continued much as before, as it had to do if the nation were to avoid total disruption.

The new rulers were oddly assorted. They could not be called either conservatives or liberals, as those abused terms had been understood throughout most of the twentieth century. They believed in an activist government philosophy, strong on public works and central planning, which might qualify them as Marxists or at least as New Deal liberals. But they also believed in the suppression of dissent for the sake of harmonious endeavor, which had never been a New Deal policy, though it was inherent in the Leninist-Stalinist-Maoist perversions of Marxism. On the other hand, they were unreconstructed capitalists, most of them, who insisted on the supremacy of the business sector of the economy and devoted much energy to restoring the business climate of, say, 1885. In foreign affairs they were starkly reactionary, isolationist, and anti-Communist to the point of xenophobia. It was, to put it mildly, a highly mixed governmental philosophy.

"It isn't a philosophy at all," Jack Bernstein maintained, hammering fist against palm. "It's just a gang of strong-arm men who happened to find a power vacuum and moved right in. They've got no overriding program of government. They simply do what they think is necessary to perpetuate their own rule and keep things from blowing up again. They grabbed power, and now they improvise from day to day."

"Then they're bound to fall," Janet said mildly. "Without a central vision of government, a power bloc is certain to collapse, in time. They'll make critical mistakes and find that there's no drawing back from the gulf."

"They've been in power for three years, now," Barrett said. "They don't show any sign of falling. I'd say they're stronger than ever. They're settling in for a thousand years."

"No," Janet insisted. "They're launched on a self-destructive course. It may be another three years, it may be ten, it may be just a matter of months, but they'll fall apart. They don't know what they're doing. You can't paste together McKinley capitalism and Roosevelt socialism and call it syndicalist capitalism and hope to rule a country this size with it. It's inevitable—"

"Who says Roosevelt was a socialist?" someone in the back of the room demanded.

"Side issue," Norman Pleyel warned. "Let's not get into side issues."

"I disagree with Janet," Jack Bernstein said. "I don't think the present government is inherently unstable. As Barrett says, they're stronger than ever. And here we sit talking. We talked right along while they took over, and we've been talking for three more years—"

"We've done more than talk," Barrett cut in.

Bernstein paced the room, hunched, tense, throbbing with inner energy. "Handbills! Petitions! Manifestoes! Calls for a general strike! What good, what good, what good?" At nineteen, Bernstein was no taller than he had been in the year of the great upheaval, but the baby fat was gone from his face. He was gaunt, fleshless, with savage cheekbones and sallow skin against which the pockmarks and scars of his skin malady gleamed like beacons. He affected a straggly mustache now. Under the pressure of events, they were all transforming themselves; Janet had dieted away her blubber, Barrett had let his hair grow long, even the imperturbable Pleyel had grown a wispy beard that he stroked as though it were a talisman. Bernstein glowered at the little group assembled in the apartment that Barrett and Janet shared. "Do you know why this illegal government has been able to sustain itself in power? Two reasons. First, it maintains an immoral secret police network through which it stifles opposition. Second, it maintains firm control over all the media of communication, and thereby perpetuates itself by persuading the citizens that they've got no alternative except three cheers for syndicalism. Do you know what's going to happen in another generation? This nation will be so firmly wedded to syndicalism that it'll settle down with it for the next few centuries!"

"Impossible, Jack," Janet said. "A system of government needs more to sustain itself than a secret police. It—"

"Shut up and let me finish," Bernstein said. There was a snarl in his tone. He rarely troubled to conceal his intense hatred for her any longer. Sparks flew when he was in the same room with her, which in the nature of things was quite often.

"Go ahead, then. Finish."

He drew a deep breath. "This is basically a conservative country," he said. "Always has been. Always will be. The Revolution of 1776 was a conservative revolution in defense of property rights. For the next two hundred years there were no fundamental changes in the political structure here. France had a revolution and six, seven constitutions, Russia had a revolution, Germany and Italy and Austria turned into entirely different countries, even England quietly transformed its whole arrangement, but the United States didn't budge. Oh, I know, there were changes in the electoral law, little touch-up jobs, and the franchise was extended to women and Negroes, and the powers of the President gradually expanded, but all that was within the original framework. And in the schools the kids were taught that there was something sacred about that framework. It was a built-in stability factor: the citizens wanted the system to remain as it was, because it had always been that way, and so on, round and round and round in an eternal circle. This nation *couldn't* change because it didn't have the capacity to change. It had been schooled to hate change. That's why incumbent Presidents always got re-elected unless they were absolute dogs. That's why the constitution was amended maybe twenty times in two centuries, tops. That's why whenever a man came along who wanted to change things in a big way, like Henry Wallace, like Goldwater, he got stepped on by the power structure. Did you study the Goldwater election? He was supposed to be a conservative, yes? But he lost, and who fought him the hardest but the conservatives, because they knew he was a radical, and they feared letting a radical in."

"Jack, I think you're exaggerating the——"

"Damn you, *let me finish*." Bernstein's face was red. Sweat rolled down his haggard cheeks. "It was a country conditioned from birth against fundamental change. But eventually the existing government overextended itself and lost control, and the radicals finally did get in, and they changed things so much that everything fell apart and we got the constitutional crisis of 1982-84, followed by the syndicalist takeover. Okay. The takeover was such a trauma that millions of people are still in shock over it. They open up their newspapers and they see that there's no President any more, there's something called a Chancellor, and instead of Congress passing laws there's a Council of Syndics, and they say, what are these crazy names, what country is this, it can't be the good old U.S. of A., can it? But it is. And they're so stunned that they go into retrogression and start thinking they're hedgehogs. Okay. Okay. But the discontinuity has occurred. The old system's been replaced with something new. Kids are still being born. The schools are open, and the teachers are teaching syndicalism, because they'd goddam better well teach syndicalism if they want to keep their jobs. The fifth graders today think of Presidents as dangerous dictators. They smile at the big tridims of Chancellor Arnold every morning. The third-graders don't even know what Presidents were. In ten more years, those kids will be adults. In twenty more years, they'll be running society. They'll have a vested interest in the status quo, the way American adults always have, and to them *the status quo will be the syndicalists*. Don't you see? Don't you see? We're going to lose unless we grab the kids growing up! The syndicalists are getting them, and educating them to think that syndicalism is true and good and beautiful, and the longer that goes on, the longer it's *going* to go on. It's self-perpetuating. Anybody who wants the old constitution back, or who wants the new constitution amended, is going to look like a dangerous fire-breathing radical, and the syndicalists will be the nice, safe, conservative boys we've always had and always want. At which point everything is over and done with." Bernstein subsided. "Give me a drink, somebody. Fast!"

Pleyel's soft voice cut across the hubbub. "That's well reasoned, Jack. But I'd like to hear some suggestions from you, some plan of positive action."

"I've got plenty of suggestions," Bernstein said. "And they all start by scrapping the existing counter-revolutionary structure we've established. We're using methods appropriate to 1917, or maybe to 1848, and the syndicalists are using 1987 methods and they're killing us. We're still passing out handbills and asking people to sign petitions. And they've got the television stations, the whole damned nexus of communications, all turned into a big propaganda network. And the schools." He held out a hand and ticked off programs on his fingers. "One. Establish electronic means for tying into computer channels and other media to scramble government propaganda. Two. Insert our own counterrevolutionary propaganda wherever possible, not in printed form but on the media. Three. Assemble a cadre of clever ten-year-olds to spread discontent in the fifth grade. And stop snickering! Four. A program of selected assassinations to remove—"

"Hold it," Barrett said. "No assassinations."

"Jim's right," said Pleyel. "Assassination isn't a valid method of political discourse. It's also futile and self-defeating, since it brings new and hungrier leaders to the fore, and makes martyrs out of villains."

"Have it your own way, then. You asked me for suggestions. Kill off ten syndics and we'd be that much closer to freedom, but all right. Five. Formulate a coherent schematic plan for a take-over of the government, at least as clear-cut and well organized as the syndicalist bunch used in '84-'85. That is, find out how many men are needed at the key points, what kind of job it would be to take over the communications media, how we can immobilize the existing leadership, how we can induce the strategic defections among the general staff of the armed forces. The syndicalists used computers to do it. The least we can do is imitate them. Where's our master plan? Suppose Chancellor Arnold resigned tomorrow and said he was turning the country over to the underground, would we be able to form a government, or would we just be a bunch of fragmented cells spouting stale theories?"

Pleyel said, "There is a master plan, Jack. I'm in contact with many groups."

"A computer-programmed plan?" Bernstein pressed. Pleyel spread his long hands out eloquently in the gesture that meant he would rather not reply.

"It ought to be," Bernstein said. "We've got a man right in our group who's the greatest mathematical genius since Descartes, for God's sake. Hawksbill ought to be plotting templates for us. Where the hell is he, anyway?"

"He doesn't come around much any more," Barrett said.

"I know that. But why not?"

"He's busy, Jack. He's trying to build a time machine, or some such thing."

Bernstein gaped. A burst of bitter laughter, harsh and grinding, erupted from his throat. "*A time machine?* You mean, a literal and actual thing for traveling in time?"

"1 think that's what he said," Barrett murmured. "He didn't exactly call it that. I'm no mathematician, and I couldn't follow too much of what he was saying, but—"

"There's a genius for you." Bernstein cracked his knuckles furiously. "A dictatorship in control, the secret police making arrests daily, the situation deteriorating all the time, and he sits around inventing time machines. Where's his common sense? If he wants to be an inventor, why doesn't he invent some way of tossing out the government?"

"Perhaps," Pleyel said gently, "this machine of his can be of some use to us. If, say, we could go back in time to 1980 or 1982, and take corrective action to forestall the causes of the constitutional crisis—"

"You're really serious, aren't you?" Bernstein asked. "While the crisis was going on, we sat on our cans and deplored the sad state of the cosmos, and eventually the thing we all predicted was going to happen happened, and we hadn't done a damned thing to prevent it. And now you talk about taking a crazy machine and going back and changing the past. I'll be damned. I'll be absolutely damned."

"We know much more about the vectors of the revolution, Jack," Pleyel said. "It might just work."

"With judicious assassinations, maybe. But you've already ruled out assassination as a means of political discourse. So what will you do with Hawksbill's machine? Send Barrett back to 1980 to wave banners at rallies? Oh, this is crazy. Pardon me, but you all make me sick. I'm going to go over to Union Square and puke, I think." He stormed out of the room.

"He's unstable," Barrett said to Pleyel. "He was practically frothing at the mouth. I wish he'd quit the movement, you know? One of these days he'll get so disgusted with our stick-in-the-mud ways that he'll denounce us all to the secret police."

"I doubt that, Jim. He's excitable, yes. But he's tremendously brilliant. He spouts ideas of all sorts, some of them worthless, some of them not. We've got to see him through the rough moments, because we need him. You should know that better than any of us, Jim. He's your childhood friend, isn't he?"

Barrett shook his head. "Whatever there was between Jack and me, I don't think it could have been called friendship. And it's been over for years, anyway. He hates my guts. He'd love to see me trampled in the gutter."

The meeting broke up soon afterward. There were the usual motions to investigate the recommendations put forth, and there were the customary assignments to prepare special reports on the findings. And that was that. The members of the counterrevolutionary cell drifted out. At last only Janet and Barrett were left, emptying ashtrays, straightening chairs.

She said, "It was frightening to watch Jack tonight. He seemed to be possessed by demons. He could have talked for hours without running out of words."

"What he said made some sense."

"Some of it, yes, Jim. He's right that we ought to be planning in greater detail, and that we ought to be putting Ed Hawksbill to more use. But it's the way he spoke, not what he said, that scared me. He was like a little demagogue, standing up there, pacing back and forth, spitting out words. I imagine Hitler must have been like that when he was starting out. Napoleon, maybe."

"Well, then, we're lucky Jack's on our side," Barrett said.

"Are you sure he is?"

"Did he sound like a syndicalist tonight?"

Janet gathered a bundle of discarded papers and stuffed them in the disposall. "No, but I could imagine him going over to the other side very easily. As you yourself said, he's unstable. Brilliant but unstable. Given the right sort of motivation, he could very well switch sides. He's restless here.

He wants to challenge Pleyel for the leadership of the group, but he's afraid to hurt Norm's feelings, so he's stymied, and someone like Jack doesn't take well to being stymied."

"Besides which, he hates us."

"He only hates you and me," Janet said. "I don't think he's got anything personal against the others."

"Yet."

"He might transfer his hatred of us to the whole group," Janet conceded.

Barrett scowled. "I haven't been able to talk rationally with him in two years. I keep getting this tremendous surge of jealousy from him. Loathing. All because I happened to move in on his girlfriend, without knowing what I was doing. There are other women in the world."

"And I was never his girlfriend," Janet said. "Haven't you realized that by now? I dated him three, four times before you joined the group. But there was nothing serious going between him and me. Nothing."

"You slept with him, didn't you?"

Her cool dark eyes rose and leveled with his. "Once. Because he begged me. It was like sleeping with a dentist's drill. I never let him touch me again. He had no claim on me. Even if he thinks he did, it's his own fault for what happened. He introduced you to me."

"Yes," Barrett said. "He begged me to join the group. He harangued me. He accused me of having no commitment to humanity, and I suppose he was right. I was just a big naïve sixteen-year-old clod who liked sex and beer and bowling, and now and then looked at a newspaper and wondered what the hell all the headlines meant. Well, he set out to awaken my conscience, and he did, and in the course of events I found a girl, and now—"

"Now you're a big naïve nineteen-year-old clod who likes sex and beer and bowling and counterrevolutionary activities."

"Right."

"So to hell with Jack Bernstein," Janet said. "One of these days he'll grow up and stop envying you, and we can all start working together to fix up the mess that the world's gotten itself into. Meanwhile we just go along from day to day and do our best. What else is there?"

"I suppose," Barrett said.

He walked to the window and nudged the control. The opaquing faded, and he looked out through the darkness to the street fifteen stories below. Two bottle-green police cars were angle-parked across the street; they had stopped a small blue-

and-gold electric runabout, and the police were questioning its driver. From this far up, Barrett couldn't see much, but the man's high-pitched protests of innocence rose to window level. After a moment a third police car arrived. Still protesting, the man was shoved into it and taken away. Barrett opaqued the window again. As it turned gray and clouded, it showed him the reflection of Janet, standing nude behind him, the full globes of her breasts rising and falling expectantly. He turned. She looked immensely better, now that she had taken off that weight, but he couldn't find any delicate way of telling her that without implying that she had been a slob before.

"Come to bed," she said. "Stop staring out windows." He moved toward her. He was well over a foot taller than she was, and when he stood beside her he felt like a tree above a shrub. His arms enclosed her, and he felt the soft warmth of her against him, and as they sank into the mattress he imagined he could hear Jack Bernstein's reedy, angry voice howling through the night, and he reached for her and pulled her fiercely into a tight embrace.

## SEVEN

RUDIGER'S CATCH WAS spread out in front of the main building the next morning when Barrett came up for breakfast. Rudiger had had a good night's fishing, obviously. He usually did. Rudiger went out into the Atlantic three or four nights a week when the weather was good, using the little dinghy that he had cobbled together a few years ago from salvaged packing crates and other miscellaneous materials, and he took with him a team of friends whom he had trained in the deft use of the trawling nets. They generally returned with a good haul of seafood.

It was an irony that Rudiger, the anarchist, the man who profoundly believed in individualism and the abolition of all political institutions, should be so good at leading a team of fishermen. Rudiger didn't care for the concept of teamwork in the abstract. But it was hard to manipulate the nets alone, he had quickly discovered, and he had begun to assemble his little microcosm of a society. Hawksbill Station had many small ironies of that sort. Political theorists, Barrett knew well, tend to swallow their theories when forced back on pragmatic matters of survival.

The prize of the catch was a cephalopod about a dozen feet long—a rigid greenish conical tube out of which some limp orange squid-like tentacles dangled, throbbing fitfully. There was plenty of meat on that one, Barrett thought. Rubbery but good, if you cultivated a taste for it. Dozens of trilobites were arrayed around the cephalopod. They ranged in size from the inch-long kind that went into trilobite cocktails to the three-footers with baroquely involuted exoskeletons. Rudiger fished both for food and for knowledge; evidently these trilobites were discards, representatives of species that he had already studied, or he wouldn't have left them here to go into the food hoppers. His hut was stacked ceiling-high with trilobites, classified and sorted according to genus and species. It kept Rudiger sane to collect and analyze and write about them, and no one here begrudged him his hobby.

Near the heap of trilobites were some clusters of hinged brachiopods, looking like scallops that had gone awry, and a pile of snails. The warm, shallow waters just off the coastal shelf teemed with invertebrate life, in striking contrast to the barren land. Rudiger had also brought in a mound of shiny black seaweed for salads. Barrett hoped that someone would gather all this stuff up and get it into the Station's heat-sink cooler before it spoiled. The bacteria of decay worked a lot slower here than they did Up Front, but a few hours in the mild air would do Rudiger's haul no good. Barrett hobbled into the kitchen and found three men on morning mess duty. They nodded respectfully to him.

"There's food lying by the door," Barrett said. "Rudiger's back, and he dumped a load."

"He could have told somebody, huh?"

"Perhaps there was nobody here to tell when he came by. Will you collect it and get it under refrigeration?"

"Sure, Jim. Sure."

Today Barrett planned to recruit some men for the annual Inland Sea expedition. Traditionally, it was a trek that he always had led himself, but the injury to his foot made it impossible for him even to consider going on the trip this year, or ever again.

Each year, a dozen or so able-bodied men went out on a wide-ranging reconnaissance that took them in a big circular arc, looping northwestward until they reached the Inland Sea, then coming around to the south and back up the strip of land to the Station. One purpose of the trip was to gather any temporal garbage that might have materialized in the vicinity of the Station during the past year. There was no way of knowing how wide a margin of error had been allowed during the early attempts to set the Station up, and the scattershot technique of hurling material into the past had been pretty unreliable.

New stuff was turning up all the time. It had been aimed for Minus One Billion, Two Thousand Oh Five A.D., but didn't arrive until a few decades later. Now, in

## Hawksbill Times Two

A.D. Minus One Billion, Two Thousand Twenty-Nine, things were still appearing that had been intended to arrive in the Station's first year of operation. Hawksbill Station needed all the spare equipment it could get, and Barrett didn't miss a chance to round up any of the debris from the future.

There was another and subtler reason for making the Inland Sea expeditions, though. They served as a focus for the year, an annual ritual, something to peg a custom to. The expedition was the local rite of spring. The dozen strongest men, going on foot to the distant rock-rimmed shores of the tepid sea that drowned the heart of North America, were performing the closest thing Hawksbill Station had to a religious function, although they did nothing more mystical when they reached the Inland Sea than to net a few trilobites and eat them.

The trip meant more to Barrett himself than he had ever suspected, also. He realized that now, when he was unable to go. He had led every such expedition for twenty years. Across the changeless, monotonous scenery, beyond the slippery slopes, down to the sea, eyes ranging the horizon at all times for the tell-tale signs of temporal garbage. Trilobite stew cooked over midnight fires far from the dreary huts of Hawksbill Station. A rainbow lancing into the sea somewhere over what was to be Ohio. The stunning crackle of distant lightning, the tang of ozone in the nostrils, the rewarding sensation of aching muscles at the end of a day's march. The pilgrimage was the pivot on which the year turned, for Barrett. And to see the grayish-green waters of the Inland Sea come into view was strangely like coming home to him.

Hawksbill Times Two

But last year at the edge of the sea Barrett had gone scrabbling over boulders loosened by the tireless action of the waves, venturing into risky territory for no rational reason that he could name, and his aging muscles had betrayed him. Often at night he woke sweating and trembling to escape from the dream in which he relived that ugly moment: slipping and sliding, clawing at the rocks, a mass of stone dislodged from somewhere and crashing down with improbably agonizing impact against his foot, pinning him, crushing him.

He could not forget that sound of grinding bones. Nor was he likely to lose the memory of the homeward march, across hundreds of miles of bare rock under a huge sun, his bulky body slung between the bowed forms of his companions. He had never been a burden to anyone before. "Leave me behind," he had said, not really meaning it, and they knew he was making only a formalized gesture of apology for troubling them, and they said, "Don't be a fool," and hauled him onward. But they worked hard to carry him along and in the moments when the pain allowed him to think clearly, he felt guilty about troubling them in this way. He was so big. If any of the others had suffered such an accident, it would not have been such a chore to transport him. But he was the biggest one.

Barrett thought he would have to lose the foot. But Quesada had spared him from the amputation. The foot would stay, though Barrett would not be able to touch it to the ground and put weight on it, not now or ever again. It might have been simpler to have the dead appendage sliced off; Quesada had vetoed that, though.

"Who knows," he had said, "someday they might send us a transplant kit. I can't rebuild a leg that's been amputated. Once we cut it off, all I can do is give you a prosthetic, and I don't have any prosthetics here."

So Barrett had kept his crushed foot. But he had never been quite the same since the accident. More than blood had leaked from him as he lay on the glistening rocks beside the Inland Sea. And now someone else would have to lead this year's march.

Who would it be, he wondered?

Quesada was the likeliest choice. Next to Barrett, he was the strongest man here, in all the ways that it was important to be strong. But Quesada couldn't be spared from his responsibilities at the Station. It might be handy to have a medic along on the trip, but it was vital to have one here.

After some reflection Barrett put down Charley Norton as the leader of the expedition. Norton was bouncy and talkative and got worked up too easily, but he was basically a sensible man capable of commanding respect. Barrett added Ken Belardi to the list—someone for Norton to talk to during the long dull hours of trekking from nowhere to nowhere. Let them go on debating—an endless ballet of fixed postures.

Rudiger? Rudiger had been a tower of strength on the journey last year after Barrett had been injured. He had taken charge beautifully while the others dithered around and gaped at the sight of their fallen, battered leader. Barrett didn't particularly want to let Rudiger leave the Station so long, though. He needed able men for the expedition, true, but he didn't care to strip the home base down to a population of invalids, crackpots, and psychotics.

So Rudiger stayed behind. Barrett put two members of his fishing team on the list, Dave Burch and Mort Kasten. Then he added the names of Sid Hutchett and Arny Jean-Claude.

Barrett thought about putting Don Latimer in the group. Latimer was coming to be something of a borderline mental case, but he was rational enough except when he lapsed into his psionic meditations, and he'd pull his own weight on the expedition. On the other hand, Latimer was Lew Hahn's bunkmate, and Barrett wanted Latimer around to observe Hahn at close range. He toyed with the idea of sending both of them out, but nixed it. Hahn was still an unknown quantity. It was too risky to let him go with the Inland Sea party this year. Probably he'd be in next year's group, though. It would be foolish not to take advantage of Hahn's youthful vigor. Let him get to know the ropes, and he'd be an ideal expedition leader for years to come.

Finally Barrett had chosen a dozen men. A dozen would be enough. He chalked their names on the slate in front of the mess hall, and went inside to find Charley Norton.

Norton was sitting alone, breakfasting. Barrett eased himself into the bench opposite him, going through the complex series of motions that constituted his way of sitting down without letting go of his crutch.

"You pick the men?" Norton asked. Barrett nodded. "The list's posted outside."

"Am I going?"

"You're in command."

Norton looked flattered. "That sounds strange, Jim. I mean, for anyone else but you to be in command—"

"I'm not making the trip this year, Charley."

"It takes some getting used to. Who's going?"

"Hutchett. Belardi. Burch. Kasten. Jean-Claude. And some others."

"Rudiger?"

"No, not Rudiger. Not Quesada either, Charley. I need them here."

"All right, Jim. You have any special instructions for us?"

"Just come back in one piece, is all I ask." Barrett picked up a water flask and cupped it in his huge hands. "Maybe we should call it off, this time. We don't have all that many able-bodied men."

Norton's eyes flashed. "What are you saying, Jim? Call off the trip?"

"Why not? We know what's between here and the sea: nothing."

"But the salvage—"

"It can wait. We're not running short of material right at the moment."

"Jim, I've never heard you talk this way before. You've always been big on the trip. The highlight of the year, you said. And now—"

"I'm not going on this one, Charley."

Norton was silent a moment, but his eyes did not leave Barrett's. Then he said, "All right, you're not going. I know how that must hurt you. But there are other men here. They *need* the trip. Just because you can't go, you've got no right to say we ought to call it off as pointless. It isn't pointless."

"I'm sorry, Charley," Barrett said heavily. "I didn't mean any of that. Of course there'll be a trip. I was just running off at the mouth again."

"It must be tough for you, Jim."

"It is. But not *that* tough. You have any ideas of the route you'll take?"

"Northwest route out, I guess. That's the usual distribution line for the odd-year garbage, isn't it? And then down to the Inland Sea. We'll follow the shoreline for, oh, a hundred miles, I guess. And come home via the lower path."

"Good enough," Barrett said. In the eye of his mind he saw the rippling surface of the shallow sea, stretching off to the distant western land zone. Year after year he had come to the edge of that sea and peered off toward the place where the Midwest would someday rise above the water. Each year, he had dreamed of a voyage across the continental heart to the other side. But he had never found the time to organize such a voyage. And now it was too late . . . too late. . . .

We would never have found anything much over there anyway, Barrett told himself. Just more of the same. Rock, seaweed, trilobites. But it might have been worth it . . . to see the sun drop into the Pacific one last time. . . . Norton said, "I'll get the men together after breakfast. We'll be on our way fast."

"Right. Good luck, Charley."

"We'll make out."

Barrett clapped Norton on the shoulder, a gesture that struck him instantly as stagy and false, and went out. It was odd and more than odd to know that he'd have to stay home while the others went. It was an admission that he was beginning to abdicate after running this place so long. He was still king of Hawksbill Station, but the throne was getting rickety beneath him.

A crippled old man was what he was now, hobbling around snooping here and there. Whether he liked to admit it to himself or not, that was the story. It was something he'd have to come to terms with soon.

After breakfast, the men chosen for the Inland Sea expedition gathered to select their gear and plan the logistics of their route. Barrett carefully kept away from the meeting. This was Charley Norton's show, now. He'd made eight or ten trips, and he would know what to do, without getting any hints from the previous management. Barrett didn't want to interfere, to seem to be vicariously running things even now.

But some masochistic compulsion in him drove him to take a trek of his own. If he couldn't see the western waters this year, the least he could do was pay a visit to the Atlantic, in his own back yard.

Barrett stopped off in the infirmary. Hansen, one of the orderlies, came out—a bald, cheerful man of about seventy who had been part of the California anarchist bunch. The only training Hansen had ever had was as a low-grade computer technician for a freight railroad, but he had shown some knack for medicine, and these days he was Quesada's chief helper. He flashed his usual dazzling smile.

"Is Quesada around?" Barrett asked.

"No, sorry. Doc's gone over to talk about the trip. He's giving them some medical pointers. But if it's important, I could get him for you—"

"Don't," Barrett said. "I just wanted to check with him on our drug inventory. It can wait. You mind if I take a quick look at the supplies?"

"Whatever you'd like."

Hawksbill Times Two

Hansen stepped back, ushering Barrett into the supply room. The barricade was down for the morning. Since there was no way of locking the drugstore, Barrett and Quesada had devised an intricate barricade that was guaranteed to set off a ton of noise if anyone meddled with it. Whenever the infirmary was left unattended, the barricade had to be put in place. An intruder would inevitably upset the whole thing, creating enough loud bangs and crashes to summon a warder. That was the only way they had been able to guard against unauthorized raiding of their drug supplies by moody residents. They couldn't afford wasting their precious and irreplaceable drugs on would-be suicides, Barrett reasoned. If a man wanted to kill himself, let him jump into the sea; at least that didn't impose a hardship on the other residents of the Station.

Barrett looked down the rows of drugs. It was an unbalanced assortment, dependent as they were on the random largesse from Up Front. Right now they were heavy on tranquilizers and digestive aids, low on pain-killers and anti-infectants. Which made Barrett feel even guiltier about what he was going to do. The man who had imposed the rules on drug-stealing was now going to take advantage of his privileged position and help himself to a drug. So much for morality, he thought. But he had known men to betray much more sacred trusts, in his time. And he needed the drug, and he didn't want to get into a lengthy fuss with Quesada over his use of it. This was simplest. Wrong, but simplest. He waited until Hansen's back was turned. Then he slipped one hand into the cabinet and palmed a slim gray tube of neural depressant, pocketing it quickly.

# Hawksbill Times Two

"Everything seems in order," he said to Hansen, as he left the infirmary. "Tell Quesada I'll stop by and talk to him later."

He was using the neural depressant more and more often nowadays to soothe his legs. Quesada didn't like it. He said, not quite in those words, that Barrett was developing an addiction. Well, to hell with Quesada. Let Doc try to walk around these paths on a foot like this, and he'll start reaching for the drugs too, Barrett told himself.

Scrambling along the eastern trail, Barrett halted when he was a few hundred yards from the main building. He stepped behind a low hump of rock, dropped his trousers, and quickly gave each thigh a jolt of the drug, first the good leg, then the gimpy one. That would numb the muscles just enough so that he'd be able to take an extended hike without feeling the fire of fatigue in his protesting joints. He'd pay for it, he knew, eight hours from now, when the depressant wore off and the full impact of his exertion hit him like a million daggers. But he was willing to accept that price.

The road to the sea was a long, lonely one. Hawksbill Station was perched on the eastern rim of Appalachia, more than eight hundred feet above sea level. During the first half dozen years here, the men of the Station had reached the ocean by a suicidal route across sheer rock faces. Barrett had incited a project to carve a path. It had taken ten years to do the job, but now wide, safe steps descended to the Atlantic. Chopping those steps out of the living rock had kept a lot of men busy for a long time—too busy to worry about loved ones Up Front, or to slip into the insanity that was so easily entered here. Barrett regretted that he couldn't conceive some comparable works project to occupy the idle men nowadays.

The steps formed a succession of shallow platforms that switch-backed to the edge of the water. Even for a healthy man it was a strenuous walk. For Barrett in his present condition it was an ordeal. It took him close to two hours to descend a distance that normally could be traversed in less than a quarter of that time.

When he reached the bottom of the path, he sank down exhausted on a flat rock licked by the waves, and dropped his crutch. The fingers of his left hand were cramped and gnarled from gripping the crutch, and his entire body was bathed in sweat.

The water of the ocean looked gray and somehow oily. Barrett could not explain the prevailing colorlessness of the Late Cambrian world, with its somber sky and somber land and somber sea, but his heart quietly ached for a glimpse of green vegetation again. He missed chlorophyll. The dark wavelets lapped against his rock, pushing a mass of floating black seaweed back and forth.

The sea stretched to infinity. He didn't have the faintest idea how much of Europe, if any, might be above water in this particular epoch. At the best of times most of the planet was submerged; here, only a few hundred million years after the white-hot rocks of the first land had pushed into view, it was likely that not much was above water on Earth except a strip of territory here and there.

Had the Himalayas been born yet? The Rockies? The Andes? Barrett knew the approximate outlines of Late Cambrian North America, but the rest was a mystery. Blanks in knowledge were not easy to fill when the only link with Up Front was by one-way transport; Hawksbill Station had to rely on the unpredictable assortment of reading matter that came back in time, and it was furiously frustrating to lack information that any college geology text could supply.

As he watched, a big trilobite unexpectedly came scuttering up out of the water. It was the spike-tailed kind, about a yard long, with a glossy eggplant-purple shell and a bristling arrangement of slender yellow spines along the margins. There seemed to be a lot of legs underneath. The trilobite crawled up on the shore—no sand, no beach, just a shelf of rock—and advanced landward until it was eight or ten feet from the waves.

*Good for you*, Barrett thought. *Maybe you're the first one who ever came out on land to see what it was like. The pioneer. The trail blazer.*

It occurred to him that this adventurous trilobite might very well be the ancestor of all the land-dwelling creatures of the eons to come. The thought was biological nonsense, and Barrett knew it. But his weary mind conjured a picture of a long evolutionary procession, with fish and amphibians and reptiles and mammals and man all stemming in unbroken sequence from this grotesque armored thing that moved in uncertain circles near his feet.

And if I were to step on you, he thought?

A quick motion—the sound of crunching chitin—the wild scrabbling of a host of little legs—and the whole chain of life snapped right in its first link.

Evolution undone. No land creatures ever to emerge. With the brutal descent of that heavy foot all the future would instantly change, and there would never have been a human race, no Hawksbill

Station, no James Edward Barrett (1968-?). In a single instant he would have both revenge on those who had condemned him to live out his days in this barren place, and release from his sentence.

He did nothing. The trilobite completed its slow perambulation of the shoreline rocks and scuttered back into the sea unharmed.

Then the soft voice of Don Latimer said, "I saw you sitting alone down here, Jim. Do you mind if I join you?" The intrusion jolted Barrett. He swung around rapidly, sucking in his stomach in surprise. Latimer had come down from his hilltop but so quietly that Barrett hadn't heard him approaching. But he recovered and grinned and beckoned Latimer to an adjoining rock.

"You fishing?" Latimer asked.

"Just sitting. An old man sunning himself."

"You took a hike way the devil down here just to sun yourself ?" Latimer laughed. "Come off it. You're trying to get away from it all, and you probably wish I hadn't disturbed you, but you were too polite to tell me to go away. I'm sorry. I'll leave if—"

"That's not so. Stay here. Talk to me, Don."

"You can give it to me straight if you'd prefer to be left in peace."

"I don't prefer to be left in peace," said Barrett. "And I wanted to see you, anyway. How are you getting along with your new bunkmate Hahn?"

Latimer's high forehead corrugated into a complex frown. "It's been strange," he said. "That's one reason I came down here to talk to you, when I saw you." He leaned forward and peered searchingly into

Barrett's eyes. "Jim, tell me straight: do you think I'm a madman?"

"Why should I think that?"

"The esping business. My attempt to break through to another realm of consciousness. I know you're tough-minded and skeptical of anything you can't grab hold of and measure and squeeze. You probably think it's all a lot of nonsense, this extrasensory stuff."

Barrett shrugged and said, "If you want the blunt truth, I do. I don't have the remotest belief that you're going to get us anywhere, Don. Call me a materialist if you like, and I admit that I haven't done much homework on the subject, but it all seems like pure black magic to me, and I've never known magic to work worth a damn. I think it's a complete waste of time and energy for you to sit there for hours trying to harness your psionic powers, or whatever it is you think you're doing. But no, I don't think you're crazy. I think you're entitled to your obsession and that you're going about a basically futile thing in a reasonably levelheaded way. Fair enough?"

"More than fair. 1 don't ask you to put any credence at all in the assumptions of my research—but I don't want you to write me off as a total lunatic because I'm trying to find a psionic escape hatch from this place. It's important that you regard me as a sane man, or else what I want to tell you about Hahn won't be valid to you."

"I don't see the connection."

"It's this," said Latimer. "On the basis of one evening's acquaintance, I've formed an opinion about Hahn. It's the kind of an opinion that might be formed by any garden-variety paranoid, and if you think I'm nuts you're likely to discount my ideas about Hahn. So I want to establish that you think I'm sane before I try to communicate my feelings about him."

"I don't think you're nuts. What's your idea?"

"That he's spying on us."

Barrett had to work hard to keep from emitting the savage guffaw that he knew would shatter Latimer's fragile self-esteem. "Spying?" he said casually. "Don, you can't mean that. How can anyone spy here? I mean, even if we had a spy, how could he report his findings to anyone?"

"I don't know," Latimer said. "But he asked me a million questions last night.. About you, about Quesada, about some of the sick men like Valdosto. He wanted to know everything."

"So? It's the normal curiosity of a new man trying to relate to his environment."

"Jim, he was taking notes. I saw him after he thought I was asleep. He sat up for two hours writing all my answers down in a little book."

Barrett frowned. "Maybe Hahn's going to write a novel about us."

"I'm serious," Latimer said. His hand traveled tensely to his ear. "Questions—notes. And he's shifty. Just try to get him to talk about himself!"

"I did. I didn't learn much."

"Do you know why he's been sent here?"

"No."

"Neither do I," said Latimer. "Political crimes, he told me, but he was vague as hell about them. He hardly seemed to know what the present government was up to, let alone what his own opinions were toward it. I don't detect any passionate philosophical convictions in Mr. Hahn. And you know as well as I do that Hawksbill Station is the refuse heap for revolutionaries and agitators and subversives and all sorts of similar trash, but that we've never had any other kind of prisoner here."

Barrett said coolly, "I agree that Hahn's a puzzle. But who could he possibly be spying for? He's got no way to file a report, if he's a government agent. He's stranded here for keeps, same as the rest of us."

"Maybe he was sent to keep an eye on us—to make sure we aren't cooking up some way to escape. Maybe he's a volunteer who willingly gave up his life in the twenty first century so he could come among us and thwart anything we might be hatching. The dedicated sort, a willing martyr to society. You know the type, I think."

"Yes, but—"

"Perhaps they're afraid we've invented forward time travel. Or that we've become a threat to the ordained sequence of the timelines. Anything. So Hahn comes among us to scout around and block any dangerous activity before it turns into something really troublesome. For example, like my own psionic research, Jim."

Barrett felt a cold twinge of alarm. He saw how close to paranoia Latimer was hewing, now: in half a dozen quiet sentences, Latimer had journeyed from the rational expression of some justifiable suspicions to the fretful fear that the men from Up Front were going to take steps to choke off the escape route that he was so close to perfecting.

He kept his voice level as he told Latimer, "I don't think you need to worry, Don. Hahn seems like an odd one, but he's not here to make trouble for us. The fellows Up Front have already made all the trouble for us they ever will. Unless they've repealed the Hawksbill Equations, there's no chance that we can bother anybody ever again, so why would they waste a man spying on us?"

"Would you keep an eye on him, anyway?" Latimer asked.

"You know I will. And don't hesitate to let me know if Hahn does anything else out of the ordinary. You're in a better spot to notice than anyone else."

"I'll be watching, Jim. We can't tolerate any spies from Up Front among us." Latimer got to his feet and gave Barrett a pleasant smile that almost seemed to cancel the paranoia. "I'll let you get back to your sunning now," he said.

Latimer went up the path. Barrett eyed him until he was close to the top, only a faint dot against the stony backdrop. After a long while Barrett seized his crutch and levered himself to a standing position. He stood staring down at the surf, dipping the tip of the crutch into the water to send a couple of little crawling things scurrying away. At length he turned and began the long, slow climb back to the Station.

# EIGHT

BARRETT WASN'T SURE of the exact point in time when it happened, but somewhere along the way they had all stopped thinking of themselves as counterrevolutionaries, and now regarded themselves as revolutionaries in their own right. The semantic shift had occurred early in the 1990's, happening in a gradual, processless manner. For the first few years after the upheavals of 1984-85, the syndicalists had been the revolutionaries, and rightly so, since they had overthrown an establishment more than two centuries old. Thus the conspirators of the antisyndicalist underground were of necessity counterrevolutionaries. But after a while the syndicalist revolution had institutionalized itself. It had ceased to be a revolution and had become an establishment itself.

So Barrett was a revolutionary, now. And the goal of the underground had subtly capitalized itself into The Revolution. The Revolution was coming any day now, any month, any year. . . . All it took was further planning, and then The Word would be given, and all over the nation the revolutionaries would rise. . . .

He did not question the truth of those propositions. Not yet. He did his work, and went through the round of days, and waited hopefully for the downfall of the entrenched and ever more confident syndicalists.

The Revolution had become Barrett's whole career. He had slipped easily and without regret out of college without finishing; the college had been syndicalist dominated, anyway; and the daily dollop of propaganda offended him. Then he had come to Pleyel, and Pleyel had given him a job. Officially, Pleyel ran an employment agency; at least, that was the cover story. In a small office far downtown in Manhattan he screened applicants for the underground while managing also to operate legitimately part of the time. Janet was his secretary; Hawksbill dropped in now and then to program the agency's computer; Barrett was taken on as assistant manager. His salary was small, but it allowed him to keep eating regularly and to pay the rent on the cramped apartment he shared with Janet. Thirty hours a week he dealt with innocent seeming activities of the employment agency, freeing Pleyel for more delicate work in other quarters.

Barrett actually enjoyed the cover job. It gave him a chance to deal with people, and he liked that. All sorts of unemployed New

Yorkers drifted through the office, some of them radicals in search of an underground, others merely hunting for jobs, and Barrett did what he could for them. They didn't realize that he was barely out of his teens, and some of them came to look upon him as a source of all their guidance and direction. That made him a little uncomfortable, but he helped them where he could.

The work of the underground went on steadily during those years.

That phrase, Barrett knew, was a high-order abstraction nearly empty of content: "the work of the underground." What did it amount to, this work? Endless planning for an often-postponed day of uprising. Transcontinental telephone calls conducted entirely in oblique jargon that decoded out into subversive scheming. The surreptitious publication of anti-syndicalist propaganda. The daring distribution of undoctored history books. The organization of protest meetings. An infinite series of small actions, amounting in the long run to very little indeed. But Barrett, in the full flush of his youthful enthusiasm, was willing to be patient. One day all the scattered threads would come together, he told himself. One day The Revolution would arrive.

On behalf of the movement he traveled all over the country. The economy had revived under the syndicalists, and the airports once again were busy places; Barrett got to know them well. He spent most of the summer of 1991 in Albuquerque, New Mexico, working with a group of revolutionaries who in the old order of things would have been called extremist right-wingers. Barrett found most of their philosophy unpalatable, but they hated the syndicalists as much as he did, and in their separate ways he and the New Mexico group shared a love for the Revolution of 1776 and all the symbolism that went with it. He came close to being arrested a few times that summer.

In the winter of 1991-92 he commuted weekly to Oregon to coordinate an outfit in Portland that was setting up a northwest propaganda office. The two-hour trip became wearily familiar after a while, but Barrett kept to his routine, dutifully huddling with the Portland people on Wednesday nights, then hustling back to New York. The following spring he worked mostly in New Orleans, and that summer he was in St. Louis. Pleyel kept moving the pawns about. The theory was that you had to stay at least three jumps ahead of the police agents. Actually, there were few arrests of any importance.

The syndicalists had ceased to take the underground seriously, and they picked up a leader every now and then purely to maintain form. Generally, the revolutionaries were regarded as harmless cranks and were allowed to go through the motions of conspiracy, so long as they didn't venture into sabotage or assassination. Who could object to syndicalist rule, after all? The country was thriving. Most people were working regularly again. Taxes were low. The interrupted flow of technological wonders was no longer interrupted, and each year produced its new marvel: weather conditioning, color telephone picture transmission, tridim video, organ transplants, instafax newspapers, and more. Why gripe? Had things ever been any better under the old system? There was even talk of the restoration of the two-party system by the year 2000. Free elections had come back into vogue in 1990, though of course the Council of Syndics exercised a right of veto over the choice of candidates. No one talked any more of the "stopgap" nature of the Constitution of 1985, because that constitution looked like it was on its way to becoming a permanent feature, but in small ways the government was amending the constitution to bring it more in line with past national traditions.

Thus the revolutionaries were thwarted at the root. Jack Bernstein's gloomy prediction was coming true: the syndicalists were turning into the familiar, beloved, traditional incumbent government, and the vast center of the nation had come to accept them as though they had always been there. There were fewer and fewer malcontents. Who wanted to join an underground movement when, if everybody was patient, the present government would transform itself into an even more benevolent institution? Only the embittered, the incurably angry, the dedicated destroyers, cared to involve themselves in revolutionary activities. By late 1993, it looked as though the underground and not the syndicalist government would wither away as America's basic conservatism reasserted itself even in these transformed conditions. But the last month of 1993 brought a transfer of power within the government. Chancellor Arnold, who had ruled the country for all eight years under the new constitution, died of a ruptured aortic aneurysm. He had been only forty-nine years old, and there was talk that he had been murdered; but in any event Arnold was gone, and after a brief internal crisis the Syndics thrust forward one of their number as the new Chancellor. Thomas Dantell of Ohio took command, and there was a general tightening of security up and down the line. Dantell's responsibility as a Syndic had been to run the national police: and now, with the top cop in office, the genial tolerance of the underground movements abruptly ended. There were arrests.

"We may have to disband for a while," Pleyel said dismally in the snowy spring of '94. "They're coming too close. We've had seven critical arrests so far, and they're moving toward our leadership cadre now."

"If we disband," said Barrett, "we'll never get the movement organized again."

"Better to lay low now and come out of hiding in six months or a year," Pleyel argued, "than to have everyone go to jail on twenty-year sedition terms."

They fought the matter out in a formal session of the underground. Pleyel lost. He took his defeat mildly, and pledged to keep working until the police dragged him away. But the episode demonstrated how Barrett was moving toward an ever more important position in the group. Pleyel was still the leader, but he seemed too remote, too unworldly. In matters of real crisis everyone turned to Barrett.

Barrett was twenty-six years old, now, and he towered over the others literally and figuratively. Enormous, powerful, tireless, he drew on hidden reserves of strength in the most direct way: he had broken up one nasty street incident singlehanded, when a dozen young toughs attacked three girls distributing revolutionary leaflets. Barrett had happened along to find the leaflets fluttering through the air and the girls on the verge of suffering a nonideological rape, and he had scattered live bodies in all directions, like Samson among the

Philistines. But under ordinary circumstances he tried to restrain himself.

His relationship with Janet lasted nearly a decade; he had lived with her for seven years. Neither of them had ever considered legalizing the arrangement, but in most ways it amounted to a marriage. They reserved the right to have separate adventures, and occasionally they did. Janet had set the trend in that, but Barrett had taken advantage of his freedom when the opportunity presented itself. Yet generally they felt themselves bound by a tie deeper than the government's marriage certificate alone could create. So it hurt him deeply when she was arrested one scorching day in the summer of '94.

He was in Boston that day, checking into reports that a Cambridge cell had been infiltrated by government informers. Late in the afternoon he headed for the tube station to return to New York. The telephone he carried behind his left ear bleeped its signal, and Jack Bernstein's thin voice said, "Where are you now, Jim?"

"On my way home. I'm about to take a tube. What's wrong?"

"Don't take the Forty-second Street tube. Make sure you get off in White Plains. I'll meet you there."

"What's wrong, Jack? What happened?"

"I'll tell you about it when I see you."

"Tell me now."

"It's best if I don't," Bernstein said. "I'll see you in an hour or two."

The contact broke. As he boarded the tube, Barrett tried to reach Bernstein in New York, but got no answer. He called Pleyel, and the line was silent. He dialed his home number, and Janet did not answer. Frightened now, Barrett gave up. He might be making trouble for himself or the others by putting through this call. He tried to wait for the time to elapse, as the tube rammed him at two hundred miles an hour down the Boston—New York corridor. It was very much like Bernstein to call him and bait him this way, sadistically hinting at a dire emergency and then clamming up on the details. Jack always seemed to take a peculiar pleasure in inflicting little tortures of that sort. And he did not grow mellower as he grew older.

Barrett left the tube as instructed at the suburban station. He stood at the exit lip for a long moment, staring warily in all directions and reflecting, not for the first time, that a man his size was really too conspicuous to be a successful revolutionary. Then Bernstein appeared and tapped his elbow and said, "Follow me. I've got a car in the lot out back. Don't say anything until we get there."

They walked grimly to the car. Bernstein thumbed the door panel and opened it on the driver's side, letting Barrett wait a moment before his door was opened too. The car was a rental job, green and black, low-slung, somehow sinister. Barrett got in and turned toward the pale, slight figure beside him, feeling as always a kind of revulsion for Bernstein's scarred cheeks, his bushy united eyebrows, his cold, mocking expression. But for Jack Bernstein, Barrett might never had joined the underground in the first place, yet it seemed incomprehensible to him that he could have chosen such a person as his most intimate boyhood friend. Now their relationship was purely business: they were professional revolutionaries, working together for the common cause, but they were not friends at all.

"Well?" Barrett blurted.

Bernstein smiled a death's-head smile. "They got Janet this afternoon."

"Who got her? What are you talking about?"

"The *polizei*. Your apartment was raided at three o'clock. Janet was there, and Nick Morris. They were planning the Canada operation. Suddenly the door opens and four of the boys in green rush in. They accuse Janet and Nick of subversive activities and start searching the place."

Barrett closed his eyes. "There's nothing in the place that could upset anyone. We've been very careful that way."

"Nevertheless, the police didn't know that until they had searched the place." Bernstein steered the car out onto the highway bound for Manhattan and locked it into the electronic control system. As the master computer took over, Bernstein released the steering knobs, took a pack of cigarettes from his breast pocket, and lit one without offering any to Barrett. He crossed his legs and turned cozily to Barrett, saying, "They also searched Janet and Nick very thoroughly while on the premises. Nick told me about it. They made Janet strip completely, and then they went over her from top to bottom. You know that business out in Chicago last month, the girl with the suicide bomb in her vagina? Well, they made sure Janet wasn't about to blow herself up. The way they do it, they put her ankles into interrogation loops and spread-eagle her on the floor, and then—"

"I know how they do it," Barrett said tightly. "You don't need to draw a picture for me." He struggled to stay cool. It was a powerful temptation to seize Bernstein and bat his head against the windshield a few times. The little louse is telling me this deliberately to torture me, Barrett thought.

He said, "Skip the atrocities and tell me what else happened."

"They finished with Janet and stripped Nick and examined him too. That was Nick's thrill for the year, I guess, watching them work Janet over, and then putting on a display himself." Barrett's scowl deepened; Nick Morris was a maidenly little fellow of doubtful heterosexuality for whom this had surely been a scarifying ordeal, and Bernstein's pleasure was all too close to the surface. "Then they took Janet and Nick down to Foley Square for close interrogation. About four-thirty they let Nick go. He called me and I called you."

"And Janet?"

"They kept her."

"They've got no more evidence on her than they had on Nick. So why didn't they let her go too?"

"I can't tell you that," said Bernstein. "Nevertheless, they kept her."

Barrett knotted his hands together to keep them from shaking. "Where's Pleyel?"

"He's in Baltimore. I called him and told him to stay there until the heat was off."

"But you invited me to come back."

"Someone's got to be in charge," Bernstein said. "It isn't going to be me, so it's got to be you. Don't worry, you aren't in any real danger. I've got a contact in an important place, and he checked the data sheets and said that the only pickup order was for Janet. Just to make sure, I staked Bill Klein out at your apartment, and he says they haven't come back looking for you in the past two hours. So the coast is clear."

"But Janet's in jail!"

"It happens," Bernstein said. "It's the risk we run." The little man's dry silent laughter was all too audible. For months, now, Bernstein had seemed to be withdrawing from the movement, skipping meetings, regretfully declining out-of-town assignments. He had seemed aloof, alienated, scarcely interested in the underground. Barrett hadn't spoken to him in three weeks. But suddenly he was back in circulation, hooked into the movement's communication nexus. Why? So he could cackle with glee at Janet's arrest?

The car plunged into Manhattan at a hundred twenty miles an hour. Bernstein resumed manual control once they were past 125th Street, and took the car down the East River Tunnel, emerging at the vehicular overpass on Fourteenth Street. A few minutes later they were at the building where Barrett and Janet had lived. Bernstein called upstairs to the man he had left on watch there. "The coast is clear," he told Barrett after a moment. They went upstairs. The apartment had been left just as it had been after the police visit, and it was a somber sight. They had been very thorough. Every drawer had been opened, every book taken down from the shelves, every tape given a quick scan. Of course, they had found nothing, since Barrett was inflexible about keeping revolutionary propaganda out of his apartment, but in the course of the ransacking they had managed to get their grimy hands on every piece of property in the place. Janet's underclothes lay fanned out in pathetic array; Barrett glowered when he saw Bernstein staring wolfishly at the flimsy garments. The visitors had been neither gentle nor careful with the contents of the apartment. Barrett wondered how much was missing, but he did not have the stomach to take an inventory now. He felt as though the interior of his body had been laid open by a surgeon's knife, and all his organs removed, examined, and left scattered about.

Stooping, Barrett picked up a book whose backbone had been split, carefully closed it, and set it on a shelf. Then he clamped his hand against the shelf and leaned forward, closing his eyes, waiting for the anger and fear to subside.

In a moment he said, "Get hold of your contact in an important place, Jack. We've got to have her released."

"I can't do a thing for you."

Barrett whirled. He seized Bernstein by the shoulders. His fingers dug in, and he felt the sharp bones beneath the scanty flesh. The blood drained from Bernstein's face, and the stigmata of his acne glowed like beacons. Barrett shook him furiously; Bernstein's head lolled on the thin neck.

"What do you mean, you can't do a thing? You can find her! You can get her out!"

"Jim—Jim, stop—"

"You and your contacts! Damn you, they've arrested Janet! Doesn't that mean anything to you?"

Bernstein clawed feebly at Barrett's wrists, trying to pull them from his shoulders. Shortly Barrett grew calm and released him. Gasping, red-faced, Bernstein stepped back and adjusted his clothing. He dabbed at his forehead with a handkerchief. He looked badly frightened; but yet his eyes glowed with sullen resentment.

In a low voice he said, "You ape, don't ever grab me like that again."

"I'm sorry, Jack. I'm under stress. Right now they might be torturing Janet— beating her—lining up for a mass rape, even—"

"There's nothing we can do. She's in their hands. We have no official channel of legal protest, and no unofficial one, either. They'll interrogate her and maybe then they'll release her, and it's out of our control."

"No. We'll find her and we'll spring her somehow."

"You're not thinking this through, Jim. Each individual member of this group is expendable. We can't risk personnel in the hope of getting Janet free. Unless you want to think of yourself as someone privileged, who can risk the lives or freedom of your comrades simply to recover someone you're emotionally involved with, even if her usefulness to the organization has ended—"

"You make me sick," Barrett snapped.

But he knew that Bernstein was speaking sense. No one in their immediate group had ever been arrested before, yet Barrett was aware of the general pattern of events that followed such an arrest. It was hopeless to think of forcing the government to disgorge a prisoner unless it wanted to. There were a dozen interrogation camps scattered about the country, and at this moment Janet might be in Kentucky or North Dakota or Nevada, no telling where, facing an uncertain prison sentence on an undefined charge. On the other hand, she might already be free and on her way home. Capriciousness is of the essence of things, in running a totalitarian government; this government was nothing if not capricious. Janet was gone, and no action of his could undo that, only the mysterious mercies of the government.

"Maybe you ought to have a drink," Bernstein suggested. "Get yourself settled down a little. You aren't even remotely thinking straight, Jim."

Barrett nodded. He went to the liquor cabinet. They kept a meager supply there, a couple of bottles of scotch, some gin, light rum for the daiquiris Janet liked so much. But the cabinet was empty. The visitors had cleaned it out. Barrett peered at the bare shelves for a long while, idly following the dance of dust motes within.

"The liquor's gone," he said at length. "It figures. Come on, let's get out of here. I can't stand the sight of this place any more."

"Where are you going?"

"Pleyel's office."

"They may have guards posted there waiting to arrest anyone who shows up," Bernstein said.

"So they'll arrest me. Why fool ourselves? They can arrest any of us, whenever the mood takes them. Will you come with me?"

Bernstein shook his head. "I don't think so. You're in charge, Jim. You do what you think is proper. I'll keep in touch, okay?"

"Yeah."

"And I'd advise you to be less emotional, if you want to stay free much longer."

They went out. Barrett crossed town to the employment agency, checked the building cautiously from the street, saw nothing amiss, and entered it. The office was undisturbed. He locked himself in and began making calls to cell chiefs in other districts: Jersey City, Greenwich, Nyack, Suffern. The reports he got showed a distinct pattern of sudden simultaneous arrests, not necessarily of top leaders at all. Two or three members of each cell had been picked up in midafternoon. Some had been questioned and released unharmed; others remained in custody. No one had any clear idea of where anybody was, although Valkenburg of the Greenwich group had learned from an unidentified source that the prisoners were being distributed among four interrogation camps in the South and Southwest. He had no specific news of Janet. None of them did. They all sounded badly shaken.

Barrett spent the night on a couch in Pleyel's office. In the morning he went back to the apartment and started the dreary job of cleaning it up, hoping that Janet would appear. He kept picturing her in custody, a plump, dark-eyed girl with strands of white prematurely streaking her black hair, twisting and writhing in agony as the interrogators went to work on her, demanding names,, dates, goals. He knew how they questioned women. There was always a component of sexual indignity in their approach; their theory, and it was a sound one, was that a naked woman being questioned by six or seven men wasn't likely to put up much resistance. Janet was tough, but how much pinching and prodding and leering could she take? Interrogators didn't have to use red-hot pokers, thumbscrews, or the rack to extract information. Simply transform a person into so much metabolizing meat, handle her flesh until she loses sight of her soul, and the will crumbles.

Not that Janet could tell them anything they didn't already know. The underground was scarcely a secret organization, despite the passwords and pretense. The police already knew names, dates, goals. These arrests were made purely to shatter morale, the government's sly way of letting its opponents know that they weren't fooling anybody. Capriciousness: it was the essence. Keep the enemy off balance. Arrest, interrogate, imprison, possibly even execute—but always in an amiable, impersonal way, with no aspect of vindictiveness. No doubt a government computer had suggested picking up X members of the underground today, as a strategic move in the continuing subterranean struggle. And so it had been done. And so Janet was gone.

She was not released that day. Nor the next.

Pleyel came back from Baltimore, grim, bleak-faced. He had been working on the problem from down there. He had learned that Janet had been taken to the Louisville interrogation camp the first day, transferred to Bismarck on the second, to Santa Fe on the third. After that the trail fizzled out. This, too, was part of the government's campaign of psychological warfare: move the prisoners about, shuttle them here, shuttle them there, baffle the rubes with the old shell game. Where was she? No one knew. Somehow life went on. A long-planned protest meeting was held in Detroit; government police stood benignly by, smugly tolerating the event but ready to suppress it if it grew violent. New leaflets were distributed in Los Angeles, Evansville, Atlanta, and Boise. Ten days after Janet's disappearance, Barrett cleared out of the apartment and took another one a block away.

It was as though the sea had closed over her and swallowed her up.

For a while, he continued to hope that she would be released, or that at the very least his information network would be able to tell him where she was being kept. But no news of her was forthcoming. In its impersonally arbitrary way, the government had chosen a small group of victims that day. Perhaps they were dead, perhaps they were merely hidden in the lowest level of some maximum-security dungeon. It did not matter. They were gone.

Barrett never saw her again. He never found out what they had done to her.

The pain became an ache, and in time, to his surprise, even the ache went away, and the work of the underground went on steadily, a ceaseless striving toward an always more distant goal.

# NINE

A COUPLE OF days passed before Barrett had the chance to draw Lew Hahn aside for a spot of political discussion. The Inland Sea party had set out by then, and in a way that was too bad, for Barrett could have used Charley Norton's services in penetrating Hahn's armor. Norton was the most gifted theorist at the Station, a man who could weave a tissue of dialectic from the least promising material. If anyone could find out the depth of Hahn's revolutionary commitment, it was Norton.

But Norton was away leading the expedition, and so Barrett had to do the interrogating himself. His Marxism was a trifle rusty, and he couldn't thread a path through the Leninist, Stalinist, Trotskyite, Khrushchevist, Maoist, Berenkovskyite and Mgumbweist schools with Charley Norton's skills. Yet he knew what questions to ask. He had served his time on the ideological battlefront, though it had been a long while past.

He picked a rainy evening when Hahn seemed to be in a fairly outgoing mood. There had been an hour's entertainment at the Station that night, an ingenious computer-composed film that Sid Hutchett had programmed the week before. Up Front had been kind enough to ship back a modest computer, and Hutchett had rigged it to do animations by specifying line widths, shades of gray, and progressions of raster units. It was a simple but remarkably clever business, and it brightened the dull nights. He was able to produce cartoons, satiric lampoons, erotic amusements, anything at all.

Afterward, sensing that Hahn was relaxed enough tonight to lower his guard a bit, Barrett sat down beside him and said, "Good show tonight?"

"Very entertaining."

"It's Sid Hutchett's work. He's a rare one, that Hutchett. Did you get a chance to meet him before he went off on the Inland Sea trip?"

"Tall fellow with a sharp nose and no chin?"

"That's the one," Barrett said. "A clever boy. He was the top computer man for the Continental Liberation Front until they caught him back in '19. He programmed that fake broadcast in which Chancellor Dantell denounced his own regime. God, I wish I had been there to hear that one! Remember it?"

"I'm not sure I do." Hahn frowned. "How long ago was this?"

"The broadcast was in 2018. Would that be before your time? Only eleven years ago—"

"I was nineteen, then. I guess I wasn't very politically oriented. I was an unsophisticated kid, you might say. Slow to awaken."

"A lot of us were. Still, you were nineteen, that's pretty grown up. Too busy studying economics, I suppose."

Hahn grinned. "That's right. I was deep in the dismal science."

"And you never heard the broadcast? Or even heard of it?"

"I must have forgotten."

"The biggest hoax of the century," Barrett said, "and you forgot it. The greatest achievement of the Continental Liberation Front. You're familiar with the Continental Liberation Front, of course."

"Of course." Hahn looked uneasy.

"Which group did you say you were with?"

"The People's Crusade for Liberty."

"I don't know it, I'm afraid. One of the newer groups?"

"Less than five years old. It started in California in the summer of '25."

"What's its program?"

"Oh, the usual revolutionary line," Hahn said. "Free elections, representative government, an opening of the security files, an end to preventive detention, restoration of the habeas corpus and other civil liberties."

"And the economic orientation? Pure Marxist or one of the offshoots?"

"Not really any, I guess. We believed in a kind of—well, capitalism with some government restraints."

"A little to the right of state socialism, and a little to the left of *pure laissez faire?*" Barrett suggested.

"Something like that."

"But they tried that system and it failed, didn't it, in the middle of the twentieth century? It had its day. It led inevitably to total socialism, which produced the compensating backlash of total capitalism, followed by collapse and the birth of syndicalist capitalism. Which gave us a government that pretended to be libertarian while actually stifling all individual liberties in the name of freedom. So if your group simply wanted to turn the economic clock back to 1955, say, there couldn't be much substance to its ideas."

Hahn looked bored at the string of dry abstractions. "You've got to understand that I wasn't in the top ideological councils," he said.

"Just an economist?"

"That's it."

"What were your particular party responsibilities?"

"I drew up plans for the ultimate conversion to our system."

"Basing your procedures on the modified liberalism of Ricardo?"

"Well, in a sense."

"And avoiding, I hope, the tendency to fascism that was found in the thinking of Keynes?"

"You could say so," Hahn said. He stood up, flashing a quick, vague smile. "Look, Jim, I'd love to argue this further with you some other time, but I've really got to go now. Ned Altman talked me into coming around and helping him do a lightning-dance in the hopes of bringing that pile of dirt of his to life. So if you don't mind—" Hahn beat a hasty retreat.

Barrett was more perplexed than ever. Hahn hadn't been "arguing" anything. What he had been doing was carrying on a lame and feeble and evasive conversation, letting himself be pushed hither and thither by Barrett's questions. And he had spouted a lot of nonsense. He didn't seem to know Keynes from Ricardo, nor to care about the difference between them, which was an odd attitude for a self-professed economist to have. He didn't appear to have a shred of an idea what his own political party stood for. He hadn't protested while Barrett had uttered a lot of deliberately inane doctrinaire talk. He had so little revolutionary background that he was unaware even of Hutchett's astonishing hoax of eleven years ago. He seemed phony from top to bottom.

How was it possible that this thirtyish kid had been deemed worthy of exile to

Hawksbill Station, anyhow? Only the top firebrands and most effective opponents of the government were sent to the Station. Sentencing a man to Hawksbill was very much like sentencing him to death, and it wasn't a step that was taken lightly by a government that was now so very concerned with appearing benevolent, respectable, and tolerant.

Barrett couldn't imagine why Hahn was here at all. He seemed genuinely distressed at having been exiled, and evidently he had left a beloved young wife behind, but nothing else rang true about the man.

Was he—as Don Latimer had suggested—some kind of spy?

Barrett rejected the idea out of hand. He didn't want Latimer's paranoia infecting him. The government wasn't likely to send anyone on a one-way trip to the Late Cambrian just to spy on a bunch of aging revolutionaries who could never possibly make trouble again. But what was Hahn doing here, then?

He would bear further watching, Barrett decided. Barrett took care of some of the watching himself. But he saw to it that he had plenty of assistance. If nothing else, the Hahn-watching project could serve as a kind of therapy for the ambulatory psycho cases, the ones who were superficially functional but were full of all kinds of fears and credulities. They could harness those fears and credulities and play detective, which would give them an enhanced sense of their own value, and also perhaps help Barrett come to understand the meaning of Hahn's presence at the station.

The next day, at lunch, Barrett called Don Latimer aside.

"I had a little talk with your friend Hahn last night," Barrett said. "The things he said sounded mighty peculiar to me, you know?"

Latimer brightened. "Peculiar? How?"

"I checked him out on economics and political theory. Either he doesn't know a thing about either, or else he thinks I'm such a damned fool that he doesn't need to bother making sense when he talks to me. Either way it's strange."

"I told you he was a fishy one!"

"Well, now I believe you," Barrett said. "What are you going to do about him?"

"Nothing yet. Just keep tabs on him and try to find out why he's here."

"And if he's a spy from the government?"

Barrett shook his head. "We'll take whatever action is necessary to protect ourselves, Don. But the important thing is not to act hastily. It may very well be that we're misjudging Hahn, and I don't want to do anything that would make it awkward to go on living with him here. In a group like this we've got to avoid tensions in advance, or else we're likely to split apart altogether. So we'll go easy on Hahn. But we won't lay off him. I want you to report to me regularly, Don. Watch him carefully. Pretend to be asleep and see what he does. If possible, sneak a look at those notes he's been taking, but if you do, do it subtly and without arousing his suspicion."

Latimer glowed with pride. "You can count on me, Jim."

"Another thing. Get help. Organize a little team of Hahn-watchers. Ned Altman seems to be getting along well with Hahn; put him to work too. Get a few of the other boys—some of the sicker ones, who need responsibilities. You know the ones. I'm putting you in charge of this project. Recruit your men and give them their assignments. Gather your information and transmit it to me. All right?"

"Will do," Latimer said.

And so they kept an eye on the new man.

The day after that was the fifth day after Hahn's arrival. Mel Rudiger needed two new men for his fishing crew, to make up for the pair who had gone on the Inland Sea trek. "Take Hahn," Barrett suggested. Rudiger spoke to Hahn, who seemed delighted by the offer. "I don't know much about fishing with nets," he said, "but I'd love to go."

"I'll teach you what you need to know," Rudiger said. "In half an hour you'll be a master fisherman. You've got to remember, we're not actually dealing with *fish* out here. What we're netting are a bunch of dumb invertebrates, and it doesn't take much to fool them. Come along and I'll show you."

# Hawksbill Times Two

Barrett stood for a long time on the edge of the world, watching the little boat bobbing in the surging Atlantic. For the next couple of hours Hahn would be away from Hawksbill Station, with no chance of getting back until Rudiger was ready to come back. Which gave Latimer a perfect chance to scout through Hahn's notebook. Barrett didn't precisely suggest to Latimer that he ought to infringe on his bunkmate's privacy in this way, but he did let Latimer know that Hahn would be out at sea for, a while. He could count on Latimer to draw the right conclusion.

Rudiger never went far from shore— eight hundred, a thousand yards out—but the water was rough enough there. The waves came rolling in with X thousand miles of gathered impact behind them, and they hit hard even where outlying fangs of rock served as breakwaters. A continental shelf sloped off at a wide angle from the land, so that even at a substantial distance offshore the water wasn't exceptionally deep. Rudiger had taken soundings up to a mile out, and had reported depths no greater than a hundred sixty feet. Nobody had gone past a mile out to sea.

It wasn't that they were afraid of falling off the side of the world if they should go too far east. What motivated their caution was simply that a mile was a long distance for aging men to row in an open boat, using stubby oars made from old packing cases. Up Front hadn't thought to spare an outboard motor for them.

Looking toward the horizon, Barrett had an odd thought. He had been told that the women's equivalent of Hawksbill Station was safely segregated out of reach, a couple of hundred million years up the time-line. But how could he be sure that was true?

## Hawksbill Times Two

The government Up Front didn't issue press releases on its time-line prison camps, and, anyway, it was foolhardy to believe anything that came, however indirectly, from a government source. In Barrett's day, the public had not even known of the existence of Hawksbill Station. He had found out about it only during the course of his own interrogation, when as part of the process of breaking his will they had let him know where he was likely to be sent. Later, some details had leaked—probably not by chance. The nation discovered that incorrigible politicals were sent off to the beginning of time, yes, and subsequently it was made clear that the men went to one era and the women to another, but Barrett had no real reason to believe it was true.

For all he knew, there could be another Hawksbill Station somewhere else in this very year, and no one living here would have any way of knowing about it. A camp of women living on the far side of the Atlantic, say, or perhaps just across the Inland Sea.

It wasn't very likely, Barrett realized. With the entire past to dump the exiles into, the edgy men Up Front wouldn't take any chance that the two groups of deportees might somehow get together and spawn a tribe of little subversives. They'd take every precaution to put an impenetrable barrier of epochs between the men and the women.

Yet it was a tempting thing to consider. From time to time Barrett wondered if Janet might not be at that other Hawksbill Station.

When he examined the idea rationally, he knew it was impossible. Janet had been arrested in the summer of 1994, and had never been traced thereafter. The first deportations to Hawksbill Station had not begun until 2005. Hawksbill himself hadn't perfected the time-transfer process when Barrett had discussed it with him as late as 1998. Which meant that a minimum of four years, and more probably eleven, had elapsed between the time of Janet's arrest and the beginning of the shipments to the Late Cambrian era.

If Janet had been in a government prison that long, the underground would surely have found out about it, one way or another. But there hadn't been any news of her at all. And therefore it was logical to conclude that the government had disposed of her, in all likelihood within a few days after her arrest. It was folly to think that Janet had lived to see 1995, let alone that she had been kept incommunicado by the government until Hawksbill had finished his research, then had been shot back into this segment of the past.

No, Janet was dead. But Barrett allowed himself the luxury of a few illusions, like anyone else. So he permitted himself sometimes to enjoy the fantasy that she had been sent back, which led him to the even more gargantuan fantasy that he might find her right here in this very epoch. She would be nearly seventy now, he thought. He had not seen her for thirty-five years. He tried and failed to picture her as a fat little old lady. The Janet who had lived in his memory all these decades was quite different, he knew, from any conceivable Janet who might possibly have survived. Better to be realistic and admit she's dead, he thought. Better not to hope to find her again, because the wish might just come true, and a dream would die a terrible death if it did.

Hawksbill Times Two

But the idea of a female Hawksbill Station on this time-level raised interesting possibilities of a more useful sort. Barrett wondered if he could make the concept sound convincing to the other men. Perhaps. Perhaps with a little effort he could get them to believe in the existence of two simultaneous Hawksbill Stations on this level of time, separated not by epochs but merely by geography.

If they'd believe that, he thought, it could be our salvation.

The instances of degenerative psychosis were beginning to snowball, now. Too many men had been here too long, and one crackup was starting to feed the next. The strain of dwelling in this blank lifeless world where humans were never meant to live was eroding one after another of the Station's inmates. What had happened to Valdosto and Altman and the other psychos would ultimately overtake the rest. The men needed sustained projects to keep them going, to hold back the deadly boredom. As it was, they were starting to slip off into schizophrenia, like Valdosto, or else they were beginning to involve themselves in harebrained enterprises like Altman's Frankenstein girlfriend and Latimer's pursuit of a psionic gateway.

Suppose, Barrett thought, I could get them steamed up about reaching the other continents?

A round-the-world expedition. Maybe they could construct some kind of big ship. That would keep a lot of men busy for a long time. And they'd need to work up some navigational equipment—compasses, sextants, chronometers, whatnot. Somebody would have to design an improvised radio, too. Of course, the Phoenicians had got along pretty well without radios and chronometers, but they hadn't done open-sea voyaging, had they? They had kept close to the coast. But in this world there was hardly any coast, and the Station inmates weren't Phoenicians, either. They'd need navigational aids.

It was the kind of project that might take thirty or forty years, designing and building the ship and its equipment. A long-term focus for our energies, Barrett thought. Of course, I won't live to see the ship set sail, but that's all right. Even so, it's a way of staving off collapse. I don't really care what's across the sea, but I care very much about what's happening to my people here. We've built our staircase to the sea, but it's finished. Now we need something bigger to do. Idle hands make for idle minds . . . sick minds. . . .

He liked the idea he had hatched. He had been worrying for weeks, now, about the deteriorating state of affairs at the Station, and looking for some fresh way to cope with it. Now he thought he had his way. A voyage! Barrett's ark!

Turning, he saw Don Latimer and Ned Altman standing behind him.

"How long have you been there?" he asked.

"Two minutes," said Latimer. "We didn't want to interrupt you. You seemed to be thinking so hard."

"Just dreaming," Barrett said.

"We brought you something to look at," Latimer told him. Barrett saw the papers now, clutched in his hand. Altman nodded vigorously. "You ought to read it. We brought it for you to read."

"What is it?" Barrett asked.

"Hahn's notes," said Latimer.

# TEN

BARRETT HESITATED FOR a moment, saying nothing, making no attempt to take the papers from Latimer's hand. He was pleased that Latimer had done this, but yet he had to be delicate about it. Private property was sacred at Hawksbill Station. It was very much a breach of ethics to meddle with something another man had written. That was why Barrett had not specifically ordered Latimer to search Hahn's bunk. He could not afford to implicate himself in so flagrant a misdeed.

But of course he had to know what Hahn thought he was doing here. His responsibilities as leader of the Station transcended the moral code, he told himself. So he had asked Latimer to keep an eye on Hahn. And he had asked Rudiger to take Hahn out on a fishing trip. Latimer had taken the next step without needing to be prodded.

Barrett said finally, "I'm not sure I like this, Don. To disturb his belongings—"

"We have to know about this man, Jim."

"Yes, but a society has to obey its own morality, even when it's defending itself against possible enemies. That was our gripe against the syndicalists, remember? They didn't play fair."

Latimer said, "Are we a society?"

"We sure as hell are. We're the whole population of the world. A microcosm. And I represent the State, which has to keep its rules. I don't know if I want to look at those papers you've got there, Don."

"I think you ought to. When important evidence falls into the State's hands, the State has an obligation to examine it,. I mean, you aren't just watching out for

Hahn's welfare. You've got the rest of us to look after too."

"Is there anything significant in Hahn's papers?"

"You bet there is," Altman put in. "He's guilty as hell!"

Barrett said calmly, "Remember, I never requested you to bring these documents to my attention. The fact that you went snooping is a matter between you and Hahn, at least until I see if there's cause to take action against him. Do we have that much clear?"

Latimer looked a little hurt. "I suppose. I found the papers tucked away in Hahn's bunk after he went out in Rudiger's boat. I know I'm not supposed to be invading his privacy, but I had to have a look at what he's been writing. There it is. He's a spy, all right."

He offered the folded sheaf of papers to Barrett. Barrett took them, glanced quickly at them without reading them, and tucked the sheaf into his hand. "I'll look them over a little later," he said. "What's Hahn been writing, anyway? In a few words."

"It's a description of the Station, and a profile of most of the men in it that he's met," said Latimer. He smiled frostily. "The profiles are very detailed and not very complimentary. Hahn's private opinion of me is that I've gone mad and won't admit it. His private opinion of you is a little more flattering, Jim, but not much."

"The man's opinions aren't all that important," said Barrett. "He's entitled to think that we're nothing but a bunch of cockeyed old crackpots. Very likely we are. All right, so he's been having a bit of literary exercise at our expense, but I don't see that that's any cause for alarm. We—"

Altman said flatly, "He's also been hanging around the Hammer."

"What?"

"I saw him going there late last night. He went into the building. I followed him, and he didn't notice me. He was looking at the Hammer for a long time. Walking around it, studying it. He didn't touch it."

"Why the devil didn't you tell me that right away?" Barrett snapped.

Altman looked confused and terrified. He blinked his eyes five or six times and backed nervously away from Barrett, running his hands through his yellow hair. "I wasn't sure it was important," he said finally. "Maybe he was just curious about it, I mean. I had to talk things over with Don first. And I couldn't do that until Hahn had gone out fishing."

Sweat burst out on Barrett's face. He reminded himself that he was dealing with a mildly psychotic individual, and he kept his voice as steady as he could, masking the sudden alarm that gripped him. "Listen, Ned, if you ever catch Hahn going near the time-travel equipment again, you let me know in a hurry. You come right to me, whether I'm awake or asleep, eating, resting. Without consulting Don or anyone else. Clear?"

"Clear," said Altman.

"You knew about this?" Barrett asked Latimer.

Latimer nodded. "Ned told me just before we came down here. But I figured it was more urgent to give you the papers, first. That is, Hahn couldn't damage the Hammer while he's out in the boat, anyway, and whatever he might have done last night is already done."

Barrett had to admit that that made sense. But he could not easily shake off his distress. The Hammer was their only contact point, unsatisfactory though it was, with the world that had cast them out. They were dependent on it for their supplies, for their fresh personnel, for such shards of news about the world Up Front as the new men brought. Let some disturbed individual wreck the Hammer, and the choking silence of total isolation would descend on them. Cut off from everything, living in a world without vegetation, without raw materials, without machines, they'd be back to savagery within months.

But why would Hahn be fooling with the Hammer, Barrett wondered?

Altman giggled. "You know what I think? They've decided to exterminate us, Up Front. They want to get rid of us. Hahn's been sent here as a suicide volunteer. He's checking us out, getting everything ready. Then they're going to send a cobalt bomb through the Hammer and blow the Station up. We ought to wreck the Hammer and Anvil before they get a chance."

"But why would they send a suicide volunteer?" Latimer asked reasonably. "If their aim was to wipe us out, they could simply transmit a bomb, without wasting an agent. Unless they've got some way to rescue their spy—"

"In any case, we shouldn't take chances," Altman argued. "Wreck the Hammer, first thing. Make it impossible for them to bomb us from Up Front."

"That might be a good idea. Jim, what do you think?"

Barrett thought that Altman was crazy and that Latimer was far down the same road. But he said simply, "I'm inclined not to worry much about this bomb theory of yours, Ned. Up Front's got no reason to want to wipe us out. And if they did, Don's right—they wouldn't send an agent to us. Just a bomb."

"Even so, perhaps we should disable the Hammer on the possibility that—"

"No," Barrett said. He made it emphatic. "If we do anything to the Hammer, we're chopping off our own heads. That's why it's so serious that Hahn's been messing with it. And don't you get any ideas about the Hammer either, Ned. The Hammer sends us food and clothing. Not bombs."

"But—"

"And yet—"

"Shut up, both of you," Barrett growled. "Let me look at these papers."

The Hammer, he thought, would have to be protected. He and Quesada would have to rig some kind of guardian system for it, the way they had done for the drug supplies. But a more effective one, he added.

Hawksbill Times Two

He walked a few steps away from Altman and Latimer and sat down on a shelf of rock. He unfolded the sheaf of papers.

He began to read.

Hahn had a cramped, crabbed handwriting that enabled him to pack a maximum of information into a minimum of space, as though he regarded it as a mortal sin to waste paper. Fair enough; paper was a scarce commodity here. Evidently Hahn had brought these sheets with him from Up Front, though. They were thin and had a metallic texture. When one piece slid against another, a soft whispering sound was produced.

Small though the writing was, Barrett had no difficulty in deciphering it. Hahn's script was clear. So were his opinions.

Painfully so.

He had written a detailed analysis of conditions at Hawksbill Station, and it was an impressive job. In about five thousand well-organized words Hahn had set forth everything that Barrett knew was going sour here. His objectivity was merciless. He had neatly ticked off the men as aging revolutionaries in whom the old fervor had turned rancid; he listed the ones who were certifiably psychotic, and the ones who were on the edge, and in a separate category he noted the ones who were hanging on, like Quesada and Norton and Rudiger. Barrett was interested to see that Hahn rated even those three as suffering from severe strain and likely to fly apart at any moment. To him, Quesada and Norton and Rudiger seemed to be just about as stable as when they had first dropped onto the Anvil of Hawksbill Station; but that was possibly the distorting effect of his own blurred perceptions. To an outsider like

Hahn, the view was different and perhaps more accurate.

Barrett forced himself not to skip ahead to Hahn's evaluation of him.

He read doggedly on through Hahn's assessment of the likely future of Hawksbill's population: not bright. Hahn thought that the process of deterioration was cumulative and self-generating, and that any man who had been in the place more than a year or two would shortly be brought to his knees by the pressures of loneliness and rootlessness. Barrett thought so too, although he believed it would take a little longer for the younger men to cave in. But Hahn's reasoning was inexorable and his evaluation of the possibilities sounded convincing. How has he learned so much about us so fast, Barrett wondered? Is he that sharp? Or are we so totally transparent?

On the fifth page, Barrett found Hahn's description of him. He wasn't pleased when he came to it.

"The Station," Hahn had written, "is nominally under the authority of Jim Barrett, an old-line revolutionary who's been here about twenty years. Barrett is the ranking prisoner in terms of seniority. He makes the administrative decisions and seems to act as a stabilizing force. Some of the men worship him, but I am not convinced that he would be able to exert any real influence in the event of a serious challenge to his rule, such as a blood feud in the Station or an attempt to depose him. In the loose-knit anarchy of Hawksbill Station society, Barrett rules very much by the consent of the governed, and since the Station is lacking in weapons he would have no actual recourse if that consent were to be withdrawn. However, I see no likelihood of that, since the men here are generally devitalized and demoralized, and an anti-Barrett insurrection would be beyond their capabilities even if they had any need to mount one.

"By and large Barrett has been a positive force within the Station. Though some of the other men here have qualities of leadership, doubtless the place would have fragmented into disastrous confusion long ago without him. However, Barrett is like a mighty beam that's been gnawed from within by termites. He looks solid, but one good push would break him apart. A recent injury to his foot has evidently had a bad effect on him. The other men say he used to be physically vigorous and derived much of his authority from his size and strength. Now Barrett can hardly walk. But I feel that the trouble with Barrett is inherent in the life of Hawksbill Station, and does not have much to do with his lameness. He's been cut off from normal human drives for too many years. The exercise of power here has provided the illusion of stability for him and allowed him to keep functioning, but it's power in a vacuum, and things have happened within him of which he's totally unaware. He's in bad need of therapy. He may be beyond help."

Stunned, Barrett read that passage several times. Words stuck to him like clinging burrs.

*Gnawed from within by termites . . .*

*. . . one good push . . .*

*. . . things have happened within him . . .*

*. . . bad need of therapy . . .*

*. . . beyond help . . .*

Barrett was less angered by Hahn's words than he thought he should have been. Hahn was entitled to his views. He might even be right. Barrett had lived too long as a man apart from the others here; no one dared to speak bluntly to him. Had he decayed? Were the others being too kind to him?

Finally Barrett stopped going over and over Hahn's profile of him, and pushed his way to the last page of the notes. The essay ended with the words, "Therefore I recommend prompt termination of the Hawksbill Station penal colony and, where possible, the therapeutic rehabilitation of its inmates."

What the hell was this?

It sounded like the report of a parole commissioner! But there was no parole from Hawksbill Station. That final insane sentence let all the viability of what had gone before bleed away. No matter that Hahn's insight into the Station was keen and deeply penetrating. A man who could write, "I recommend prompt termination of the Hawksbill Station penal colony," was a man who was insane.

Hahn was pretending to be composing a report to the government Up Front, obviously. In brisk and capable prose he had dissected the Station and provided a full analysis. But a wall a billion years thick made the filing of that report an impossibility. So Hahn was suffering from delusions, just like Altman and Valdosto and the others. In his fevered mind he believed he could send messages to those Up Front, pompous documents delineating the flaws and foibles of his fellow prisoners.

That raised a chilling prospect. Hahn might be crazy, but he hadn't been in the Station long enough to have gone crazy there. He must have brought his insanity with him from Up Front.

Hawksbill Times Two

What if they had stopped using Hawksbill Station as a camp for political prisoners, Barrett asked himself, and were starting to use it as an insane asylum?

It was a somber thing to consider: a cascade of psychos descending on them. Human debris of all sorts would rain from the Hammer. Men who had gone honorably buggy under the stress of long confinement would have to make room at the Station for ordinary Bedlamites.

Barrett shivered. He folded up Hahn's papers and handed them back to Latimer, who was sitting a few yards away, watching him intently.

"What did you think of that?" Latimer asked.

"I think it's hard to evaluate at one reading." He rubbed his hand over his face, pressing heavily against it. "But possibly friend Hahn is emotionally disturbed in some way. I don't think this is the work of a healthy man."

"You think he's a spy from Up Front?"

"No," said Barrett. "I don't. But I think he thinks he's a spy from Up Front. That's what I find so disturbing about this stuff."

"What are you going to do to him?" Altman wanted to know.

Gently Barrett said, "For the moment, just watch and wait." He folded the thin, crinkling sheaf of papers and pressed it into Latimer's hands. "Put this stuff back exactly where you got it, Don. And don't give Hahn the faintest inkling that you've read it or removed it."

"Right."

"And come to me the moment you think there's something I ought to know about him," Barrett said. "He may be a very sick boy. He may need all the help we can give."

# ELEVEN

ARRETT DIDN'T HAVE any steady women after Janet was arrested. He lived alone, although there was plenty of transient company in his bed. Somehow he regarded himself as guilty for Janet's disappearance, and he didn't want to bring the same fate on some other girl.

It was phony guilt, he knew. Janet had been in the underground before he'd ever heard of it, and doubtless the police had been watching her for a long time. When they had picked her up, it had probably been because they regarded her as dangerous in her own right, not because they were trying to reach through to Barrett. But he couldn't help that feeling of responsibility, that sense that he'd jeopardize the freedom of any other girl who moved in with him.

He had no difficulty finding companions, though. He was the virtual leader of the New York group, now, and that invested him with a kind of charismatic appeal that seemed irresistible to girls. Pleyel, ever more ascetic and saintly, had retired to the role of a pure theoretician. Barrett handled the day-by-day routine of the organization. Barrett dispatched the couriers, coordinated the activities of the adjoining areas, and planned the coups. And, like a lightning rod drawing energy, he became the focus for the yearnings of a bunch of kids of all sexes. To them, he was a famed hero of revolt, an Old Revolutionary. He was becoming a legend. He was almost thirty years old.

So the girls trooped through the little apartment. Sometimes he'd let one live with him for as much as two weeks at a time. Then he'd suggest that it was time for her to move on.

"Why are you throwing me out?" she'd ask, in effect. "Don't you like me? Don't I make you happy, Jim?"

And he would reply, essentially, "You're wonderful, doll. But one of these days the police are going to come for you, if you stay here. It's happened before. They'll take you away and you'll never be seen again."

"I'm small fry. Why should they want me?"

"To harass me," Barrett would explain. "So you'd better go. Please. For your own safety."

Eventually he would get them to leave. And then would come a week or two of monastic solitude, which was good for his soul, but as the laundry began to pile up and the linens started to need changing he'd realize that the monastic life has its disadvantages, and some other thrilled young revolutionary in her late teens would move into his apartment and dedicate herself to his earthly needs for a while. Barrett had trouble keeping his memories of them distinct from one another. Generally they were leggy kids, dressed in whatever was the current nonconformist fashion, and most of them had plain faces and good bodies. The Revolution tended to attract the sort of girl who couldn't wait to get her clothes off, so that she could prove that her breasts and thighs and buttocks made up for the deficiencies of her face.

There was always plenty of new young blood coming along, now. The police-state psychology introduced by Chancellor Dantell had seen to that. He ran a tight ship of state, but every time his minions came around to knock on a door at midnight, new revolutionaries were created. Jack Bernstein's fears that the underground would shrivel into impotence as a result of the government's wise benevolence had not quite come to pass. The government was not altogether infallible, and could not entirely resist being totalitarian; and so the resistance movement survived in a straggling way, and grew slightly from year to year. Chancellor Arnold's government had been shrewder. But Chancellor Arnold was dead.

Among the new people who came into the movement during those tougher years in the late 1990's was Bruce Valdosto. He showed up in New York City one day in the early part of 1997, knowing no one, full of unfocused hatreds and seething angers. He was from Los Angeles. His father had run a tavern there, and, when goaded too far by a government tax collector, had spit in the collector's face and hurled him out into the street. (The syndicalist government, notoriously puritan, was almost as tough with the makers and vendors of alcoholic drinks as it was with artists and writers.) Later that day, the tax collector had returned with six of his colleagues, and they had methodically beaten the elder Valdosto to death. His son, unable to halt the slaughter, had been arrested for interference with the functions of government officers, and was released only after a month of high-grade interrogation, the translation of which was torture. Then Valdosto set out on the confused transcontinental hegira that brought him to Jim Barrett's apartment in lower Manhattan.

He was little more than seventeen years old. Barrett didn't know that. To him, Valdosto was a short, swarthy man of about his own age, with immense shoulders and a powerful torso and strangely malproportioned little legs. He had thick tangled hair and the burning, ferocious eyes of a born terrorist, but nothing about his looks or his words or his actions betrayed his youthfulness. Barrett never did find out whether Valdosto had simply been born that way or had undergone accelerated aging in the crucible of the Los Angeles interrogation tank.

"When does The Revolution start?" Valdosto wanted to know. "When does the killing begin?"

"There won't be any killing," Barrett told him. "The coup will be bloodless when it comes."

"Impossible! We've got to remove the head of the enemy. *Whack*, like killing a snake."

# Hawksbill Times Two

Barrett showed him the flow charts of The Revolution: the scheme whereby the Chancellor and the Council of Syndics would be taken into custody, the junior officers of the army would proclaim martial law, and a reconstituted Supreme Court would announce the restoration of the overthrown 1789 Constitution. Valdosto peered at the charts, picked his nose, scratched his hairy chest, clenched his fists, and grunted. "Nah. It'll never come off. You can't hope to take over a country by arresting maybe two dozen key men."

"It happened in 1984," Barrett pointed out.

"That was different. The government was in ruins anyway. Christ, there wasn't even any President that year, huh? But now we got a government of real pros. The head of the snake is bigger than you think, Barrett. You've got to reach behind the Syndics.

Down to the bureaucrats. The little Fuhrers, the two-bit tyrants who love their jobs so much they'll do anything to keep them. The sort of guys who killed my father. They've got to go."

"There are thousands of them," Barrett said, alarmed. "Are you saying we should execute the entire civil service?"

"Not all. But most. Clean out the tainted ones. Start with a fresh slate."

The most frightening thing about Valdosto, Barrett thought, was not that he was fond of spouting bombastic, vehemently violent ideas, but that he sincerely believed in them and was fully ready to carry them out. Within an hour after meeting Valdosto for the first time, Barrett was convinced that he must have committed at least a dozen murders already. Later, Barrett found out that Valdosto was only a kid dreaming of avenging his father, but he never lost the uncomfortable feeling that Val was wholly lacking in the usual scruples. He could remember nineteen-year-old Jack Bernstein insisting, nearly a decade earlier, that the best way to overthrow the government was through a judicious campaign of assassination. And Pleyel, mild as ever, remarking, "Assassination isn't a valid method of political discourse." So far as Barrett knew, Bernstein's bloodlust had never passed the theoretical stage; but here was young Valdosto, offering himself as the Angel of Death to fulfill Jack's dreams of revolution. A good thing that Bernstein wasn't very deeply involved in underground activities any more, Barrett told himself. With the right encouragement, Valdosto could become a one-man terror squad.

Instead he became Barrett's roommate. The arrangement was an accidental one. Valdosto needed a place to stay on his first night in the city, and Barrett offered him a couch. Since Val had no money, he was in no position to find himself an apartment, and even after he had gone onto the payroll of what they now were calling the Continental Liberation Front, he continued to live with Barrett. Barrett didn't mind. After the third week he said, "Forget about looking for a place of your own. You might as well just go on living here."

They got along beautifully, despite the gulf in age and temperament. Barrett found that Valdosto had a rejuvenating effect on him. Though he was just coming up on thirty himself, Barrett felt older than that— ancient, sometimes. He had been active in the underground for nearly half his life, so that The Revolution had become a pure abstraction to him, a matter of unending meetings and secret messages and leaflets. A doctor healing one runny nose after another does not find it easy to think of himself as working step by step toward a world in which disease is extinct; and Barrett, immersed in the trifling rituals of the revolutionary bureaucracy, all too often lost sight of the main goal, or forgot that there was any such goal. He was beginning to slide into the rarefied realm inhabited by Pleyel and the other original agitators—a realm in which all fervor is dead and idealism is transmuted into ideology. Valdosto rescued him from that.

To Val there was nothing abstract about The Revolution. For him The Revolution was a matter of splitting skulls and twisting necks and bombing offices. He regarded the faceless officials of the government as his special enemies, knew their names, dreamed of the punishments he would inflict on each one of them. His intensity was contagious. Barrett, while drawing back from Valdosto's lust for destructiveness, began to remember that there was a central purpose fundamental to his network of daily routines. Valdosto revived in him the revolutionary dreams that were so difficult to sustain, week in and week out, across years and decades.

And when he was not brooding of bloodshed, Valdosto was a lively, uproarious companion. He took some getting accustomed to, of course. He lacked almost all inhibitions, and liked to wander about the apartment naked, even when there were visitors; the first time he emerged that way he seemed like an impossibly grotesque anthropoid apparition, his barrel-thick body densely matted with coarse black hair, his legs so dwarfed that it could not have been too difficult for him to press his knuckles against the floor. And a few days later, when he had a girl in his room, the two of them emerged in a helter-skelter scramble, both of them bare, Val chasing her about the living-room while Barrett, Pleyel, and two others looked on in astonishment. The panicky girl, all white thighs and jiggling breasts, finally found herself trapped in a corner, and Val hauled her off in triumph for the consummation.

"He's the primordial kind," Barrett explained in embarrassment.

Soon Valdosto abandoned his more flagrantly bizarre antics, but there was never any predicting what he might do next. He appeared to be sublimating his terrorist urges in erotic gymnastics, and sometimes took his women on two and three at a time, tossing the castoffs to

Barrett. It was a wild few months at the outset for Barrett, but in time he adjusted to the fact that the place was likely to be stacked with sprawling exhausted naked females at any given time, and he joined the fun with unfeigned enthusiasm, telling himself that a revolutionary's life didn't necessarily *have* to be a dour one.

Barrett's apartment once again became a social center for the underground group, as it had been in the days when Janet had been living with him. The climate of fear had been eased again, and there was no need for exaggerated caution; although Barrett knew he was under surveillance, he did not hesitate to allow others to visit him.

Hawksbill came a few times. Barrett met him quite incidentally, on one of his rare ventures into nonrevolutionary social circles. Columbia University had been reopened after a three-year forced suspension of classes, and Barrett found himself journeying to Morningside Heights on a frosty spring evening in '98 to attend a party given by a man he knew vaguely, a professor of applied information technology named Golkin. Through the thick haze of smoke he spied Edmond Hawksbill across the room, and their eyes met, and they exchanged remote nods, and Barrett debated going over to say hello to him, and Hawksbill seemed to be debating the same thing, and after a moment Barrett thought, what the hell, I will, and he started to shoulder his way through the crowd.

They met in the middle. Barrett had not seen the mathematician for nearly two years, and he was startled by the change in his appearance. Hawksbill had never been a handsome man, but now it looked as though he had undergone some kind of glandular collapse, and the effects were unsettling to behold. He was completely bald. His cheeks, which had always had a grubby, unshaven look, were strangely pink. His lips and nose had thickened; his eyes were lost in orbits of flesh; his belly was enormous, and his entire frame seemed to have been embedded in new layers of fat. They shook hands briefly; his touch was moist; his fingers were soft and limp. Hawksbill, Barrett remembered, was only nine years his senior, and so not yet forty years old. He looked like a man at the edge of the grave.

"What are you doing here?" they both said at once. Barrett laughed and outlined his tenuous friendship with Golkin, their host. Hawksbill explained that he had recently been co-opted for Columbia's faculty of advanced mathematics.

"I thought you hated teaching," Barrett said.

"I do. I'm not. I've been given a research appointment. Government work."

"Classified?"

"Is there any other kind?" Hawksbill asked, smiling faintly.

The sight of him made Barrett's flesh crawl. Behind the thick glasses, Hawksbill's eyes looked cold and alien; some effect of myopia robbed his gaze of all humanity, and staring into those eyes was like trading glances with a being from another world. Chilled, Barrett said, "I didn't realize you were taking the governmental shilling."

"Perhaps I shouldn't be talking to you, then. I might be compromising you."

"You mean, you're still plugging away at The Revolution?" Hawksbill asked.

"Still plugging away, yes."

The mathematician favored him with a fluid smile. "I would think a man of your intelligence would have seen through that bunch of bores and misfits by now."

"I'm not as bright as you think I am, Ed," Barrett said quietly. "I don't even have a college degree, remember? I'm stupid enough to think that there's a meaning in what we're working toward. You once thought so yourself."

"I still do."

"You oppose the government and yet you work for the government?" Barrett asked.

Hawksbill jiggled the ice-cubes in his drink. "Is that so hard for you to accept? The government and I have arranged a marriage of convenience. They know that I'm polluted with a revolutionary background, of course. And I know that they're a bunch of fascist bastards. However, I'm conducting certain research which is simply impossible for me to perform without financial assistance amounting to millions of dollars a year, and that obliges me to seek government grants. And the government is interested enough in my project, and aware enough of my special gifts, so that they're willing to back me without worrying about my ideology. I loathe them, they mistrust me, and we come to an arm's-length working agreement."

"Orwell called that doublethink."

"Oh, no," Hawksbill said. "It's *Realpolitik*, it's cynicism, but it isn't doublethink. Neither part is operating under any kind of illusion about the other. We're using each other, my friend. I need their money, they need my brains. But I continue to abominate the philosophy of this government, and they know it."

"In that case," said Barrett, "you could still be working with us, without jeopardizing your research grant."

"I suppose."

"Then why have you stayed away? We need your gifts, Ed. We have no one whose mind can juggle fifty factors at once, as you do so easily. We've missed you. Can I lure you back to our group?"

"No," Hawksbill said. "Let's sweeten our drinks and I'll explain why."

"Good enough."

They went through the ritual of refilling. Hawksbill took a long, deep gulp. Some driblets of liquor appeared at the edge of his mouth and trickled down his fleshy chin, disappearing into the stained folds of his collar. Barrett looked away, taking a deep pull of his own drink. Then Hawksbill said, "I haven't withdrawn from your group out of fear of arrest. Nor is it that I've lost my disdain for the syndicalists, or that I've sold out to them. No. I left, if you must know, out of boredom and contempt. I decided that the Continental Liberation Front wasn't worthy of my energy."

"That's blunt enough," Barrett agreed.

"Do you know why? It's because the leadership of the movement fell into the hands of genial delayers like yourself. Where is The Revolution? It's 1998, Jim. The syndicalists have been in power fourteen years, nearly. There's been not one visible attempt to push them aside."

"Revolutions aren't planned in a week, Ed."

"But fourteen years? *Fourteen years?* Perhaps if Jack Bernstein had been running things, we'd have had some action. But Jack got bitter and drifted away. Very well: Edmond Hawksbill has but one life to live, and he wants to spend it validly. 1 got tired of serious economic debates and procedural parliamentarianism. I became more involved in my own research. I withdrew."

"I'm sorry we bored you so, Ed."

"I'm sorry too. For a while, I thought the country stood a chance of getting its freedom back. Then I realized it was hopeless."

"Would you come to visit me anyway? Maybe you can help us get moving again," Barrett said. "We've got young people joining us all the time. There's a chap named Valdosto out of California with enough fervor for ten of us. And others. If you came, and lent your prestige—"

Hawksbill was skeptical. He could barely conceal his total scorn for the Continental Liberation Front. But yet he could not deny that he still supported the ideals for which the Front stood, and so Barrett maneuvered him into coming around. Hawksbill came to the apartment the next week. There were a dozen people there, most of them girls. They sat at Hawksbill's feet, eyeing him adoringly while he gripped his glass and exuded perspiration and weary sarcasm. He was, Barrett thought, like a great white slug in the armchair, damp, epicene, repulsive. But his appeal to these girls was frankly sexual. Barrett noticed that Hawksbill took good care to fend off their advances before they 'went too far. Hawksbill enjoyed being the focus of their desires—that was, Barrett suspected, why he came around so frequently—but he showed no interest in capitalizing on his opportunities. Hawksbill consumed a good deal of Barrett's filtered rum, and offered a great many opinions on why the Continental Liberation Front was doomed to fail. Tact had never been Hawksbill's strong point, and he was often savagely incisive in his analysis of the underground's shortcomings. For a while Barrett thought it might be a mistake to expose the neophyte revolutionaries to him, since his raw pessimism might tend to dismay or permanently discourage them. But Barrett discovered that none of Hawksbill's young admirers took his dire accusations seriously. They worshiped the mathematician for his brilliance as a mathematician, but they assumed that his pessimism was simply part of his general eccentricity, along with his sloppiness and his fat and his flaccidity. So it was worth the risk of keeping Hawksbill around, spinning out his long streams of unresonant declamations, in the hope of seducing him somehow back into the movement.

In an unguarded moment when he was brimming with filtered rum, Hawksbill allowed Barrett to question him about the secret research he was doing on behalf of the government.

"I'm building a time transport," Hawksbill said.

"Still? I thought you'd given that up a long time ago."

"Why should I? The initial equations of 1983 are valid, Jim. My work's been assailed for a whole generation and no weak spot has developed. So it's merely a matter of translating theory into practice."

"You always used to look down your nose on experimental work. You were the pure theoretician."

"I change," Hawksbill said. "I've carried the theory as far as it needs to go." He leaned forward and ponderously clasped his interlaced fingers, pudgy and pink, across his gut. "Time reversal is an accomplished fact on the subatomic level,

Jim. The Russians showed the way toward that at least forty years ago. My equations confirmed their wild guesses. In laboratory work it's been possible to reverse the time-path of an electron and send it back close to a full second."

"Are you serious?"

"It's old stuff. When we flip the electron around, it alters its charge and becomes a positron. That would be all right, except that it tends to seek out an electron moving forward up its track, and they annihilate each other."

"Causing an atomic explosion?" Barrett asked.

"Hardly." Hawksbill smiled. "There's a release of energy, but it's only a gamma ray. Well, at least we've succeeded in prolonging the lifetime of our backward-traveling positron by a factor of about a billion, but that still comes only to something short of one second. However, if we can send a single electron back in time for a single second, we know that there are no theoretical objections to sending an elephant back a trillion years. There are merely technical difficulties. We must learn to increase the transmission mass. We must get around the reversal of charge, or we'll simply be shipping antimatter bombs into our own past and wrecking our laboratories. We must find out, too, what it does to a living thing to have its charge reversed. But these are trivialities. Five, ten, twenty years and we'll solve them. The theory is what counts. And the theory is sound." Hawksbill burped grandly. "My glass is empty again, Jim."

Barrett filled it. "Why does the government want to sponsor your time-machine research?"

"Who knows? What concerns me is the mere fact that they authorize my expenditures. Mine not to reason why. I do my work and hope for the best."

"Incredible," Barrett said softly.

"A time machine? Not really. Not if you've studied my equations."

"I don't mean the time machine is incredible, Ed. Not if you say you can build it. What's incredible to me is that you're willing to let the government get hold of it. Don't you see what power this gives them? To go back and forth through time as they please, snuffing out the grandparents of people who trouble them? To edit the past, to—"

"Oh," said Hawksbill, "no one will be able to go back *and forth* through time. The equations deal only with going back in time. I haven't considered forward movement at all. I don't believe it would be possible, anyway. Entropy is entropy, and it can't be reversed, not in the sense I employ. The journey through time will be one way only, just as it is for all us poor mortals today. A different direction, is all."

To Barrett, much of what Hawksbill said about the time machine was incomprehensible, and the rest was infuriating in its smugness. But he emerged with the uncomfortable feeling that the mathematician was close to succeeding, and that, in another few years, a process for reversing the flow of time would be perfected and in the hands of the government. Well, he thought, the world had survived Albert Einstein. It had survived J. Robert Oppenheimer. It would survive Edmond Hawksbill, too, somehow.

He wanted to know more about Hawksbill's research. But just then Jack Bernstein arrived, and Hawksbill, belatedly remembering that he was under a security blanket, abruptly changed the subject.

Bemstein, like Hawksbill, had wandered far from the underground movement in recent years. To all intents and purposes, he had dropped out after the wave of arrests in the summer of '94. During the four years that followed, Barrett had seen him perhaps a dozen times. Their meetings were cold and remote. It had come to seem to Barrett that he had dreamed those afternoons when he and Jack had been fifteen, and had furiously debated every topic of any intellectual interest in Jack's small, book-crammed bedroom. Their long walks together in the snow—their collaborations on class assignments--their early days together in the underground--had any of that really happened? The past, for Barrett, was breaking off and sloughing away like dead skin, and his boyhood friendship with Jack Bernstein had been the first to go.

Bernstein was hard and cold, now, a compact, spare little man who might well have been carved from stone. He had never married. Since leaving the underground, he had gone into the practice of law; he had an apartment somewhere far uptown, and spent much of his time traveling on business. Barrett did not understand why Bernstein had begun dropping in on him again. Not out of sentiment, surely. Nor did he show any interest in the Continental Liberation Front's spasmodic activities. Perhaps it was the figure of Hawksbill that drew him, Barrett thought. It was hard to view anyone as frosty and self-contained as Jack as a hero worshiper, but maybe he

had never shaken off his adolescent admiration for Hawksbill.

He came, he sat, he drank, occasionally he talked. He spoke as if every word cost him a pound of flesh. His lips seemed to close like clippers between each syllable. His eyes, small and red-rimmed, flickered with what might have been suppressed pain. Bernstein made Barrett acutely uncomfortable. He had always thought of Jack as a man ridden by demons, but now the demons appeared too close to the surface, too capable of bursting forth to seize innocent bystanders.

And Barrett felt the tingle of Jack's unvoiced mockery. As an ex-revolutionary, Bernstein seemed to share Hawksbill's idea that the Front was futile and its members self-deceivers. Without doing more than smiling secretively, Bernstein seemed to be passing judgment on the group to which he had devoted so many years of his own life. Only once did he let his contempt show, though. Pleyel entered the room, a dreamy figure in a flowing white beard, lost in calculations of the coming millennium. He nodded to Bernstein as if he had forgotten who he was. "Good evening, Comrade," Bernstein said. "How goes The Revolution?"

"Our plans are maturing," said Pleyel mildly.

"Yes. Yes. It's a fine strategy, Comrade. Wait patiently, until the syndicalists die out unto the tenth generation. Then strike, strike like hawks!"

Pleyel looked puzzled. He smiled and turned away to confer with Valdosto, obviously unwounded by Bernstein's bitter sarcasm. Barrett was annoyed. "If you're looking for a target, Jack, aim at me instead."

Bernstein laughed harshly. "You're too big, Jim. I couldn't possibly miss, so where's the sport? Besides, it's cruel to shoot at sitting ducks."

That night—late in November 1998—was the last time Bernstein came to Barrett's apartment. Hawksbill paid only one more visit himself, three months later. Barrett asked him, "Have you heard anything from Jack?"

"Jacob, he calls himself now. Jacob Bernstein."

"He always used to hate that name. He kept it a secret."

Hawksbill blinked amiably. "That's his problem. When I met  him and called him Jack, he instructed me that his name was Jacob. He was quite sharp about it."

"I haven't seen him since that night in November. What's he been up to?"

"You mean you haven't heard?"

"No," Barrett said. "Something I should know?"

"I suppose," Hawksbill said, and snickered. "Jacob has a new job, and he's not likely to be paying social calls on leaders of the Front any more. Professional calls, maybe. But not social ones."

"What kind of new job?" said Barrett tightly.

Hawksbill seemed to enjoy saying it. "He's an interrogator, now. For the government police. It's a job that fits his personality quite well, wouldn't you say? He should make an outstanding success of it."

# TWELVE

THE FISHING EXPEDITION returned to the Station early in the afternoon. Barrett saw that Rudiger's dinghy was overflowing with the haul, and Hahn, coming ashore with his arms full of gaffed trilobites, looked sunburned and pleased with his outing.

Barrett went over to inspect the catch. Rudiger was in an effusive mood, and held up a bright red crustacean that might have been the great-great-grandfather of all boiled lobsters, except that it had no front claws, and sprouted a wicked-looking triple spike where a tail should have been. It was about two feet long, and ugly.

"A new species!" Rudiger crowed. "There's nothing like it in any museum. God, I wish I could put it where it would be found. Some mountaintop, maybe."

"If it could be found, it *would* have been found," Barrett reminded him. "The odds are a twentieth-century paleontologist would have dug it out and put it on display, and you'd have known all about it. So forget it, Mel."

Hahn said, "I've been wondering about that point. Just how is it that nobody Up Front ever dug up the fossil remains of Hawksbill Station? Aren't they worried that one of the early fossil-hunters will find it in the Cambrian strata and raise a fuss? Say, one of the nineteenth-century dinosaur diggers? That would be something, if he turned up huts and human bones and tools in a stratum older than dinosaurs."

Barrett shook his head. "For one thing, no paleontologist from the beginning of the science to the founding of the Station in 2005 ever *did* dig up Hawksbill. That's a matter of record—it hadn't happened, so there was nothing to worry about. And if the Station came to light after 2005, why, everyone would know what it was. No paradox there."

"Besides," said Rudiger sadly, "In another billion years this whole strip of rock will be on the floor of the Atlantic, with a couple of miles of sediment sitting on top of it. There's not a chance we'll be found. Or that anyone Up Front will ever see this guy I caught today. Not that I give a damn. I've seen him. I'll dissect him. Their loss."

"But you regret the fact that science will never know of this species," Hahn said. "Twenty-first century science."

"Sure I do. But is it my fault? Science does know of this species. Me. I'm science. I'm the leading paleontologist of this epoch. Can I help it if I can't publish my discoveries in the professional journals?"

He scowled and walked away, carrying the big red crustacean.

Hahn and Barrett looked at each other. They smiled, in a natural mutual response to Rudiger's grumbled outburst. Then Barrett's smile faded.

*. . . termites . . . one good push . . . therapy . . .*

"Something wrong?" Hahn asked.

"Why?"

"You looked so bleak, all of a sudden."

"My foot gave me a twinge," Barrett said. "It does that, you know. Here. I'll lend you a hand carrying those things. We'll have fresh trilobite cocktail tonight."

They started up the steps toward the Station itself. Suddenly there came a wild shout from up above, Quesada's voice: "Catch him! He's heading for you! Catch him!"

Jerking his head upward in alarm, Barrett saw Bruce Valdosto plunging down the steps along the face of the cliff, stark naked and trailing the shreds of the webfoam cradle in which he had been gently imprisoned. Perhaps a hundred feet farther up the cliff stood Quesada, blood streaming from his nose, looking dazed and battered.

Valdosto was a shattering sight as he stormed toward them. He had never been an agile man, because of his legs, but now, after weeks under sedation, he could scarcely stand upright at all. He lurched along, stumbling and dropping, scrambling to his feet and hurtling another few steps before he fell again. His hairy body glistened with sweat, and his eyes were wild; his lips were drawn back in a rigid grin. He seemed like some animal that had thrown its leash and was rushing pell-mell toward freedom and destruction together.

Barrett and Hahn had barely enough time to set down their load of trilobites when Valdosto was upon them. Hahn said, "Put your shoulder against mine and we'll block him." Barrett nodded; but he could not move fast enough, and Hahn seized him by the arm and pulled him into position. Barrett braced himself against his crutch. Valdosto hit them like a plummeting stone.

Half running, half falling, he rushed down the steps and threw himself into the air when he was still ten feet above them. "Val!" Barrett gasped, and reached for him, but then Valdosto struck him, between chest and waist. Barrett absorbed the full momentum. His crutch was driven deep into his armpit, and he pivoted on his knees, twisting his good leg and sending a blazing message of pain the full length of his body. To avoid a dislocated shoulder he let go of the crutch, and as it fell backward he felt himself falling, and caught it again before he toppled. The net effect of his change of position was to slew him around sideways, creating a gap between Hahn and himself. Valdosto shot through that gap like a bounding ball. He eluded Hahn's clutching grasp and sped down the steps.

"Val, come back!" Barrett boomed. "Val!"

But he could do no more than shout. He watched helplessly as Valdosto reached the edge of the sea and, now slipping, now diving, launched himself into the water. His arms beat wildly in a madman's crawl. His dark head bobbed for a moment; then a towering wave fell on him and swept him under. When Barrett saw him again, he was fifty yards out to sea.

By then Hahn had reached Rudiger's beached dinghy and was pulling it free of its moorings. He waded out and began to row desperately. But the tide was in, and the tide was merciless; the waves flipped the boat about like a twig. For every yard Hahn rowed away from shore, he was hurled half a yard back. All the while Valdosto grew more distant, lashing the waves with his splayed hands, rising briefly above the surface, then vanishing again to reappear long moments later.

Barrett, stunned, stood frozen and aching at the place on the steps where Valdosto had burst past him. Quesada had joined him, now.

"What happened?" Barrett asked.

"I was giving him sedation and he went berserk. The cradle was open and he ripped his way out of it and knocked me down. And started to run. Toward the sea . . . he kept yelling that he was going to swim home. . . ."

"He will," Barrett said.

They watched the struggle. Hahn, exhausted, was furiously trying to row a boat too heavy for a solitary oarsman in waves too rough to conquer. Valdosto, unleashing his last energies, was beyond the inner breakers and swimming steadily for the open sea. But the sloping shelf of rock turned upward in the area just ahead of him, and white water splashed against jutting stony teeth. At high tide there were whirlpools there. Valdosto headed unerringly for the roughest stretch of water. The waves took him, tossed him high, pulled him down again. Soon he was only a line against the horizon.

The others were coming, now, attracted by the shouts. One by one they arrayed themselves along the shore or down the stone steps. Altman, Rudiger, Latimer, Schultz, the sane and the sick, the dreamers, the old, the weary, they stood motionless as

Hahn lashed the sea with his oars and Valdosto leaped through the waves. Hahn was coming in, now. He fought his way through the surf, and Rudiger and two or three of the others broke from their stasis, seizing the boat, hauling it ashore, mooring it. Hahn stumbled out, white-faced with fatigue. He dropped to his knees and retched against the rocks while the waves licked at his boots. When he was through, he got shakily to his feet and walked over to Barrett.

"I tried," he said. "The boat wouldn't move. But I tried to get to him."

"It's all right," Barrett told him gently. "No one could have made it. The water was too rough."

"Maybe if I had tried to swim after him instead—"

"No," said Doc Quesada. "Valdosto was insane. And terribly strong. He'd have pulled you under if the waves didn't get you first."

"Where is he?" Barrett asked. "Can anybody see him?"

"Out by the rocks," said Latimer. "Isn't that him?"

Rudiger said, "He's gone under. He's been under three, four minutes now. It's better this way. For him, for us, for everybody."

Barrett turned away from the sea. No one approached him. They knew his relationship with Valdosto, the thirty years of it, the apartment shared, the wild nights and stormy days. Some of them had been here on the day, not so many years ago, when Valdosto had dropped onto the Anvil and Barrett, who had not seen him in more than a decade, let out a whoop of delight and pleasure. One of the last ties to a distant past had just been severed; but,

Barrett told himself, Valdosto had been gone for a long time before today.

It was growing dark. Slowly Barrett began to climb the cliff to the Station. Half an hour later Rudiger came to him.

"The sea's calmer now. Val's been washed ashore."

"Where is he?"

"A couple of the boys are bringing him up here for the services. Then we'll take him out in the boat and give him the burial."

"All right," Barrett said. There was only one form of burial at Hawksbill Station, and that was burial at sea. They could hardly dig graves into the living rock for their dead. So Valdosto would be interred twice. Cast up by the waves, he would have to be taken out again, properly weighted, and sent to his resting place. Ordinarily they would have held the funeral by the shore, but now, as a tacit concession to Barrett's handicap, they were bringing Valdosto all the way up here rather than subject Barrett to another strenuous climb along the cliff steps. It seemed pointless, somehow, this dragging back and forth of lifeless flesh. It would have been better, Barrett thought, if Val had simply been swept out to sea ` the first time.

Hahn and several others appeared soon afterward, carrying the body wrapped in a sheet of blue plastic. They laid it out on the ground in front of Barrett's hut. It was one of his self-imposed tasks here to deliver the valedictories; it seemed to him that he had delivered fifty such speeches in the last year alone. About thirty of the men were present. The rest were beyond caring about the dead, or else cared so much that they could not attend.

## Hawksbill Times Two

Barrett kept it simple. He spoke briefly of his friendship with Valdosto, of their days together at the turn of the century, of Valdosto's revolutionary activities. He outlined some of Valdosto's heroic acts. Most of them Barrett had learned about at second hand, for he himself had been a prisoner at Hawksbill during Valdosto's years of fame. Between 2006 and 2015, Val had almost singlehandedly reduced the government to a condition of battle fatigue, bombing and mining and killing.

"They knew who he was," Barrett said, "but they couldn't find him. They chased him for years, and one day they caught him, and they put him on trial—*you* know what sort of trial—and they sent him to us in Hawksbill Station. And for many years Val was a leader here. But he wasn't meant to be a prisoner. He couldn't adapt to a world where he was unable to fight against the government. And so he came apart. We had to watch it, and it was not easy for us. Or for him. May he rest in peace."

Barrett gestured. The pallbearers lifted the body and walked toward the east. Most of the mourners followed. Barrett did not. He stood watching until the funeral procession had begun to wind down the steps that led to the sea; then he turned and went into his hut. After a while he slept.

A little before midnight, Barrett was awakened by the sound of hasty footsteps outside his hut. As he sat up, groping for the luminescence switch, Ned Altman came blundering through the door.

Barrett blinked at him. "What's the matter, Ned?"

# Hawksbill Times Two

"It's Hahn!" Altman rasped. "He's fooling around with the Hammer again. We just saw him go into the building." Barrett shed his drowsiness like a seal bursting out of water. Ignoring the insistent throb in his left leg, he pulled himself from his bed and grabbed some clothing. He was more apprehensive than he wanted Altman to see, and he kept his face frozen, masklike. If Hahn, fooling around with the temporal mechanism, smashed the Hammer accidentally or deliberately, they might never receive replacement equipment from Up Front. Which would mean that all future shipments—if there were to be any—would come as random shoots that might land in any old year and at great distances from the Station. What business did Hahn have with the machine, anyway?

As Barrett pulled on his trousers, Altman said, "Latimer's up there keeping an eye on him. He got suspicious when Hahn didn't come back to the but at bedtime, and he got me, and we went looking for him. And there he was, sniffing around the Hammer."

"Doing what?"

"I don't know. As soon as we saw him go into the building, I came right down here to get you. That's what I was supposed to do, wasn't it?"

"Yes," Barrett said. "Come on!"

He stumped his way out of the but and did his best to trot toward the main building. Pain shot like trails of hot acid up the whole lower half of his body. The crutch dug mercilessly into his left armpit as he leaned all his weight into it. His crippled foot, swinging freely, burned with a cold glow. His right leg, which had to bear most of the burden, creaked and popped. Altman ran breathlessly alongside him. The

# Hawksbill Times Two

Station looked dreamlike in the salmon moonlight. It was terribly silent at this hour.

They jogged past Quesada's hut. Barrett considered waking the medic and taking him along. He decided against it. Whatever trouble Hahn might be up to, Barrett felt that he could handle it himself. There was some strength left in the old gnawed beam, after all. Latimer stood waiting for them at the entrance to the main dome. He was right at the edge of panic, or perhaps he was over the edge. He seemed to be gibbering with fear and shock. Barrett had never seen a man gibber before. He clamped a big paw on Latimer's thin shoulder and said harshly, "Well, where is he? Where's Hahn?"

"He—disappeared."

"What the hell do you mean? Which way did he go?" Latimer moaned. His angular face was fish-belly white. His lips trembled and flickered before words would emerge.

"He got onto the Anvil," Latimer blurted at length. "The light came on—the glow. And then Hahn disappeared!"

Altman giggled. "Can you beat that! He disappeared! Powie, right into the machine, eh?"

"No," Barrett said. "It isn't possible. The machine's only equipped for receiving, not for transmitting. You must be mistaken, Don."

"I saw him go!"

"He's hiding somewhere in the building," Barrett insisted doggedly. "He's got to be. Close that door! Search the place until you find him!"

Altman said mildly, "He probably did disappear, Jim. If Don says he disappeared—"

"Yes," said Latimer, equally mildly. "That's true, you know. He climbed right on top of the Anvil. Then everything turned red in the room and he was gone."

Barrett clenched his fists and pressed his knuckles against his aching temples. There was a white-hot blaze just behind his forehead that almost made him forget about the pain in his foot. He saw his mistake clearly now. He had depended for his espionage on two men who were patently and unmistakably insane, and that had been itself a not very sane thing to do. A man is known by his choice of lieutenants. Well, he had relied on Altman and Latimer, and now they were giving him precisely the sort of information that such spies could be counted on to supply.

"You're hallucinating," Barrett told Latimer curtly. "Ned, go wake up Quesada and get him over here right away. You, Don, you stand here by the entrance, and if Hahn shows up I want you to sing out at the top of your lungs. I'm going to search the building for him."

"Wait," Latimer said, catching Barrett's wrist. He seemed to be making an effort to gain control of himself again. "Jim, do you remember when I asked you if you thought I was crazy? You said you didn't. You said you trusted me."

"So?"

"Well, don't stop trusting me now. I tell you I'm not hallucinating. I saw Hahn disappear. I can't explain it, but I'm rational enough to know what I saw."

Barrett stared intently at him. Sure, he thought. Take a crazy man's word for it, when the crazy man tells you in a nice calm voice that he's perfectly sane. Sure.

He said in a milder tone, "All right, Don. Maybe so. I want you to stay by the door, anyway. I'll run a quick check, just to see what's what."

He went into the building, planning to make a circuit of the dome, beginning with the room where the Hammer was mounted. He entered it. Everything seemed to be in perfect order there. No Hawksbill Field glow was in evidence, nor could Barrett see any indication that anything had been disturbed.

The receiving room had no closets or cupboards or alcoves or crannies in which Hahn could be hiding. When he had inspected the room thoroughly, Barrett moved on down the corridor, looking into the infirmary, the mess hall, the kitchen, the reception room. He checked every likely hiding place. He looked high and he looked low. No Hahn. Not anywhere.

Of course, there were plenty of places in those rooms where Hahn might have secreted himself. Maybe he was sitting in the refrigerator on top of a pile of frigid trilobites. Maybe he was under all the equipment in the recreation room. Maybe he was in the drug closet.

But Barrett doubted that Hahn was in the building at all. Very likely he was down by the waterfront, taking a moody stroll, and hadn't set foot in the place since evening. Very likely this entire episode had been some feverish fantasy of Latimer's, nothing more. Knowing that Barrett was worried about Hahn's interest in the Hammer, Latimer and Altman had nudged themselves into imagining that they saw him snooping here, and had succeeded in convincing themselves of it.

Barrett completed the route through the building's circling corridor and found himself back at the main entrance. Latimer still stood guard there. He had been joined by a sleepy Quesada, his face bruised and puffy from his battle with Valdosto.

Altman, pale and shaky-looking, was just outside the door.

"What's going on?" Quesada asked.

"I'm not sure," Barrett said. "Don and Ned had the idea that they saw Lew Hahn fooling around with the time equipment. I've checked through the whole building, and he doesn't seem to be in here, so maybe they made a little mistake. I suggest you take them both into the infirmary and give them a shot of something to settle their nerves, and then we'll all try to get back to sleep."

Latimer said thinly, "I tell you, I swear I saw—"

"Shut up!" Altman broke in. "Listen! Listen! What's that noise?"

Barrett listened. The sound was clear and loud: the hissing whine of ionization. It was the sound produced by a functioning

Hawksbill Field. Suddenly goose-pimples were breaking out on his skin.

In a low voice, he said, "The Field's on. We're probably getting some supplies."

"At this hour?" said Latimer.

"We don't know what time it is Up Front. All of you stay here. I'll check the Hammer."

"Perhaps I ought to go with you, Jim," Quesada suggested gently.

"*Stay here!*" Barrett thundered. He paused, embarrassed at his own explosive show of wrath. Nerves. Nerves. He said more quietly, "It only takes one of us to check things. You wait. I'll be right back."

Without staying around to hear further dissent, Barrett pivoted and limped down the hall to the Hammer room. He shouldered the door open and looked in. There was no need for him to switch on the light. The deep red glow of the Hawksbill Field illuminated everything.

He stationed himself just within the door. Hardly daring to breathe, he stared fixedly at the metallic bulk of the Hammer, watching the play of colors against its shafts and power rods and fuses. The glow of the Field deepened through various shades of pink toward crimson, and then spread until it enfolded the waiting Anvil beneath it. An endless moment passed.

Then came the implosive thunderclap, and Lew Hahn dropped out of nowhere and lay for a moment in temporal shock on the broad plate of the Anvil.

# THIRTEEN

T HEY HAD ARRESTED Barrett on a beautiful day in October 2006, when the leaves were crisp and yellowing, when the air was clear and cool, when the cloudless blue sky seemed to reflect all the glory of autumn. He was in Boston that day, as he had been on a day ten years previous when they had arrested Janet at his New York apartment. He was walking down Boylston Street on his way to an appointment when two alert-looking young men in neutral gray business suits matched their strides to his, kept pace with him for perhaps ten feet, and moved in to flank him.

"James Edward Barrett?" the one on the left said.

"That's right." Why pretend?

"We'd like you to come with us," said the one on the right.

"Please don't attempt any violence," said his partner.

"It'll be better for all of us if you don't. Especially for you."

"I won't make trouble," Barrett said.

They had a car parked on the corner. Keeping close to him at every step, they walked him to the car and guided him within it. When they closed the doors, they didn't just lock them, but sealed them with a radio block.

"May I make a phone call?" Barrett asked.

"Sorry. No."

The agent who sat at his left produced a degausser and quickly voided any recording device Barrett might be carrying. The agent at his right checked him out for communication instruments, found the telephone mounted against his ear, and deftly removed it. They locked Barrett in place with a microwave restraining field that left him enough freedom to yawn or stretch, but not enough to touch either of the agents beside him. The car moved away from the curb.

"So this is it," Barrett said. "I've been expecting it for so long that I began to believe it would never happen."

"It happens eventually," said the left-hand one.

"To all of you," said the right-hand one. "It just takes time."

Time. Yes. In '85, '86, '87, the first years of the resistance movement, an adolescent Jim Barrett had lived in perpetual expectation of arrest. Arrest or worse: a laser beam whistling out of nowhere to penetrate his skull, maybe. In those years he saw the new government as omniscient and all-threatening, and saw himself in constant peril. But the arrests had been few, and in time Barrett had swung to the opposite extreme, confidently assuming that the secret police would leave him untouched. He had even convinced himself that a decision had been taken not to molest him—that he was being spared deliberately, as a symbol of the regime's tolerance of dissent. After Chancellor Dantell had replaced Chancellor Arnold, Barrett had lost some of that naïve confidence of personal grace. But yet he had not fully come to terms with the possibility of arrest until the day they took Janet away. One does not believe one can be struck by lightning until a bolt blasts the person at one's side. And after that one expects the heavens to open again whenever a cloud appears.

There had been arrests all through the harsh years of the middle '90s, but he had never even been called in for questioning. Eventually he came once again to believe that he was immune. Having lived with the possibility of arrest, on and off, for more than twenty years, Barrett simply pushed that possibility into a distant corner of his mind and forgot about it. And now they had come for him at last.

He searched his soul for a reaction, and was puzzled at the only reaction he found: relief. The suspense was over. So was the toil. Now he could rest.

He was thirty-eight years old. He was Supreme Commander of the Eastern Division of the Continental Liberation Front. Since boyhood he had labored to bring about the overthrow of the government, taking a million tiny steps that covered no territory whatever. Of those who had been present at his first underground meeting, that day in 1984, he alone remained. Janet was missing and presumed dead. Jack Bernstein, his mentor in revolutionary affairs, had gone over cheerfully to the enemy. Hawksbill had died, bloated and hypothyroid at forty-three, just a few years ago. His work on time travel, so they said, had been a success. He had built a workable time machine and turned it over to the government. There was a rumor that the government was conducting experiments with the machine, using political prisoners as subjects. Barrett had heard that old Norman Pleyel had been one of the subjects. They had arrested him in March of '05, at any rate, and no one knew where he was now. Pleyel's arrest had left Barrett in command of the sector in title as well as in fact; but he had expected to have a little more time before they picked him up too.

So they were all gone, those revolutionaries of '84, dead or missing or on the other side. He alone was left, and now he was about to be dead or missing too.

Strangely, he had few regrets. He was willing to let others carry on the dreary task of preparing for The Revolution. The Revolution that would never come, he thought bitterly. The Revolution had been lost before it ever began. Jack Bernstein's words drifted across time to him out of 1987: "We're going to lose unless we grab the kids growing up! The syndicalists are getting them, and educating them to think that syndicalism is true and good and beautiful, and the longer that goes on, the longer it's *going* to go on. It's self-perpetuating. Anybody who wants the old constitution back, or who wants the new constitution amended, is going to look like a dangerous fire-breathing radical, and the syndicalists will be the nice, safe, conservative boys we've always had and always want. At which point everything is over and done with." Yes. Jack had been right. The Front had grabbed some of the kids growing up, but not enough. Despite an ever more sophisticated propaganda campaign, despite a cunning interleaving of revolutionary agitation with popular entertainment, despite the financial support of some of the nation's finest minds, they had achieved nothing. They had been unable to move that vast placid mass of citizens, the ones who were satisfied with the government, whatever sort of government it might happen to be, the ones who feared rocking the boat more than they feared being devoured by the boat.

They might as well arrest me, then, Barrett told himself. I'm used up. I've got nothing left to offer the Front. I've admitted inward defeat, and if I stick around, I'll poison all the younger ones with my pessimism.

It was true. He had ceased to be a revolutionary agitator years ago. He was nothing but a bureaucrat of revolution now, a shuffler of papers, a representative of entrenched interests. If The Revolution actually broke out, now, would he rejoice or would he be terrified of it? He had grown accustomed to living on the brink of revolution. He was comfortable there. His commitment to change had eroded.

"You're very quiet," said the agent at his left.

"Should I be screaming and sobbing?"

"We expected more trouble with you," said the agent at his right. "A top leader like you—"

"You don't know me very well," Barrett said. "I'm past the stage of caring what you do with me."

"Oh, really? That's not the profile we've got on you. You're a dedicated revolutionary from way back, Barrett. You're a dangerous radical. We've been watching you."

"Why did you wait so long to arrest me, then?"

"We don't believe in picking up everybody right away. We have a long-range program of arrest. Everything's programmed for impact. We get one leader this year, one the next, one five years afterward—"

"Sure," Barrett said. "You can afford to wait, because we don't represent any real threat anyway. We're just a bunch of frauds."

"You sound almost serious," said the agent at his left. Barrett laughed.

"You're a funny one," said the agent at his right. "We've never had one quite like you before. You don't even look like an agitator. You could almost be a lawyer, or something. Something respectable."

"Are you sure you've got the right man, then?" Barrett asked.

The two agents eyed each other. The man on Barrett's right stopped the car and deactivated the restraining field in which Barrett was caged. He seized Barrett's right hand and pushed it against the data plate on the dashboard. He punched for computer time. A moment passed while the central computer checked Barrett's fingerprints against its master files.

"You're Barrett, all right," the agent said in obvious relief.

"I never denied it, did I? I just asked if you were sure."

"Well, now we're even surer."

"Good."

"You're a funny one, Barrett."

They took him to the airport. A small government plane was waiting there. The flight lasted two hours, which would have been enough to take him nearly across the continent, but Barrett had no assurance that he had gone any such distance. They could have been flying in circles over Boston all that time; the government, he knew, did things like that. When the plane landed, nightfall had come. He did not catch more than a glimpse of the airport, for a sealed transport capsule was pushed up against the plane and he was hustled into it. That single glimpse was not enough to tell Barrett where he might be.

But he did not need to be told his destination. He ended his journey in one of the government's interrogation camps. A blank, smooth black metal door closed behind him. Within, all was sleek, brightly lit, antiseptic. It might have been a hospital. Corridors receded in many directions; recessed lighting gave a pleasant greenish-yellow glow.

They fed him. They gave him a seamless uniform made of some imperishable-looking fabric.

They put him in a cell.

Barrett was surprised and vaguely pleased to discover that he had not landed in a maximum-security block. His cell was a comfortable room, about ten by fourteen, with a bunk, a toilet, an ultrasonic bath, and a video eye behind a nearly invisible barrier in the ceiling. There was a grillwork in the cell door through which he could carry on conversations with the prisoners in the facing cells. He did not recognize their names; some of them belonged to underground groups he had never heard of, and he thought he had heard of them all. Probably at least a few of his neighbors here were government spies, but Barrett did not mind that, since he expected it.

"How often do the interrogators come?" Barrett asked.

"They don't," said the stocky, bearded man across the way. His name was Fulks. "I've been here a month and I haven't been interrogated yet."

"They don't come here to interrogate," said the man next to Fulks. "They take you away and question you somewhere else. Then you never come back here. They're in no hurry, either. I've been here a month and a half."

A week passed, and no one took official notice of Barrett. He was fed regularly, allowed to requisition certain reading matter, and taken from his cell every third day for exercise in the courtyard. But there was no indication that he was going to be interrogated or placed on trial or even indicted. Under the law of preventive detention, he could be held indefinitely without an arraignment, if he were deemed dangerous to the continuity of the state.

Some of the prisoners were led away. They did not return. New prisoners arrived each day.

A good deal of the talk was about the time-travel program. "They're doing the experiments," reported a thin, tough-faced newcomer named Anderson. "They got a process, it lets them send back rabbits and monkeys a couple of years in time. They got it almost perfect now. And then they're going to start sending prisoners back. They'll send us a million years back and let us get eaten by dinosaurs."

It sounded unlikely to Barrett, even though he had discussed this project with its inventor six years before. Well, Hawksbill was dead now, and his work was the property of those who had footed the bill for it, and God help us all if these wild stories are true. A million years into the past? The government piously declared that it had renounced capital punishment; but perhaps it could stick a man into Hawksbill's machine, ship him off to who knew where or when, and maintain a clear conscience. Barrett thought he had been in custody for four weeks when they took him from his cell and transferred him to the interrogation department. He was not sure, because he had been having some difficulty keeping an accurate count of the passing days, but he thought it was about four weeks. He had never known twenty-eight days to pass so slowly. He would not have been amazed at all to learn that he had been in his cell four years before they came for him.

A snub-nosed little electric runabout took him through endless mazes and delivered him to a cheerful office, where he went through an elaborate registration process. When the routines were completed, two monitors escorted him to a small, austere room containing a desk, a couch, and a chair.

"Lie down," one monitor said.

Barrett obeyed. He was aware of a restraining shield taking form about him. He studied the ceiling. It was gray and perfectly smooth, as though the entire room had been squirted from a nozzle as, a single bubble. They let him examine the perfection of the ceiling for several hours, and then, just as he was beginning to get hungry, a section of the wall slid away long enough to admit the lean figure of Jack Bernstein. "I knew it would be you, Jack," Barrett said calmly.

"Please call me Jacob."

"You never let anyone call you Jacob when we were kids," Barrett said. "You insisted your name was Jack, right on your birth certificate. Remember when a bunch of our classmates got bothered with you and chased you halfway across the schoolyard, yelling, *Jacob, Jacob, Jacob?* I had to save you then. That was, how long, Jack, twenty-five years ago? Two thirds of our lives ago, Jack."

"Jacob."

"Do you mind if I go on calling you Jack? I can't break the habit after all this time."

"You'd be wiser to call me Jacob," Bernstein said. "I have great power over your future."

"I've got no future. I'm a prisoner for keeps."

"That isn't necessarily so."

"Don't tease me, Jack. The only power you have is to decide, maybe, whether I'll get tortured or just left to rot in boredom. And, frankly, I don't give a damn. I'm beyond your reach, Jack. There's nothing you can do to me that matters."

"Nevertheless," Bernstein said, "it might prove to your advantage to cooperate with me, in the small things as well as in the big ones. Regardless of how desperate you think your present situation is, you're still alive, and you might conceivably discover that we mean you no harm. But it all depends on your attitude. I find that it pleases me to be called Jacob these days, and it shouldn't be that difficult for you to adapt."

"As long as you wanted to change your name, Jack," said Barrett amiably, "why didn't you make it Judas?" Bernstein did not reply at once. He crossed the room and stood beside the couch on which Barrett lay, and stared down at him in an impersonal, abstracted manner. His face, thought Barrett, looks calm and relaxed for the first time I can recall. But he's lost more weight. His cheekbones are like knives. He can't weigh more than a hundred pounds. And his eyes are so bright . . . so bright. . . .

Bernstein said, "You were always such a big fool, Jim."

"Yes. I didn't have the sense to be radical when you were joining the underground. Then I didn't have the sense to jump to the other side when the jumping was good."

"And now you don't have the sense to accommodate yourself to your interrogator."

"I'm not much on selling out, Jack. *Jacob*."

"To save yourself?"

"Suppose I'm not interested in saving myself?"

"The Revolution needs you, doesn't it?" Bernstein asked. "It's your duty to get out of our clutches and continue your sacred task of working toward the overthrow of the government."

"Is it?"

"I think so."

"I don't, Jack. I'm tired of being a revolutionary. I think I'd just like to lie here and rest for the next forty or fifty years. As prisons go, this one's pretty comfortable."

"I can arrange your release," Bernstein said. "But only if you cooperate."

Barrett smiled. "All right, *Jacob*. Tell me what you want to know, and I'll see if I can't give you the answers you want."

"I have no questions now."

"None?"

"None."

"That's a lousy way to interrogate a man, no?"

"You're still full of resistance, Jim. I'll come back another time, and we'll talk again."

Bernstein went out. They left Barrett alone for a couple of hours, until he thought he would split apart in boredom, and then they brought him a meal. He expected Bernstein to return after dinner. But, in fact, Barrett did not see the interrogator again for quite some time. They put him in an interrogation tank late that evening.

The theory, and it was a reasonable one, held that total sensory deprivation lessens a man's individuality, and hence reduces his tendency toward stubbornness. Plug his ears, cap his eyes, put him in a warm nutrient bath, pipe food and air to him along plastic conduits, let him float in idleness, in womb-like ease, day after day, until the spirit decays and the ego corrodes. Barrett entered the tank. He could not hear. He could not see. Before long, he could not sleep.

As he lay in his tank he dictated his autobiography to himself, a document several volumes long. He invented mathematical games of great intricacy. He recited the names of the states of the old United States of America, and tried to recall the names of their capitals. He re-enacted scenes that had been climactic in his life, altering the script here and there.

Then it became too much trouble even to think, and he merely drifted on the amniotic tide. He came to believe that he was dead, and that this was the afterlife, eternal relaxation. Soon his mind twitched into renewed activity, and he waited eagerly to be taken from the tank and questioned, and then he waited desperately, and then he waited furiously, and then he ceased to wait at all.

After what could have been eight hundred years, they took him from the interrogation tank.

"How do you feel?" a guard asked. His voice was like a shriek. Barrett clapped his hands to his ears and dropped to the floor. They picked him up.

"You get used to the sound of voices again eventually," the guard said.

"Stop it," Barrett whispered. "Stop talking!"

He could not abide even the sound of his own voice. His heartbeat was merciless thunder in his ears. His breathing made a ferocious rustling sound, like the tearing down of forests by gusts of wind. His eyes were numbed by the flood of visual impressions. He shivered. He quaked.

Jacob Bernstein came to him an hour after he had been brought from the tank.

"Feel rested?" Bernstein asked. "Relaxed, happy, cooperative?"

"How long was I in there?"

"I'm not prepared to tell you that."

"A week? A month? A year? What's today's date?"

"It doesn't matter, Jim."

"Please stop talking. Your voice hurts my ears."

Bernstein smiled. "You'll adjust. I hope you've been reviewing your memory while you've rested, Jim. Answer some questions, now. The names of people in your group, to begin with. Not everybody just those in positions of responsibility."

"You know all the names," Barrett murmured. "I want to hear them from you."

"What for?"

"Perhaps we took you from the tank too soon."

"So put me back," Barrett said.

"Don't be stubborn. List some names for me."

"It hurts my ears when I talk."

Bernstein folded his arms. "Let the names go, for now. I have here a statement describing the extent of your counterrevolutionary activities."

"*Counter*revolutionary?"

"Yes. In opposition to the continuing work of the founders of the Revolution of 1984."

"I haven't heard us described as counterrevolutionaries in a long time, Jack."

"Jacob."

"Jacob."

"Thank you. I'll read the statement. You may amend it if you find it incorrect in any details. Then you'll sign it, please." He opened a lengthy document and read a concise, dry account of Barrett's career in the underground, substantially accurate, covering everything from that first meeting in 1984 to date. When he finished he said, "Any criticisms or suggestions?"

"No."

"Sign it, then."

"My muscular coordination is lousy right now. I can't hold a pen. I guess I was in your tank too long."

"Dictate a verbal adherence to the statements of the confession, then. We'll take a voiceprint, and it'll serve as admissible evidence."

"No."

"You deny that this is an accurate summary of your career?"

"I take the Fifth Amendment."

"There is no such concept as the Fifth Amendment," Bernstein said. "Will you admit that you've worked for the conscious overthrow of the present legally constituted government of this nation?"

"Doesn't it make you sick to hear words like that coming out of your mouth, Jack?"

"I warn you not to launch a personal attack on my integrity," said Bernstein quietly. "You can't possibly understand the motivations that caused me to transfer my allegiance from the underground to the government, and I'm not about to discuss them with you. This is your interrogation, not mine."

"I hope your turn comes soon."

"I doubt that it will."

Barrett said, "When we were sixteen, you spoke of this government as wolves eating the world. You warned me that unless I woke up, I'd be one more slave in a world full of slaves. And I said I'd rather be a live slave than a dead subversive, remember, and you took me apart for saying something like that. Now here you are on the team of the wolves. You're a live slave and I'm going to be a dead subversive."

"This government has renounced capital punishment," said Bernstein. "I regard myself as neither a wolf nor a slave. And by your own words you've just demonstrated the fallacy of trying to uphold your opinions-aged-sixteen into adulthood."

"What do you want from me, Jack?"

"Two things. Your acceptance of the résumé I've just read you. And your cooperation in our attempt to gain information about the leadership of the Continental Liberation Front.”

“You’re forgetting one thing. You also want me to call you Jacob, Jacob.”

Bernstein did not smile. “If you cooperate, I can promise you a satisfactory end to this interrogation.”

“And if not?”

“We are not vindictive. But we take action to maintain the security of the citizens by removing from their environment those who threaten national stability.”

“But you don’t kill people,” Barrett said. “Hell, you must have awfully crowded prisons by now. Unless the time-travel business is true.”

Bernstein’s armor of self-containment seemed to be pierced for the first time.

Barrett said, "Is it? Did Hawksbill build a machine that lets you toss prisoners back in time? Are you feeding us to the dinosaurs?"

"I'll give you another opportunity to answer my questions," said Bernstein, looking nettled. "Will you tell me—"

"You know, Jack, a funny thing's been happening to me in this interrogation camp. When the police picked me up that day in Boston, I honestly didn't mind. I had lost interest in The Revolution. I was as uncommitted that day as I had been when I was sixteen and you dragged me into the whole business. What it was, my faith in the revolutionary process had burned out. I had stopped believing we could ever overthrow the government, and I saw that I was just going through the motions, getting older and older, using up my life in a futile Bolshevik dream, keeping up appearances so I wouldn't discourage the kids in the movement. I had just discovered that my whole life was empty. So what difference did it make to me if you arrested me? I was nothing. I bet that if you came and questioned me my first day in jail, I would have told you anything you wanted to know, simply because I was too bored to go on resisting. But now I've been in interrogation for six months, a year, I can't tell how long, and the effect's been quite interesting. I'm stubborn again. I came in here flaccid-willed, and you've built up my will until it's stronger than ever. Isn't that interesting, Jack? I guess it doesn't make you look like such a hotshot interrogator, and I'm sorry about that, but I thought you'd like to know how the process has been affecting me."

"Are you asking to be tortured, Jim?"

"I'm not asking anything: Just telling."

They took Barrett back to the tank. As before, he had no idea how long he was left in it, but it seemed longer this time than the first time, and he felt weaker when he came out. He could not be interrogated for three hours afterward, because he could not tolerate noise. Bernstein tried, but gave up and waited until his pain threshold had improved. Barrett failed to be cooperative. Bernstein was distressed.

They inflicted a moderate amount of physical torture on Barrett next. He withstood it.

Bernstein tried to be friendly. He offered cigarettes, had Barrett released from restraint, chatted about old times. They argued ideology from all viewpoints. They laughed together. They joked.

"Will you help me now, Jim?" Bernstein asked. "Just answer a few questions."

"You don't need the information I could give you. It's all on file. You're only after a symbolic capitulation. Well, I'm going to hold out forever. You might as well give up and bring me to trial."

"Your trial can't begin until you've signed the statement," Bernstein said.

"In that case you'll have to go on interrogating." But in the end, boredom got the better of him. He was tired of his immersions in the tank, tired of the bright lights, the electronic probes, the subcutaneous shocks, the jabbing questions, tired of Bernstein's haggard face peering into his own. Coming to trial seemed the only way out. Barrett signed the résumé Bernstein offered him. He delivered up a list of names of Continental Liberation Front officers. The names were imaginary, and Bernstein knew it; but he was satisfied. It was the appearance of capitulation they were after.

"You will be tried next week," said Bernstein.

"Congratulations," Barrett said. "You did a masterly job of breaking my spirit. I'm utterly defeated now. My will is shattered. I've surrendered in all respects. You're a credit to your profession—*Jack*."

The look that Jacob Bernstein gave him was tipped with acid.

The trial duly took place: no jury, no attorneys, merely a government functionary sitting before a bank of computer inputs and outputs. Barrett's confession was entered into the records. Barrett himself supplied a verbal statement. The interrogator's report was delivered. In the course of proceedings, it was necessary for a date to be affixed to all these reports, and so Barrett learned that it was now the summer of 2008. He had been in the interrogation camp for twenty months.

"The verdict is guilty as charged. James Edward Barrett, we sentence you to imprisonment for life, the place of your internment to be Hawksbill Station."

"Where?"

No reply. They led him away.

Hawksbill Station? What was that? Something to do with the time machine, perhaps?

Barrett found out soon enough.

He was brought to a vast room filled with improbable machinery. At the center of everything was a gleaming metallic plate twenty feet in diameter. Above it, descending from the distant ceiling, was a conglomeration of apparatus weighing many tons, an arrangement of colossal pistons and power cores that looked like a prehistoric monster about to strike . . . or perhaps like a gigantic hammer. The room was crowded with hard-eyed technicians, busy at dials and screens. No one spoke to Barrett. He was thrust up onto the huge anvil-like plate beneath the monstrous hammer. All about him, the room throbbed with activity. This was a lot of fuss, he told himself, for one weary political prisoner. Were they going to send him to Hawksbill Station now?

There was a red glow in the room.

But nothing happened for a long while. Barrett stood patiently, feeling faintly absurd. A voice said in the background, "How's the calibration?"

"Fine. We'll toss him exactly a billion years back."

"Wait a second!" Barrett yelled. "A billion years—" They ignored him. He could not move. There was a high whining sound, a strange odor in the air. And then he felt pain, the most intense, the most dislocating pain he had ever experienced. Had the hammer descended and crushed him flat? He could not see. He was nowhere. He was—

—falling—landing—

—sitting up, dazed, sweating, bewildered. He was in another room with some of the same sort of equipment around him, but the faces here were not the hard faces of impersonal technicians. He recognized these faces. Members of the Continental Liberation Front . . . men he had not seen for years, men who had been arrested, whose whereabouts had been unknown.

There was Norman Pleyel, with tears in his gentle eyes. "Jim—Jim Barrett—so they finally sent you here too, Jim! Don't try to get up. You're in temporal shock now, but it passes fast."

Barrett said hoarsely, "Is this Hawksbill Station?"

"This is Hawksbill Station. Such that it is."

"Where is it?"

"Not where, Jim. *When*. We're a billion years back in time."

"No. No." He shook his foggy head. So Hawksbill's machine did work, and the rumors were true, and this was where they sent the troublesome ones. Was Janet here too? He asked. No, Pleyel said. There were only men here. Twenty or thirty prisoners, managing somehow to survive.

Barrett was reluctant to believe any of this. But then they helped him down from the Anvil, and took him outside to show him what the world was like, and he stared in slowly spreading wonder at the curve of bare, rock slanting into the gray sea, at the unmarred, uninhabited coast, and the reality of his exile sank in with a blow more painful than the one the Hammer had dealt him.

# FOURTEEN

IN THE DARKNESS, Hahn did not notice Barrett at first. He sat up slowly, shaking off the stunning effects of a trip through time. After a few seconds he pushed himself toward the lip of the Anvil and let his legs dangle over it. He swung them to get the circulation going. He took a series of deep breaths. Finally he slipped to the floor. The glow of the field had gone out in the moment of his arrival, and so he moved warily, as though not wanting to bump into anything.

Abruptly Barrett switched on the light and said, "What have you been up to, Hahn?"

The younger man recoiled as though he had been jabbed in the gut. He gasped, hopped backward a few steps, and flung up both hands in a defensive gesture. "Answer me," Barrett said.

Hahn seemed to regain his equilibrium. He shot a quick glance past Barrett's bulky form toward the hallway and said, "Let me go, will you? I can't explain now."

"You'd better explain now."

"It'll be easier for everyone if I don't," said Hahn. "Please. Let me pass."

Barrett continued to block the door. "I want to know where you've been this evening. And what you've been doing with the Hammer."

"Nothing. Just studying it a little."

"You weren't in this room a minute ago. Then you appeared out of nowhere. Where did you come from, Hahn?"

"You're mistaken. I was standing right behind the Hammer. I didn't—"

"I saw you drop down on the Anvil. You took a time trip, didn't you?"

"No."

"Don't lie to me! I don't know how you do it, but you've got some way of going forward in time, isn't that so? You've been spying on us, and you just went somewhere to file your report—somewhen—and now you're back."

Hahn's pale forehead was glistening. He said tautly, "I warn you, Barrett, don't ask too many questions right now. You'll know everything you want to know in due time. This isn't the time. Please, now. Let me pass."

"I want answers first," Barrett said.

He realized that he was trembling. He already knew the answers, and they were answers that shook him to the core of his soul. He knew where Hahn had been.

But Hahn had to admit it himself.

Hahn said nothing. He took a couple of hesitant steps toward Barrett, who did not move. Hahn seemed to be gathering momentum for a sudden rush at the doorway.

Barrett said, "You aren't getting out of this room until you've told me what I want to know."

Hahn charged.

Barrett planted himself squarely, crutch braced against the doorframe, his good leg flat on the floor, and waited for the younger man to reach him. He figured that he outweighed Hahn by at least eighty pounds. That might be just enough to balance the fact that he was spotting Hahn some thirty years and one leg. They came together, and Barrett drove his hands down onto Hahn's shoulders, trying to hold him, to force him back into the room.

Hahn gave an inch or two. He looked up at Barrett without saying a word and pushed forward again. "Don't—don't—" Barrett grunted. "I—won't—let—you—"

"I don't want to do this," Hahn said.

He pushed again. Barrett felt himself buckling under the impact. He dug his hands as hard as he could into Hahn's shoulders, and tried to shove the other man backward into the room. But Hahn held firm, and all of Barrett's energy was converted into a backward thrust rebounding on himself. He lost control of his crutch. It scraped along the doorframe and slithered out from under his arm. For one agonizing moment Barrett's full weight rested on the crushed uselessness of his left foot, and then, as though his limbs were melting away beneath him, he began to sink toward the floor. He landed with a reverberating crash.

Quesada, Altman, and Latimer came rushing into the room. Barrett writhed in pain on the floor, digging his fingers into the thigh of his crippled leg. Hahn stood over him, looking unhappy, his hands locked together.

"I'm sorry," he said. "You shouldn't have tried to muscle me like that."

Barrett glowered at him. "You were traveling in time, weren't you? You can answer me now!"

"Yes," Hahn said at last. "I went Up Front."

An hour later, after Quesada had pumped him with enough shots of neural depressant to keep him from jumping out of his skin with pain, Barrett got the full story. Hahn hadn't wanted to reveal it so soon, but he had changed his mind after his little scuffle.

It was all very simple. Time travel now worked in both directions. The glib, impressive noises about the flow of entropy had turned out to be just noises.

"No," Barrett said. "I discussed it with Hawksbill myself, in—let's see—it was 1998. Hawksbill and I knew each other. I said, can people go back and forth in time, with your machine, and he said no, only back. Forward motion was impossible according to his equations."

"His equations were incomplete," said Hahn. "Obviously. He never worked out the forward-motion part."

"How could a man like Hawksbill make a mistake?"

"He made at least one. There's been further research, and we know now how to move in both directions. Even Einstein had to be amended later on. Why not Hawksbill?"

## Hawksbill Times Two

Barrett shook his head. Well, why not Hawksbill, he asked himself? But he had taken it as an article of faith that Hawksbill's work had been perfect, that he was condemned to live out his days here at the dawn of time. "How long has this two-way thing been known?" Barrett asked.

"At least five years," Hahn said. "We aren't sure yet exactly when the breakthrough came. After we're finished going through all the secret records of the former government—"

"The former government?"

Hahn nodded. "The revolution came in January. Of '29. It wasn't really a violent one, either. The syndicalists just mildewed from within, and when they got the first push they fell over. There was a revolutionary government waiting in the wings to take over and restore the old constitutional guarantees."

"Was it mildew?" Barrett asked, coloring. "Or termites? Keep your metaphors straight."

Hahn glanced away. "Anyway, the old government fell. We've got a provisional liberal regime in office now, and there's going to be an open election in six months or so. Don't ask me much about the philosophy of the new administration. I'm not a political theorist. I'm not even an economist. You guessed as much."

"What are you, then?"

"A policeman," Hahn said. "Part of the commission that's investigating the prison system of the former government. Including this prison."

Barrett said, "What's happening to the prisoners Up Front? The politicals."

"They're being freed. We review their cases and generally let them go fast."

Barrett nodded. "And the syndicalists? What's becoming of them? I wonder if you could tell me about one in particular, an interrogator, name of Jacob Bernstein. Maybe you know of him."

"Bernstein? Sure. One of the Council of Syndics, he was. Head of interrogation."

"Was?"

"Committed suicide," said Hahn. "A lot of the Syndics did that when the regime fell apart. Bernstein was the first."

"It figures," Barrett said, feeling oddly moved, somehow.

There was a long moment of silence.

"There was a girl," Barrett said. "Long ago—she disappeared—they arrested her in 1994, and no one ever could find out what happened to her. I wonder if—if—"

Hahn shook his head. "I'm sorry," he said gently. "That was thirty-five years ago. We didn't find any prisoners who had been in jail more than six or seven years. The hard core opposition all got sent to Hawksbill Station, and the others—well, if she was a special friend of yours, it's not likely that she's going to turn up."

"No," Barrett said. "You're right. She's been dead a long time, probably. But I couldn't help asking just in case—"

He looked at Quesada, then at Hahn. Thoughts were streaming turbulently through him, and he could not remember when he had last been so overwhelmed by events. He had to work hard to keep from breaking into the shakes again. His voice quavered a little as he said to Hahn, "You came back to observe Hawksbill Station, right, to see how we were getting along? And you went Up Front tonight to tell them what you saw here. You must think we're a pretty sad bunch, eh?"

"You've all been under extraordinary stress here," Hahn said. "Considering the circumstances of your imprisonment—to be sent to this remote era—"

Quesada broke in. "If there's a liberal government in power, now, and it's possible to travel both ways in time, then am I right in assuming that the Hawksbill prisoners are going to be sent back Up Front?"

"Of course," said Hahn. "It'll be done as soon as possible, as soon as we can take care of the logistics end. That's been the whole purpose of my reconnaissance mission. To find out if you people were still alive, first—we didn't even know if anyone had ever survived being sent back in time. And then to see what shape you're in, how badly in need of treatment you are. You'll be given every available benefit of modern

therapy, naturally. No expense spared to—
"

Barrett scarcely paid attention to Hahn's words. He had been fearing something like this all night, ever since Altman had told him that Hahn was monkeying with the Hammer. But he had never fully allowed himself to believe that it could really be possible.

He saw his kingdom crumbling, now.

He saw himself returned to a world he could not begin to comprehend—a lame Rip van Winkle, coming back after twenty years.

And he saw himself being taken from a place that had become his home.

Barrett said tiredly, "You know, some of the men aren't going to be able to adapt to the shock of freedom. It might just kill them to be dumped into the real world again. We've got a lot of advanced psychos here. You've seen them. You saw what Valdosto did this afternoon."

"Yes," Hahn said. "I've mentioned such cases in my report."

"It'll be necessary for the sick ones to be prepared in gradual stages to the idea of going back," Barrett said. "It might even take longer than that."

"I'm no therapist," said Hahn. "Whatever the doctors think is right for them is what will be done. Maybe it'll be necessary to keep them here indefinitely, some of them. I can see where it would be a pretty potent upheaval to send them back, after they've spent all these years believing there's no return."

"More than that," said Barrett. "There's a lot of work that can be done here. I mean, scientific work. Exploration. Going across this world, and even up and down the time-lines using this place as a base of operations. I don't think Hawksbill Station ought to be closed down."

"No one said it would be. We have every intention of keeping it going, more or less as you suggest. There's going to be a tremendous program of time exploration getting under way, and a base like this in the past will be invaluable. But the Station won't be a prison any more. The prison concept is out. Completely out."

"Good," Barrett said. He fumbled for his crutch, found it, and got heavily to his feet, swaying a little. Quesada moved toward him as though to steady him, but Barrett brusquely shook him off.

"Let's go outside," he said.

They left the building. A gray mist had come in over the Station, and a fine drizzle was beginning to fall. Barrett looked around at the scattering of huts. He looked at the ocean, dimly visible to the east in the faint moonlight. He looked toward the west and the distant sea. He thought of Charley Norton and the party that had gone on the annual expedition to the Inland Sea. That bunch is going to be in for a real surprise, he thought. When they come back here in a few weeks and discover that everybody is free to go home.

Very strangely, Barrett felt a sudden pressure forming around his eyelids, as of tears trying to force their way out into the open.

He turned to Hahn and Quesada. In a low voice he said, "Have you followed what I've been trying to tell you? Someone's got to stay here and ease the transition for the sick men who won't be able to stand the shock of return. Someone's got to keep the base running. Someone's got to explain things to the new men who'll be coming back here, the scientists."

"Naturally," Hahn said.

"The one who does that—the one who stays behind after the others go—I think it ought to be someone who knows the Station well. Someone who's fit to return Up Front right away, but who's willing to make the sacrifice and stay behind. Do you follow me? A volunteer." They were smiling at him now. Barrett wondered if there might not be something patronizing about those smiles. He wondered if he might not be a little too transparent. To hell with both of them, he thought. He sucked the Cambrian air into his lungs until his chest swelled grandly.

"I'm offering to stay," Barrett said in a loud tone. He glared at them to keep them from objecting. But they wouldn't dare object, he knew. In Hawksbill Station, he was the king. And he meant to keep it that way. "I'll be the volunteer," he said. "I'll be the one who stays." They went on smiling at him. Barrett could not stand those smiles. He turned away from them.

He looked out over his kingdom from the top of the hill.

# Afterword

As I said, I expanded the 20,000-word story "Hawksbill Station" into the novel of the same name in the spring of 1967, at a time when I was once again thinking of myself as an active science-fiction writer after a prolonged period of producing it on a now-and-then basis. Lawrence P. Ashmead, the science-fiction editor at Doubleday, had recently given me a two-book contract; the first book that I delivered was a short-story collection, *Parsecs and Parables*, and the second was a novel, *To Live Again*. Ashmead wanted some revisions on that book, which I was unwilling to do at that moment, and so, to replace it in his schedule, I suggested the expansion of "Hawksbill." He read the story in March, 1967, approved the switch, and in late April

I delivered the full manuscript. (Yes, I was that fast in those days.)

There are two basic ways of turning a novella into a novel. One is to pad the existing story by inserting a few new incidents, by extending brief conversations into lengthy ones, and by using three adjectives where one had served originally; this produces a story that is essentially identical to the original but two or three times as long. The other method is to provide entirely new narrative material, either by writing extensive prologs and epilogs or by interpolating some elaborate new subplot into the body of the story. I had employed the first method more than once, and had come to regard it not only as a bit of a fraud on the reader but also a considerable bore for the writer; so this time I opted for method two. I meant to expand the Paleozoic part of the story to some degree, yes, but my primary plan, as I had told Ashmead in my letter of March 3, 1967, was "to show much more of Barrett's career 'up front' in the 21st century, and develop a picture of him as a professional revolutionary who has been going through the motions in a total lack of conviction, and who now finds a new role to engage his energies at Hawksbill Station. I'll show the world that could exile men to the remote past this way; and I'll also open out the Hawksbill Station sequences to show more of the Paleozoic world than the immediate vicinity of the Station." All of which I did, and the book was duly accepted — Ashmead, who had a background in geology, made some cogent suggestions for improving the scientific detail-work — and was published in October, 1968.

The two versions of the story, the short and the long, have very different textures, one providing a claustrophobic view of the Paleozoic and the other, while maintaining all that material, also dodging through the totalitarian and repressive world of the early 21st century. That is one good reason for this new edition, which allows you to compare and contrast the differing effects that these two versions of the same narrative make on the reader.

But the fact that the expanded version leaves the Cambrian from time to time to show the "present-day" background of the exiles brings us to the special problem that science-fiction novels, if they have a long enough publishing life, often encounter: sooner or later, as they march on through one reprint edition after another, many books are going to overlap the real dates of the period in which they are ostensibly set.

This is, after all, the 21st century right now. That century did indeed seem to be very far in the future when I set out to write the story that became Hawksbill Station in 1966, but the future has gobbled up the young man with the dark beard who wrote that story, and here we are, the aging author and his decades-old story, in the actual year of 2002 on the very morning I write this. And the history of the late 20th century has not followed the path I described. I never seriously expected that it would; my concern was telling a tale of the early Palaeozoic, not in doing a full-scale extrapolation of modern American politics. But, still. . . .

In the fourth chapter I describe the meeting of Jim Barrett and Jack Bernstein in 1980, when they were twelve years old. 1980 in our time-line was the year of the Carter-Reagan presidential election. Four years later, Bernstein, precociously political, invites Barrett to join his underground political group, which has a Libertarian program, the goal being to dismantle as much of the American government's functions as possible. But in fact Ronald Reagan, himself pretty much a Libertarian, was President of the United States in 1984, and he was working as hard as he could to dismantle the government's functions, doing it not as part of some small-time underground cabal but right out in the open, in the Oval Office itself. So we have already begun to leave real history behind, and my protagonist is still in his adolescence.

Indeed, the book began to diverge somewhat from the actual time track a lot earlier than that. Writing in 1966, when the Vietnam war was still heating up and American political discourse was starting to get unruly but had not approached the chaos level of 1968, I spoke of the breakup of the two political parties and their realignment into more clearly delineated conservative and liberal ones. This did happen, more or less, but under the old party names, the Democrats moving left and the Republicans moving right. Then I predicted that the new American Conservative Party would win the election in 1972 (Nixon, a conservative Republican, was elected that year), then a boom and bust and a financial panic in '76 (we did have something approximating a financial crash, but no boom preceded it), and the landslide victory of the new National Liberal Party in 1976. (Carter, a Democrat, was elected in 1976, but not by a landslide, and he wasn't much of a liberal, either.) After that I predicted vast disruptions in our political system, virtually of a revolutionary kind, leading to a repressive totalitarian government of the Orwellian sort, a secret political resistance, and the exiling of political prisoners to a concentration camp a billion years in the past.

Well, you'll have to forgive me. The crystal ball was a little cloudy. We didn't get the totalitarian takeover, we didn't get the underground resistance movement, and we didn't get time travel, either. What we did get is my book, *Hawksbill Station*, which not only provides a very detailed look at the landscape of the Palaeozoic but which now can be understood as a parallel-world science-fiction novel set in an alternate 21st century different in many interesting ways from the one you happen to be inhabiting right now.

I hope you enjoyed your visit there.

# About the Author

**Robert Silverberg** was born in New York City, and educated at Columbia University, graduating in the Class of 1956. He has been a resident of the San Francisco Bay Area for many years. His first book, *Revolt on Alpha C*, was pub-lished in 1955.

He has won four Hugo awards (1956, 1969, 1987, 1990) and five Nebulas (1970, 1972, 1972 again, 1975, 1986) as well as most of the other significant science fiction honors. He was the President of the Science Fiction Writers of America from 1967 to 1968, and the Guest of Honor, World Science Fiction Convention in Heidelberg, Germany, in 1970.

He is the author of over a hundred books and an un-counted number of short stories and articles, which have appeared in such magazines as *Omni, American Heritage,*

*Harper's*, *Playboy*, and *Penthouse*, and have been widely anthologized and chosen for best-of-the-year honors. He edited the New Dimensions series of anthologies from 1971 to 1980, the first volume of *The Science Fiction Hall of Fame*, and *Robert Silverberg's Worlds of Wonder*, an anthology of great science fiction that is also a collection of his essays on the art of writing science fiction. With his wife, Karen Haber, he has edited *Universe*, an anthology of original science fic-tion.

His books include *Dying Inside*, *The Book of Skulls*, *Nightwings*, *Thorns*, *Up the Line*, *Tower of Glass*, *Gilgamesh the King*, *Lord Valentine's Castle*, *Tom O'Bedlam*, *The Man in the Maze*, *Downward to the Earth*, *The World Inside*, *Shadrach in the Furnace*, *At Winter's End*, *Born with the Dead*, *Nightfall*, (with Isaac Asimov), *The Face of the Wa-ters*, *The Ugly Little Boy* (with Isaac Asimov), *Kingdoms of the Wall*,

www.ingramcontent.com/pod-product-compliance
Lightning Source LLC
Chambersburg PA
CBHW061607210726
48287CB00001B/32

Robert Silverberg

*The Positronic Man* (with Isaac Asimov), *Hot Sky at Midnight,* and *Sorcerers of Majipoor.*